BLOODLINE DESTINIES

Book II

IULIANA FOOS

*To Steve & Christina,
Enjoy the read, and thank you for your support.
iuliana Foos*

SOUL MATE PUBLISHING

New York

BLOODLINE DESTINIES

Copyright©2019

IULIANA FOOS

Cover Design by Wren Taylor

This book is a work of fiction. The names, characters, places, and incidents are the products of the author's imagination or are used fictitiously. Any resemblance to actual events, business establishments, locales, or persons, living or dead, is entirely coincidental.

All rights reserved. No part of this publication may be reproduced, stored in a retrieval system, or transmitted in any form or by any means (electronic, mechanical, photocopying, recording, or otherwise) without the prior written permission of both the copyright owner and the publisher. The only exception is brief quotations in printed reviews.

The scanning, uploading, and distribution of this book via the Internet or via any other means without the permission of the publisher is illegal and punishable by law. Please purchase only authorized electronic editions, and do not participate in or encourage electronic piracy of copyrighted materials.

Your support of the author's rights is appreciated.

Published in the United States of America by
Soul Mate Publishing
P.O. Box 24
Macedon, New York, 14502

ISBN: 978-1-68291-900-2

ebook ISBN: 978-1-68291-846-3

www.SoulMatePublishing.com

The publisher does not have any control over and does not assume any responsibility for author or third-party websites or their content.

To my love,

my rock,

my husband Marcus.

Acknowledgments

Thank you, Michelle, for teaching me things I had no idea I should know. Your friendship, guidance and patience are and will always be close and dear to my heart. Without you holding my hand on this new path I was lost on, I would have never made it.

To all my family and friends who believed in me when I didn't, thank you for your support.

Tanya, I would have never had the courage to embark on this journey without you and your encouragement. You gave me hope and I thank you for every kind word.

Brenda, your honesty, knowledge and friendship are precious and make me one of the luckiest people in the world to have you on my side. Thank you for pushing me forward.

Barbara, Cindy, S.K., thank you so much for your invaluable insight and precious advice. I took your words to heart and they helped me get better.

I would also like to thank my critique group, a mix of talented and good-natured people I was fortunate enough to know. Too many to mention, I will still try: Karen, Miranda, Kevin, Daron, Sheila, Roy, Cynthia (both of you), Kim, Dee, Fernando, and everyone else, I love you guys. Your opinions, views, and advice helped me along the way.

We all know it takes a village to raise a child, well, it takes just as many, if not more, to write a book.

Chapter 1

"If you want my people to join your coven, you will marry me."

Malvina's words echoed in Theodor's mind even now, days after the unexpected conversation.

One low growl pushed through his lips, mixing with the wet, sticky snowflakes. A soft and immaculate blanket covered the city. Tiny crystals of ice, identically shaped, joined in one by one, and thickened the growing layer.

Theodor's blood boiled. He hoped a walk in the crisp air would help restore his calm enough to come up with a plan for the upcoming meeting with Malvina.

"Who the hell does she think she is?" Theodor muttered under his breath. His long coat billowed behind him, lifted by the frigid air.

Away from the busy commercial district, the streets were empty. Long shadows broken by sparse lights swallowed him in a comforting darkness.

His heavy boots soundlessly packed the white slush. Only the footprints left behind proved his presence. He blended into the night, a true predator.

Theodor gazed into the black sky. The humming of the speeders droned in his ears. Flying vehicles replaced the Old World's cars centuries ago. *I thought the cold and snow would keep most people indoors.*

Even if humans couldn't hear them, his enhanced senses picked up the irritating noise. Far above, endless white and red ribbons of the fast-moving traffic lanes chased into the night.

Snowflakes melted on contact with his tanned skin. Minuscule droplets ran over his anger-heated flesh, tickling him. Annoyed, Theodor wiped them away with an open palm.

He scanned the surroundings and raked his hand through wet, raven-colored hair, pushing back from his forehead a couple of rebel strands. Theodor recognized the ruins and the cobblestone pavement in what used to be the historic district.

Exposed foundations and stone half-walls eroded by time stood as witnesses to the passing of centuries. The city's council decided to preserve them, as a treasure and reminder of a long-gone era.

In need of silence, Theodor walked away from the irritating noises. Taking full advantage of his increased speed and the lack of any people around to see him, he rushed, the immediate surroundings distorting around him.

The old stone bridge ahead of him was used as cover for the few homeless huddled around a timid fire, seeking refuge from falling snow and frosty winds.

Serving as a marker to the upper-class District Four, by a miracle, the structure survived the fury of the Flood.

Making sure his fangs were fully retracted, Theodor slowed to normal speed and continued his way across the worn granite squares.

Tired and sad faces turned in his direction. He could only imagine how cold the poor people must be. Some of them, barefoot, shivered in wet blankets with more holes than the fabric barely covering the tattered clothes.

Reaching in his pockets, Theodor pulled out all the credits he had with him and approached the unfortunate mortals. Without a word, he divided the money and slipped them into the waiting hands. His mother always taught him to help the ones that can't help themselves. For one fleeting moment, he wished he could smile the way she always did, with her soul.

"Thank you, thank you," one by one, the dozen or so people whispered. An older man thanked him using the sign language, and Theodor nodded toward him.

One of the women rewarded him with a toothless smile. "What do you want in exchange, handsome?" She quickly hid the credits inside her ragged sweater.

Her question made Theodor quiver.

"Nothing. Just get somewhere warm." Tears of gratitude started to run over her creased face. She hurried to wipe them with a shaking hand. Two of her fingers were missing.

Away from the still whispering humans, Theodor returned to his thoughts. The prophecy resonated in his mind as it did every day since he turned sixteen. *You will be the most powerful of our kind ever in existence, uniting vampires from Europe and parts of Asia. Unfortunately, your quest won't be easy. You will have to fight for everything. Every single one of your accomplishments will be a struggle. The New World will be a test for all of us, but you will adapt to it and lead with justice. The first five hundred years of your life will be the hardest.*

The alien descent of his kind over two millennia ago, proved and accepted by every single vampire, combined with his prestigious bloodline, prompted Theodor to make his pact. Four centuries ago, right after the Flood, he set his goal: to reach one thousand members in his coven by the time he turned five hundred years old. He signed a blood contract that day. If he failed, all his coveners oaths will be annulled, and The Old Coven would cease to exist. *I need to prove myself and everyone else I'm worthy of my legacy.*

With only a few months left until his birthday, Theodor remained ten men short of his target, his ambition.

I could use Malvina's twenty people. Another angry rumble rolled from his chest.

Young trees and bushes bowed under the strong wind, reminding Theodor of his opponents throughout time. He had built the Old Coven from the ground up, having fought hundreds of his kind to prove his worth. As dictated by prophecy, he united vampires from former Europe and Western Asia. Over and over again, he defeated and forced them to kneel before him. He still had to prove to himself he was worthy of his name and bloodline.

The scars on his coveners' bodies served as a reminder of their defeat and Theodor's dominance. They all took their oath and signed the contracts with blood.

Strong winds shrilled in the night, rivaling his anger. Only leafless branches reached to the sky, and trembled under the powerful gusts.

Houses lined both sides of the street, and their lights caused Theodor to squint. Coming from one of the darkest parts of the city, he needed a few seconds to adjust. He preferred the shadows.

In order to reach his full potential, Theodor had allowed his inner beast to overtake him. Darkness and coldness always surrounded him, his permanent companions. He had won himself the nickname Prince Theofrost.

His rushed steps continued to leave footprints in the fast-accumulating snow.

Deep inside, under layers of stone and ice, his heart sheltered the faint hope that one day he could reverse the process and rediscover his old self. Since he could remember, Theodor aspired to become as powerful and wise as his father, Prince Andree De Croix.

Every single day, every passing minute, every agonizing second, he struggled to hold on to his last remnant of humanity: the ability to fall in love. To him, love and marriage were sacred and buried deep inside a forgotten part of his being.

And Malvina thinks I'm going to marry her? She really believes I would vow myself to her? Another hiss escaped and melted into the raging winds.

The new equivalent of a police car rounded a corner, piloted by a droid. Theodor glanced behind him, toward the approaching vehicle.

The downtown area served as a background not far away. New skyscrapers, huge black spikes, poked into the sky. Oversized floating screens filled with advertising and news made the whole city pulse with animation. On one of them, a blood bank advertised their pre-portioned vials. Scarlet liquid pouring from a glass ampoule flooded the screen. Snowflakes danced and sparkled in the bright lights, miniature ballerinas in the spotlight.

Most humans lived in the new constructions in a surrogate world. Everything in those buildings, from food, to plants, to pets, was artificial. The towers didn't even have windows, the views, mere projections. *I guess I'll never understand how anyone can live like that.* Only the penthouse levels had glass walls and private landing platforms.

Theodor wasn't in the mood for identification and a nonsensical conversation with the droid in charge.

He ran, then ducked behind some nearby overgrown bushes. His long, navy-blue leather coat brushed off the snow accumulated on a few of the lower branches.

From his hiding spot through leafless twigs, he had a clear view of the house across the street.

A couple was having a late dinner behind closed but uncovered windows. *They can afford to live here, but eat synthesized food?* The rhetorical question flashed in his mind for a brief instant.

Once the speeder passed and gained a good distance, Theodor resumed his walk. The dark ample coat barely touched the heels of his boots.

A restlessness bothered him inside and out for the past couple of days since he'd arrived in Vienna. *I expect something to happen without knowing what. It's driving me crazy.* Uncertainty amplified his anger. A puff of white steam, his own breath, blurred his vision for a fraction of a second.

Theodor turned into a dark alley. On his left, a three-story building projected its dense shadow. On the right side, wooden and metal fences marked the edge of the property for a few houses and lined up at different heights.

A wind gust filled his nostrils with the familiar smell of salt and seaweed, reminding him of home.

This can't be right. The ocean is miles away. Theodor's shadow swept the pavement.

~ ~ ~

Goosebumps rose on Vivienne's skin. The icy-cold water stung her raw wrists and ankles. She couldn't remember the last time her body was unmarked. The shackles dug into her flesh every day, and her thrashing only made it worse.

Greg leaned against the doorway watching her shower, making sure she didn't turn on the hot water, just one of his punishments. Every few seconds, he drank from the bottle hanging in his hand. The alcohol affected his equilibrium.

"Hurry up. I don't have all night. You're wearing this." He dangled a set of beige undergarments.

I miss wearing comfortable, decent clothes. She lowered her gaze to her feet. Dried blood, diluted by water, swirled around the drain.

The slurred words brought more tears to her eyes. She knew he would chain her again. Her stomach growled in hunger.

I have to survive. I need to get out of here. She turned off the water. Without the icy drops pelting her body, warmth enveloped her.

Trembling legs took her to the towel. She dried herself, slipping into the lacy garments he threw at her feet. The towel was warm and soft, and she held on to it.

Greg's hand closed around her arm. He yanked her out of the bathroom and pushed her to the floor, near the heavy chains. The blood-stained towel fell on the bathroom's white tiles like a wounded dove.

"No. Please, don't chain me again." Tears streamed on her face.

"Shut up." He sat the bottle down. "You belong here." Holding her with one hand, he grabbed one of the shackles with the other. "Freaks like you don't just roam free." A loud burp burst free of his lips and interrupted his sadistic laugh.

His body wavered for an instant, the alcohol impeding his movements.

With the strength gathered more from her will than her weakened body, she kicked, pushing him away. Her resistance infuriated him. Punches and kicks hit her body. Vivienne curled in pain, tasting her own blood.

I have nothing to lose. A second wind powered by desperation took over all her senses. The man crouched in front of her, with one of the heavy shackles in his hand. Ignoring the excruciating pain, she pushed both her feet against his chest.

Greg fell backward with a puzzled look on his face. His head hit the doorframe with a loud thud.

Now. This is my chance. She rose on trembling feet. His alcohol-laden breaths, slow and heavy, assured her he was still alive, even if motionless. He could recover any second.

With no time to waste, she stumbled out of the bedroom and down the stairs. Her hands wrapped around painful ribs. The electronic display above the entrance blinked green numbers in front of her eyes: 25.11.2516. *Is this right? Has it been almost a year?* She double-checked the bright display. It was correct.

A loud pulse drummed in her ears. Heart pounding in her chest, she opened the door to a gust of freezing wind. Afraid that Greg would catch up with her, she checked the stairs. His jacket lay on the bannister.

Her body shook from the cold, and she grabbed the oversized coat. Barefoot, Vivienne ran outside.

The street seemed deserted. Snow and wind blurred her vision, but she couldn't stop. Survival instinct, stronger than the biting cold and unbearable pain, forced her legs into motion.

At least I'll die free. Sooner or later, Greg will kill me. Another street, another corner, another hope she could escape carried her away from the house where she'd been a prisoner. Fear and desperation fueled her chaotic steps.

With no sense of direction or time, she put as much distance as she could between her and the monster who had enslaved her.

Lost, tired, and half-frozen, she turned another corner, staggering into a dark alley. Barely walking, with one hand holding the jacket close to her, and the other leaning against the brick wall, she advanced in the shadows.

Strong winds screamed from every direction. All the strength gone from her weakened and starved body forced Vivienne to sit. *I'd rather die from cold than his hands.* She shivered in the jacket and curled behind the large crate serving as a dumpster.

Eyes closed, she knew it was the end of the line. *I'm free. I'm free . . .*

~ ~ ~

Halfway into the empty alley, Theodor spotted a being lying on the ground, hidden behind a container. He sniffed the air: human. A slow, faint heartbeat traveled to his ears. *Barely alive.*

From experience, he knew not to get involved with humans, but something drew him closer.

The conversation with his father, from hundreds of years ago, sparked to life in his mind—the warning about crossing paths with the one person fated to him.

A wild whirlwind froze time and shifted the world around. The whole universe dissolved into tiny molecules only to rearrange itself into a new dimension. Every tree, every blade of grass, every atom in the air pulsed with an unfamiliar energy, paralyzing him. His lungs refused to cooperate and supply much-needed air.

Inside the disruption was quiet, a deafening silence, like in the eye of a tornado. Theodor stood still. His ears picked up the soft *poofs* each snowflake made in contact with the others.

He advanced with caution, pulled by invisible chains. His heart beat as fast as the wings of a hummingbird.

This must be a mistake. My destiny is an unconscious, half-dead human? Disappointment raised the first question.

"It can't be."

First, he noticed the small, bare feet. Purplish-pale skin bore marks of restraints on the ankles. The body lay unconscious, covered in a fluffy, oversized jacket.

"Are you all right?" His voice resonated in the night. He waited a few seconds for a response, but none came.

I couldn't have asked a more stupid question if I tried. Theodor shook his head and lowered himself to one knee. His coat covered the white slush around him like a dark, mysterious pool.

He touched the thick jacket with a firm but gentle hand. Snow, accumulated on top of the dark-colored fabric, melted under his fingertips.

The ocean's hint mixed with the human scent and stirred his senses. He inhaled deeply, filling his lungs with the fresh, sweet, inviting fragrances.

Even if forbidden to kill humans for their blood, some vampires still indulged in drinking it. They used their magnetism on their victims, placing them into a controlled state of sleep. After their thirst was satisfied, they masked their bite marks with a cut.

He'd never done it, but the scent of humans, of their blood, had always attracted him.

"Go away. Leave me alone." A woman's voice rose just above a whisper.

Theodor heard the pain through her plea. At least she'd regained consciousness.

"Miss," he tried again. With one move, he rolled her onto her back.

A moan of pain escaped her lips, and the jacket became undone.

Theodor took a sharp breath at the sight before his eyes.

The woman lay beaten, her small body covered in bruises and blood. Under the oversized jacket, she wore a beige set of undergarments.

Long, honey-colored hair, wet and tangled, covered her face, and he carefully brushed it away.

Out of all days, I had to forget my gloves today. As much as he tried not to, he touched her cold, almost translucent skin. A tiny electric discharge tickled his fingertips, forcing him to retrieve his hand. The current traveled throughout his body, charging him with unexpected heat.

Unlike humans, vampires controlled their body temperature and always adjusted to their surroundings. Extreme cold or heat didn't affect them. He figured she must've been freezing. After all, it was snowing.

Her face, swollen, covered in cuts and bruises, appeared disfigured. Theodor recognized the signs of unsatisfied thirst in her bloodshot eyes: hundreds of tiny blood vessels covered the white. "You're a GeM."

She belonged to the new species, genetically modified individuals, called GeM. A virus had infected a quarter of the remaining population shortly after the devastating Flood. Only young, healthy adults had fallen victims to the smart virus released into the atmosphere when they opened the crushed, alien ship. Scientists still tried to figure out what caused the genetic mutations.

Now, four centuries later, some GeMs developed special abilities rivaling those of his own people. They were humans with a thirst for blood. The GeMs couldn't survive more than a few days without it.

"No." Her denial mixed with fear.

He hid his anger and clenched his jaw. Muscles twitched under taut skin. She had just lied to him. Theodor hated when people attempted to hide the truth.

"Yes, you are. You haven't had blood in a while, and it seems you've been in a fight." His index finger pointed to her eyes. "I'll take you to a hospital." Theodor reached for the frightened woman.

"No, please. I can't go to any clinic." Tears started to run along the bruises on her face.

Theodor hesitated and studied her with increased attention.

"You're not registered, are you?" His eyes narrowed to dark slits.

She just shook her head slowly.

Even after four centuries, some GeMs were still the subject of severe abuse. He'd heard rumors in the past about some, enslaved by heartless humans. The restraint marks on her ankles made sense now. She must've been one of the unlucky ones.

"You're not going to make it to the morning."

If he had to guess, she had at least one broken rib. Her skinny hands were stained with fresh, sweet-smelling blood, most probably hers.

"What do you care?" The woman shrugged and turned her back to him.

Theodor closed his eyes and let out a silent sigh. *She's right. I shouldn't care.*

The wind had picked up, turning into a blizzard. He gazed into the falling snow. Out of habit, his right hand made another pass through his black, wavy hair.

Great. A weak, spineless human who doesn't care if she lives or not. What a glorious future destiny reserved for me. Theodor directed his attention back to her.

"You're not safe here." He turned her again, and the unzipped jacket reopened.

At the sight of the nude-colored bra, a surge of desire spiked through his veins. He had to fight his own instincts, to stop the fangs from descending. Every muscle in his body tensed.

Theodor inherited his father's roguish air combined with a large build, as well as his mother's sharpness, which contrasted with his apparent, laid-back attitude.

The uncommon blend gave him an edge, an irresistible charm. He could bed any woman he desired with ease. None of them had ever had that effect on him. *What the hell is going on with me? How can I even think about her this way? Poor woman is half-dead.* His mental self-scolding didn't help. *She's not even that pretty. Heck. I can't tell if she's ugly. Right now, she's . . . faceless.* He struggled to control his reactions.

"The patrols will find you. Is there anywhere I can take you?"

"No. Just go away." She covered herself with the fluffy jacket and closed her eyes.

Her resigned tone bothered Theodor. He always fought for everything, never quit. Not even once in almost five hundred years.

The woman in front of him had just given up.

Heavy snowflakes continued to cover her oversized coat. A few caught in the messy hair fanned out around her like the tentacles of an underwater creature.

Theodor scanned the alley one more time. He hoped there would be somebody else around. She couldn't be the one destined to him. There wasn't another soul.

He touched her shoulder. "Can you walk?"

She reopened her eyes. "Not anymore."

He glanced at the erratic footprints half-covered in snow, leading to where she lay. *She ran until she collapsed.* Judging by the layer of fresh snow, she must've been there for at least an hour.

"Then you'll have to trust me."

Theodor lifted her light body in his arms with ease.

Her cry of pain reminded him how badly injured she was under the jacket. A weird familiarity washed over him.

"I don't trust anyone." Her bony hands tightened on his coat. "Who are you?"

"Theodor, you can call me Theo."

After the first couple of steps, she clenched her teeth, and another moan confirmed she was in pain.

For one fraction of a second, Theodor thought of leaving her there, and walking away as if nothing had happened. He knew it would be wrong. She wouldn't survive the night. Even if he refused to accept destiny's offering, he couldn't leave her to die in a deserted alley.

"Are you a GeM, too?"

The effort to speak left her gasping for air, and Theodor figured it must be important to her.

"No."

"Human," she whispered, terrified. "Please don't turn me in."

The fear in her reddened eyes, the panic in her voice made him stare at her. *She's scared of humans. I wonder how she feels about vampires.*

Theodor shook his head. "I'm not human either."

She took a few shallow breaths. "Then . . . what are you?"

"We can talk about it later. For now, you need medical attention, blood, and a safe, warm place."

The buzzing of another security speeder assured him they didn't have much time. Theodor reached to his bracer under the coat's sleeve and pressed a button. A dark blue and purple swirl appeared in front of him.

"You can open a portal?" she asked.

"Looks that way, doesn't it?"

Her head fell on his chest. Theodor wondered if she even heard his answer before falling unconscious.

The tiny fists holding on to his coat relaxed, and her arms slid back.

He took a deep breath, inhaling the ocean scent.

Out of all women in this world, it had to be this one. Why? "What have I done to deserve this?" he muttered under his breath. His gaze lifted to the black, silent sky.

Another quick glance around and he entered the swirling portal, disappearing from the dark alley.

Chapter 2

Theodor stepped out of the portal and rushed toward the couch. The woman in his arms stirred. Her eyes fluttered opened and checked her surroundings.

"Where am I? What is this place?" Her tone sounded fearful.

Theodor's residence in Vienna was the smallest of all the other properties he had spread throughout what used to be Europe. Safe and comfortable, it met his needs for the few days away from his usual life.

'Jake, I need blood and food.' Theodor used a telepathic link with his trusted assistant. *'And hurry, I found a half-dead GeM.'*

"You're safe." He tried to sound assuring, but her tiny fists closed on his coat again. *She is scared of her own shadow. She can't be the one.*

"I don't know you, I don't trust you."

Carefully, Theodor placed her on top of the soft cushions and pulled a pillow under her head. Holding her seemed natural, as if she belonged in his arms.

"You haven't told me your name." Theodor gently unclenched her hands—a bunch of tiny, fragile bones held together by pale, delicate skin—from his coat.

Fear persisted in her eyes, and she tried to stand. A cry of pain ripped from her throat.

"Try and relax. It'll hurt less."

She ground her teeth in agony. Even with her whole body hugged by the soft, warm cushions, she shook and closed her eyes.

The cold must've infused all the way to her bones.

"Vivienne . . ." Her teeth chattered. "Vivienne Ferre."

Theodor tilted his head to the side and stared at her. Attraction and an inexplicable connection caused him to forget he was supposed to blink around humans. *She's not ready to hear what I am.*

"It suits you. Now, I should take care of this pain. You have at least one broken rib—"

"Actually, there are three," she corrected him.

"Are you a doctor?"

She shook her head again. "I used to be a biochemist, before the infection." Closing her eyes, she took in another shallow breath. "I felt every single one of them breaking." Another low moan escaped her lips when she turned her head to the side. More tears found their way down her cheeks.

Theodor listened to her, and more questions rose in his mind. How did it happen? When? Where? Answers could wait. He had to ease her pain first. "I have to touch you in order to heal you."

"Are you a doctor?"

"No." The questionable glance in her bloodshot eyes assured him his answer was far from explanatory. "Like I said earlier, you need to trust me and stay still. I'm only trying to help here."

Theodor heard her thoughts loud and clear, as if she spoke to him. '*It can't get worse.*' Her mind surrendered in resignation.

With gentle movements, he opened her jacket, pushing it to the side. He wished once more he had his gloves on. The unusual attraction made skin-to-skin contact a test of self-control. Why hadn't he taken them before leaving that evening? Slowly, he placed his hand over her bruised ribcage and held his breath.

His fingers spread, trying to cover as much surface as he could.

Vivienne's sharp breath shifted his attention from her body to her eyes.

"I know it hurts, but it'll be over before you know it." Theodor focused on her bones.

Her ribs moved into the right position, fusing back together under his touch. Muscle tissue repaired, blood vessels strengthened and carried life through her body, unobstructed.

"How did you do that?" Her gaze dropped to his fingers still covering most of her torso. "You have to be a GeM. No human can heal the way you just did."

Theodor shook his head and withdrew his hand. Even the bruises disappeared.

"Don't worry, I won't tell anyone if you want to keep it a secret. I understand that way too well." She touched her ribs with one hand, as if to make sure it was real.

I did pretty good. Theodor helped her sit. He let his body sink in the comfortable sofa, beside her.

"I already told you, not a GeM." He pointed to his chest. "I'll answer your questions once we are done here."

"But—"

"Shhh, I have to take care of this split lip so you can at least drink some blood." He lightly patted the broken skin, and just like earlier, it healed under his touch. It cost him a good amount of energy, but easing her pain was all worth it.

She trembled under his fingertips. *Must be the cold. At least, as a GeM, she won't get sick like a human would.*

Theodor healed every beaten inch of her body. When she took off the jacket, he considered it a proof of trust.

The restraint marks on her wrists were still bleeding, and Theodor took care of them first, working his way up to her shoulders. The scent of her blood made him dizzy.

Avoiding his gaze, Vivienne turned sideways, letting him see her back covered in old and fresh scars. It resembled a puzzle put together by the clumsy hands of a child. Some were distinctive marks from multiple cuts, some from powerful hits.

Theodor realized it was not the first time she had been beaten, and had to control his rising anger. Unfortunately, he couldn't heal scars.

A light knock on the door made Vivienne cover herself with the puffy jacket.

"Enter." Theodor glanced toward the entrance.

"Your Majesty." Jake, his assistant, bowed and placed the black tray he carried on the table in front of them.

"Thank you. In a few minutes, send Carla in." The crimson-colored liquid in the cup Jake brought in on the serving platter produced a sweet aroma, but not as inviting and alluring as hers.

"Understood." Jake tilted his head and left the room.

"Did he just call you *Your Majesty*?"

"Yes."

"I thought the term was used in the Old World for royalty."

Theodor stood. "That's correct. Here's some blood." With shaky hands, she took the offered mug from him. "Drink up."

He realized he must've sounded harsh. Theodor was used to giving orders. After the few steps he took away from her, he turned and observed her. She drank slowly, as if she feared to finish.

"Thank you, whoever you are, you saved my life." Vivienne placed the empty cup on the tray.

Theodor followed her slow movements. He remembered buying that serving set over two centuries ago from an artisan. It was his favorite. The shiny glass had a frosted design throughout. *He used to hand craft all his goods. What did he say? Oh, that he was the last one to master the art.* He returned to the low table.

The black metal support, on which the tray sat, revealed an impressive craftsmanship. The legs, representing swords, had symbols engraved on them. Delicate chains tied the swords together around the glass.

"Are you hungry? When was the last time you ate?" He handed her the plate with a couple of oversized meat and cheese sandwiches on it. Tomato slices and a couple of lettuce leaves brought a splash of color.

"Couple of days ago." Vivienne grabbed hold of it, her hand still far from steady.

Her answer didn't surprise him. Theodor shook his head and took off his long coat, throwing it on one of the chairs.

'*He's definitely the most gorgeous, good-hearted man I've ever met.*' Vivienne's thoughts screamed in his mind.

With slow, long strides, Theodor stopped in front of the glass doors to the patio and stared out into the night.

He met his own reflection in the shiny surface. A barely perceptible smile tugged at the corner of his lips, and a few creases appeared around his eyes. When had he smiled last? Must've been centuries. Two deep dimples marked his cheeks. He clasped his hands at the small of his back.

I forgot how good it feels. His face straightened quickly. Nobody saw his smile but the white, heavy snowflakes continuing to fall into the night. He was safe. They wouldn't tell anyone. His reputation wouldn't suffer.

Theodor glanced at Vivienne over his left shoulder. She had almost finished her food.

Poor girl has no idea who or what I am.

"Are you feeling better?" He turned to face her.

She finished chewing the last bite, and placed the empty plate on the tray. "Yes, thank you."

Another knock echoed in the quiet room.

"Come in, Carla."

"Your Majesty."

Theodor gestured toward the couch. "Vivienne is our guest. Can you find some clothes for her to wear?"

He faced Carla and used his mental link with her.

"She doesn't know who we are. Avoid answering any questions that would give it away."

"Of course, Your Majesty." The trusty servant acknowledged his instructions through the same link.

"This way, Miss Vivienne." Carla smiled in her direction. "I'm sure we can come up with something."

Theodor's attention shifted to Vivienne's hesitation. Doubt laced with fear floated around her like a thick fog. He could smell it.

"You're safe. No one in this house will hurt you." His right hand rested on top of his heart. "You have my word."

Vivienne's gaze stopped on the intertwined lines creating an intricate design in the soft rug under her feet.

"May I ask you for one favor?"

"What is it?"

"Is there any way I can wash all this blood off?" She stared at her crimson-stained hands.

"Of course. Carla, make sure she's comfortable in a guest suite."

"Thank you, I really appreciate it." Vivienne followed Carla out of the room with timid steps, her head low.

Theodor pinched the bridge of his nose and sat on the same couch where Vivienne just had her dinner. The ocean scent must've been some shampoo or perfume she wore. It lingered on the pillows and Theodor inhaled, saturating his lungs.

How is she going to react when I tell her the truth? She's weak and has no backbone. I can't see myself with her.

He remembered her reaction when he took off his coat and she admired him. The way his blood rushed when he healed her. A deep sigh left his lips, and his fangs elongated. Theodor shook his head again and started to pace the room.

No. I can't let myself think like this. She isn't the one. It's just physical attraction. I can control it. Theodor retracted his fangs as if he wanted to prove his self-control.

He pressed one of the buttons on his custom bracer matching his navy outfit. No new messages. His meeting with Malvina was in a little over an hour, and he still didn't have a plan.

Preoccupied with his own thoughts, Theodor turned around startled when Vivienne opened the door. She looked so different.

Long, light-brown hair framed her delicate face in soft waves he wanted to touch. Now that she'd quenched the blood thirst, her eyes were luminous, an unusual shade of rich honey, perfectly matching her locks. *I wonder how it would feel to lose myself in them.* Full lips curved into a shy smile when she glanced at him.

The simple black leggings paired with an oversized white crisp shirt and socks were nothing glamorous, but she seemed comfortable, not cold, beaten, and half-dead. *Is that one of my shirts?*

"Thank you for everything. I owe you my life." Vivienne lowered her head. "You were right, I wouldn't have made it to the morning." She wrapped her arms around herself in a defensive stance against an invisible threat.

Theodor hesitated a couple of seconds.

"I'm glad you feel better. I promised you some answers, but I have a business meeting in an hour." He indicated to the screen above the door, displaying the time and date. "Do you think it can wait until tomorrow? You're probably tired."

"What kind of business meeting is in the middle of the night?"

Vivienne's question was unexpected. He didn't think she would care nor have the guts to ask.

"It'll make sense when I tell you who I am."

"Then tell me. It doesn't have to be a long explanation." Her gaze returned to the rug. "I doubt there is anything I haven't heard or seen before or—"

"This is different." Theodor's annoyance was clear in his tone.

"I already know you're obviously rich." Vivienne opened her arms to her surroundings. "I also know you have some incredible powers, people call you *Your Majesty*, but most important . . ." She paused for a couple of seconds as if searching for her words. "You saved my life. Whoever, whatever, you are, I'll understand."

For the first time that night, Theodor deliberately investigated her mind. All of a sudden, the human he thought weak, spineless, and afraid of everything, demanded an answer.

With his curiosity piqued, his right eyebrow arched. She still thought he was a GeM, like her, even if he denied it more than just once.

Theodor took a few steps in silence, and decided it was time for her first real test. *Let's see how she's going to react.*

He stopped a couple of feet away from her. His gaze cut through her like a laser. "I am Theodor De Croix, Prince of the Old Coven." His chin jotted up. "And I'm a vampire."

Vivienne took a step back. Her eyes opened wide with a mix of fear and doubt.

"Vampire . . . A monster . . ." she whispered in visible disbelief. "Are you going to kill me?"

"Of course not. Why would I do that?"

Theodor followed all her thoughts. As much as he detested invading anyone's mind, this time he needed to know.

"Is it not what vampires do? I never believed they even existed."

"It isn't what we do. We have, in fact, watched over humans for centuries." Theodor took a step closer to her. "In the old times, yes, my kind used to feed on human blood, but not anymore." His voice softened. "You're safe. I won't hurt you."

She continued to retreat. Her fear hit him in waves.

"I'm sorry, but I don't believe you."

She panicked. Her pupils dilated, her pulse accelerated, and her heartbeat became erratic. The attempt to put some distance between them failed.

Theodor hissed, displaying his long, white fangs.

Vivienne whirled on her heels. Her hair danced around her shoulders, and a few strands covered part of her face.

Theodor cut off her way to the exit. His hands grabbed her shoulders. *Damn, she needs to eat more.*

"Viv, I will not hurt you. I would—"

"You're a blood-sucking monster," she yelled with tears running down her face, trying to free herself from his firm hold.

Her words shouldn't have surprised or hurt him. Humans called vampires all sorts of names. He knew since the day he found out what he was how much humans feared and hated his kind. So, why did her words hurt? Why did they feel like a slap to his face?

"Funny, coming from a GeM."

His confrontation didn't stop her. She continued to squirm in his hands, trying to break free. He wasn't going to let her go.

"Look at me." Theodor's demand froze her in place, and she stared at him.

He drove deeper into her mind. For the first time, she noticed his dark blue eyes, and for a fraction of a second, to his satisfaction, she thought they were beautiful.

"Please, let me go."

He couldn't allow her to return to where she escaped from, or on the streets. *I didn't save her life to send her back to her death.*

Theodor needed more time and used his magnetism on her. She fell unconscious in his arms without another sound.

"You failed, Viv." He was the sole witness to his own words.

Disappointed, Theodor rushed into a blur, carrying Vivienne to her suite in a blink of an eye, and placed her on the bed. After he covered her with the soft comforter, he stepped back and hesitated.

He shouldn't have cared what she thought of him. She was nothing more than another human he'd saved. But he did.

This is a mistake. Destiny messed up big time.

His head hung low, and his shoulders drooped. The tiny hope that sparked deep in his heart extinguished. Something left his body, like a white, injured bird flailing about, unable to fly.

Chapter 3

Theodor skimmed his fingertips over the black stone embedded in the handle of his sword. Every touch sparked the pebble to life. An identical bright blue glow reflected back from his eyes, amplified by the mirror in front of him.

A deep sigh left his lips. The stone connected with him the day he was born. It brought him extra strength, speed, and energy, making him the most powerful vampire in the world.

Ruled by unknown powers, it reacted to him alone, in other hands remaining an ordinary black rock. It was his gift and his curse.

Theodor lifted the special scabbard and placed it on his back, adjusting the leather straps on his shoulders and over his chest.

Discovered on the crashed alien ship, blasteel, the black metal, revolutionized many aspects of life.

The indestructible material had a rare, programmable quality. The scabbard looked like a simple, elongated metal plate. When in contact with his sword, horizontal stripes of the same metal wrapped around the sharp edges, encasing the entire length.

An upward pull on the handle caused the stripes to recede, releasing the weapon. The sword placed firmly on his back, Theodor straightened his frame and stared into the ten-foot mirror.

Vivienne's reaction from earlier came to mind and brought another glow to his eyes. His fangs started to descend.

She failed. She was scared out of her mind when I told her the truth.

Used to the smell of fear, he enjoyed it most times. It empowered him. Every one of his adversaries had been afraid of him at some point. Usually fear was mixed with respect for his power, with the admittance of their defeat.

Vivienne's came across differently. Pure and dark, her fear suffocated him. It hurt him.

He tried to clear his mind and grabbed his gloves. His focus should have been on Malvina, not the terrified, soft human sleeping in one of his beds.

Gloves on, his attention returned to the shiny surface.

She thinks I have beautiful eyes. At a closer look, Theodor noted the crinkled skin around them and quickly retreated. *This is ridiculous. I haven't smiled for over two centuries, and today I do it twice.*

"In one hour," he muttered angry at himself.

He shook his head and checked his bracer again. Time ran fast. Theodor left his room and stopped in front of the door behind which Vivienne slept, debating if he should at least check to see if she was all right.

"Make sure nobody bothers her." Theodor instructed Carla before walking away.

Now, back to business.

~ ~ ~

Theodor stepped out of the portal into the dark garden.

Malvina's residence loomed in front of him. It appeared deserted, neglected, with creeping vines covering the stone walls. He had been in that house before, over two hundred years ago, when they first met. Time and deterioration left their stamp on it.

The night he met Malvina flashed into his mind. He'd had the sudden urge to go skiing and traveled to the Alps on an impulse. In the middle of the night, the slopes were empty.

He'd sensed her presence before seeing her in the moonlight, skiing a little ahead of him. Bright red hair glittered like a flame running along the slope. Intrigued, Theodor rushed to catch up. The woman flashed a challenging smile at him, prompting a careless, race down the mountain.

Two hours later, Theodor had left her bedroom. He hoped to never see her again. Until she called him a week ago with her gutsy demand.

The double doors opened before he'd even knocked. Theodor marched over the threshold into the foyer and on into a reception room.

The spacious area seemed empty and suffocating at the same time. Sparse pieces of furniture spread throughout showed the same degradation as the house.

Heavy, dust-filled draperies hung over smudged windows. Spider webs trimmed a few cheap chandeliers with missing light bulbs and rusty spots. *It can't be her permanent residence. Nothing seems updated since the distant times of the Old World.*

"Theo, I was starting to think you wouldn't come."

Her voice scratched his eardrums in a most unpleasant way, just as annoying as the night they met.

Her see-through blouse with red embroidery left little to the imagination. Theodor fought his impulse to apologize for arriving before she had a chance to get dressed. "Malvina." He tilted his head slightly. No intonation, no emotion.

Her bright red lips matched her hair. Even, sharp teeth came into view, reminding him of a fox.

He never trusted her. Malvina kept her mind shielded. She hid something.

"Please sit. Would you like a drink?"

She gestured to the golden tray placed on the dusty, chipped coffee table. Two glasses and a bottle containing some sort of wine waited for them. The acrid smell of the ruby liquid made his nose twitch.

"No thank you. I don't have much time."

Malvina's fake hurt expression and pouted lips could've been amusing under different circumstances. She continued to advance toward him and touched his arm as soon as she came close enough to do so.

"You look better than I remember," she purred.

Theodor stared into her black-trimmed, emerald eyes. The overdone, impeccable makeup only meant to hide the reality. Her proximity triggered a memory from his childhood.

He was about six years old when he saw a drawing of a witch for the first time. She'd had green skin, with a pointy hat, and a nose she could've use for a weapon. The mole on her chin had terrorized him for days. *Maybe Malvina looks just like her under all the makeup. I sure as hell don't want to find out.*

"You haven't changed. I see you are still hiding your thoughts." His index finger pointed to her temple.

Her laugh hurt his ears again. "A girl has to protect herself."

"And her true intentions?" Theodor prodded her, hoping she would at least make a mistake. "Why do you want to marry me?"

Malvina bit her lower lip with a seductive smile. "You are one of the best-looking men I've ever seen. Any woman would—"

"Cut the fluff." He didn't give her a chance to sweet-talk him. "The real reason." Theodor crossed his arms over his chest and steeled his eyes.

"You're a Veres."

He expected horns to poke through her hair.

"What can I say? I aim high."

"My last name is De Croix. If it's the Veres name you're after, I'm the wrong guy."

"Are you talking about your uncles?" She waved her hand as if she dismissed the men in discussion. "Not my type."

"They're both breathing." His sarcasm pushed her away.

On high heeled boots rising over her knees, Malvina promenaded her way to one of the rosy, discolored couches. At some point in time, the sofas might've been crimson, or perhaps a rich burgundy.

Her shiny tight pants stretched even more when she crossed her long legs with a lazy, languorous motion. Her blouse slipped a little lower.

Theodor's eyes followed the movement of the delicate fabric revealing even more of her porcelain-white skin.

"I see you are familiar with my reputation. Things will change after we marry." She opened the bottle and poured wine in one of the glasses. "I will, after all, vow myself to you."

"I didn't agree to your terms." Theodor cut the air in front of him with his gloved hand.

Her eyes feasted on his body, and her lips forced a new smile.

No woman had ever made him so uncomfortable. Theodor shifted his weight from one leg to the other and back.

"Is that a no?" Malvina sipped from her drink. "Are you rejecting my offer?"

An avalanche of thoughts flooded his mind. He'd intended to come up with some sort of strategy, earlier, during the long walk. Vivienne had messed up his plans. *Vivienne.*

"I haven't decided yet." He tracked the movement of the ruby liquid in the globe-like glass. "I need more time. It's not an easy decision."

"What is there to think about?" She leaned back. "We get married, and I bring twenty-two people into your coven, twenty-three if you count me." She played with the glass, turning it in a clockwise motion. "That will take you to over one thousand members." Another fake smile stretched her lips. "It's rather simple."

She knows about my contract. Theodor shook his head. "Not for me. I believe in marrying for love."

Her irritating laugh filled every corner of the room again. Sickening and fake, it crept around like the plague.

"Are you serious? That is so centuries ago." She placed the glass back on the tray. "Love has nothing to do with marriage."

"Maybe for you." Theodor stood his ground.

Malvina let out a sigh and rose to her feet.

"According to our laws, your people would have to join my coven if I defeat you in a duel." Theodor grasped at the first idea that crossed his mind.

"True. According to the same laws, I have the right to decline." She propped a hand on her hip. "I'm not stupid. Nobody can defeat you." With an arched brow, she stared back at him.

Damn it. She's done her homework. With her declining the duel, there is only one option left, marriage. Or, I kill her, freeing her people from their vows. Shouldn't be too hard to convince them to join me, and I only need a half of them.

She walked toward him, swaying her hips too much for his taste. "Theo darling, I'm not asking for love, I—"

"I do." Theodor noted her surprise, the first genuine reaction in a chain of lies and false pretenses.

"You are joking, right?" Malvina placed her hands on his folded arms. Her smile could have softened any heart, make any man mad with desire.

"Do I look like I'm joking?" He glanced at her hands touching his skin. *I should've worn my long-sleeve coat.*

Her high-pitched laugh grated on his brain. She might as well have dragged her nails on a chalkboard. Would've had same effect. *There has to be a way to get her people without her. I have to figure it out.*

He had killed to protect his family and his coven. Defeated others in honorable fights for domination, in duels. Taking another vampire's life without evident cause was a slippery road to self-gratification and greed.

"Do you honestly believe there's any woman in this world who would fall in love with you?" Malvina's question brought his thoughts back in full force.

"Am I so repulsive?" He couldn't help the sarcasm.

"Women don't fall in love with looks, but with feelings," she purred. "You, Prince Theofrost, are incapable of—"

"What did you call me?" Theodor closed his hand around her arm and squeezed.

"Don't tell me you've never heard your nickname before." Malvina kept her seductive air and the painted-on smile.

Theodor smelled her fear. His inner demon stirred to life. *I'm letting her get to me.* He released her. "You have no idea what I'm capable of."

Malvina glanced at her arm. Pink prints of his fingers marked her skin.

"That's where you're wrong, My Prince." She turned her seduction up a notch and slid her hands under his vest. "I know how very capable you are."

Theodor held his breath. *She's trying hard to get in my pants.* Satisfaction and pride glimmered inside him. His stroked ego inflated.

"Let me show you a small token of my honest intentions." Her hands traveled up his abdomen, and Theodor tensed.

Malvina's words raised all kind of flags and rang all possible bells in his mind.

Giving in to her advances would mean breaking his self-imposed rule. He never slept with a woman more than once. *If I play along, I might be able to find out what she's hiding. Maybe she'll drop the shield.*

"I'd like to meet your people." He stayed true to himself.

She lifted a hand to touch the side of his face, but Theodor caught it in midair.

A loud hiss flew from Malvina's lips, between sharp, elongated fangs.

He tried to probe inside her mind. The shield infuriated him. *This isn't working.* His hand tightened.

"You like it rough, My Prince?"

I'd like you dead. Adrenaline filled his body at the idea. His eyes traveled down her chest, right above her heart.

Theodor imagined his sword's sharp blade cutting through the impossibly perfect skin, tearing the muscles, and crushing her bones. The mental picture of her blood pouring out of her shallow heart, as red as her hair, brought his fangs out.

Imaginary sounds of her last heartbeat vibrating against the end of his sword sang in his mind. A little twist would end her life. But he envisioned himself holding it still, letting the burn of the silver-coated edges spread and ignite her in bright amber, before her last breath mixed with her own ashes.

He released her arm, pushing her away. Theodor's gaze fell on her red locks. *I bet it feels artificial, dried, and brittle, like a doll's hair.*

Another possible vision danced in the back of his mind. Her head, separated from the rest of her body, rolled on the ground. Ruby hair soaked with the same color liquid, burned in flames, soundlessly turning to black dust.

"This meeting is over." Theodor returned to reality.

"Are you really leaving? This soon?" Failure to hide her disappointment amused him.

"I told you I didn't have much time." Her controlled fury alerted him, and his senses stiffened.

"When will I see you next?" Malvina walked away from him, toward the sofa.

"Whenever you show me that token of your pure intentions and bring your people before me." Theodor took a step toward the door.

"You don't trust me." Malvina sat in the middle of the couch. "You don't believe I will bring you twenty-some people." All he could see were amber flames igniting her flawless body. The horns he expected earlier to rise from under her hair were now accompanied by a snapping tail.

"Trust is earned, not given freely."

That came out perfectly. I'm good at this. Just not as good at following my own advice. Why am I expecting Vivienne to trust me? Should I—?

"When will you make your decision?" Malvina's question yanked Theodor from his thoughts.

He glanced at her with disdain. "It might take a few months. Don't hold your breath."

He turned his back on her and continued toward the door. A dark energy charged the room, and danger assaulted his senses. Particles of disturbed dust floated in the heavy, stale air.

After only a couple of steps, Malvina's hiss filled his ears, and Theodor looked back at her, over his shoulder. She pulled a dagger from behind one of the decorative pillows, and in a moment of uncontrolled fury, she threw it at him.

Theodor caught the dagger in its trajectory to his heart. Blinding speed carried him to the sofa, on top of her.

With her own dagger's blade against her throat, Malvina whimpered with helplessness.

"You really thought it would be this easy?" Theodor's question sounded half-furious, half-amused.

She moaned in pain and tried to escape his hold. An amber color spread along the straight line where the silver blade burned, from under her jaw, all the way to her collarbone.

"You try this again, and I'm going to kill you." Theodor displayed his fangs. "Are we clear?"

Instead of answering his question, she tried to fight him off. Her hands pushed against his chest. Theodor immobilized her kicking legs with one knee across hers.

"Are we clear?" Theodor growled his question and dragged the blade along her once unspoiled skin all the way to her heart.

With another painful hiss she turned her head, avoiding his piercing glare. Theodor put more pressure on the blade. The pain and burn made her scream. He branded her with his power.

"It won't happen again," she whispered.

Theodor stared at her a few extra seconds. He knew she lied, and stuck the dagger in the backrest, above her head.

She lifted her wide-open eyes to see the blade plunged into the thick wood, through the dusty velvet pillow. Fear radiated from her, feeding his ego.

"If you want to stay alive, make sure it doesn't. Otherwise, if death is what you seek, feel free to try again."

~ ~ ~

Malvina expected to see icicles forming everywhere in the room. His voice sounded colder than a glacier, his eyes emptier than black holes. The man lived up to his nickname.

Theodor stopped in the doorway and immobilized her with an icy stare.

"I'll contact you when I have an answer. Good night." He closed the door behind him.

Malvina touched the painful scar on the left side of her neck. A loud, angry roar pushed through her lips.

She had to swallow her pride, hide the hate and anger fueling every thought in her mind. Malvina had been planning her revenge and ascension for centuries. She couldn't afford any mistakes this close to succeeding.

Enjoy it while you can. Your coven will be mine. All covens will be mine.

"I hate you. I can't wait to kill you." She muttered between clenched teeth. Her hand closed around the wine bottle, and she threw it against the door.

The glass broke in hundreds of pieces and scattered on the dust-covered wooden floor.

~ ~ ~

Theodor heard the noise behind him, and a satisfied smirk tugged at his lips.

Malvina's attempt on his life could've provided enough of a reason to end her. But, with no witnesses, and her group so close to joining his coven, it could've brought doubt, affecting his reputation. There had to be another way. Marriage was out of the question.

The garden, a victim of just as much degradation, greeted him with familiar darkness, and he hurried to dial his coordinates. He couldn't wait to get out of there and take a much-needed shower.

And I need to check on Viv. Why do I keep thinking of her?

"I don't like this situation."

His whisper dissipated in the frigid air, turning into microscopic particles of ice. He enjoyed the cooling effect on his heated skin when he walked right through the mini cloud and into the portal.

Chapter 4

Theodor scrubbed himself in the shower until he was convinced he'd removed the layer of skin that Malvina had tainted with her touch.

Back in the living room, he tried to conclude the night's events. The meeting with Malvina assured him he could never trust her or let his guard down around her. She definitely had a plan.

Others had tried and failed to kill him. Malvina wasn't the first, and most probably not the last either. His hands twitched nervously, with the desire to end her games.

But her people could turn his ambition into reality. She had to stay alive for a while. He had to be careful. Perhaps find a way to make her drop her shield. A peek inside her mind became more of a necessity.

Viv... The thick rug absorbed the sound of his steps. He remembered her, walking barefoot, in the same room. She'd appeared weak, fragile and her terror sent shivers through his body.

The prospect of her being his destined one didn't appeal to him. Strong enough for two, Theodor could have overlooked her weaknesses, but he couldn't ignore her distrust and fear.

Maybe he should earn her trust. Prove to her that he wasn't a monster.

Why? What's the point? Do I want her in my life? If it's true and she is the one, am I going to regret letting her go? Should I just clear this night from her mind and take her back to where I found her?

"I need to know more," Theodor muttered under his breath.

With his head turned toward the door, he resisted the temptation to go inside her mind, and find the answers he craved.

He returned his stare through the glass doors, into the night. The blizzard raged. Immaculate snow had accumulated in a generous layer.

Still fighting his own decisions, Theodor peeked over his shoulder toward the door again. On impulse, he exited the living room and stopped in front of her guest suite.

New and improved versions of the old light bulbs, illuminating globes, floated in a predesignated pattern, painting moving light cones in the hallway. The new spheres used the technology found on the alien ship. They didn't need wires or fixtures, and were independent of electricity.

Polished wooden floors glimmered to life under the yellow, soft light. A deep-blue runner covered the middle of the long corridor. *If I could only absorb this calmness in my mind.*

Floor-to-ceiling windows at the end revealed more snowflakes fighting each other in the air, in a competition to land. They all won, in their own way, adding to the thick blanket.

The wind grew stronger, whistling from the other side of the walls.

Without a sound, Theodor opened the door and stepped inside the bedroom. With extra care, he approached and sat on the edge of her bed. She appeared peaceful in the faint light. A deep sigh left his lips, mixing with the muffled song of the blizzard.

Vivienne didn't have Malvina's striking beauty. Everything about her was subdued. Theodor probed into her mind. He needed to know what had happened to her, who she truly was under all the fear surrounding her like an invisible shield.

With the morning light flooding the room, she started to stir. Theodor didn't want her to wake and see him there. It would have frightened her more. *I'll wait outside.*

~ ~ ~

Vivienne blinked her eyes opened. A huge tree with bright red leaves right in front of the window captured her attention first. Snow decorated every branch. It created a bright spot of color against the gray, gloomy morning sky.

Too beautiful to be real. She turned her attention to the unfamiliar room. Vivienne hadn't experienced the luxury of a bed in a year. The soft mattress and the silk sheets suffocated her.

Her first reaction was to fight the covers away.

"May I come in?" A deep, raspy voice from the other side of the door startled her.

Panicked, Vivienne sat, tightening her hold on the light comforter. Her fists closed on the edge of the smooth fabric, and she glanced around one more time.

The previous night came back clear in her mind, hastening the blood through her body. Her lungs fell behind, unable to supply enough air for her racing heart.

"Good morning." Theodor didn't wait for an answer and swung the bedroom door wide open. "I hope you slept well." He stepped in.

"You . . ." Vivienne jumped out of bed, trying to put as much distance as possible between them. Her pulse thrummed in her ears. "What do you want from me?" All of her questions started to roll into an avalanche. "Why did you bring me here?"

"For starters, what about breakfast?" He advanced into the room. "I'm kind of hungry, and I can't stop thinking about coffee." Theodor came to a halt a few steps away from her.

She stared at him, apprehensive with doubt, wondering if she was on the menu. Her body quivered. The word *coffee* did the trick as much as the idea of food. She didn't trust him, but she was hungry.

"You're not going to kill me?"

"I'm not the monster you think I am." Theodor covered his heart with his right hand. "Everything you think you know about me is wrong, and I'd like to prove it."

"No thanks." Vivienne shook her head.

Her tangled hair moved and tickled her cheek. With shaking hands, she tucked the few strands behind her ears.

"I saved your life. I think I deserve at least the benefit of the doubt." Theodor gestured to the open bedroom door, inviting her to follow him.

"I need a moment first. Don't you dare come near me," she warned him. Vivienne pointed her index finger at him, trying to convince him that she meant business, in spite of her being half his size.

"I'll wait for you here." Theodor lifted his arms in a surrendering motion and took a step back.

Vivienne ran into the bathroom and slammed the door behind her. To be on the safe side, she locked it. Even if she slept in the clothes Carla had given her the previous night, they had to do. It was all she had. *I wish I had my safety bag. It's not helping me much from that locker in Central Station.*

Not even ten minutes later she came out and followed him to the living room. She made sure she stayed at least a step behind. *I need to keep an eye on him.*

Breakfast waited on the table in front of the wide French doors to the terrace. The big red tree lost a few leaves in the fight with a strong gust of wind. The ruby foliage settling in the snow made her realize it was real. *Hmm, I thought for sure it was a hologram. I guess I was wrong.*

~ ~ ~

After the first sip of coffee, Theodor glanced at her. She opened the jar with raspberry jam and spread some on a slice of toast, her attention divided between the rounded knife and every one of his movements. *She wasn't joking. Her distrust is going to be a problem.*

"Where would you like me to start?"

Vivienne chewed her toast quickly and stared at him. "How come you don't melt, or burn, or whatever it is you vampires do in the daylight?"

"Because I'm a hybrid."

"What does that mean?" she took another bite from the slice of bread smothered with jam.

"Like over ninety-five percent of the vampires in the world, I'm not bothered by daylight."

"Oh. Why not?" Vivienne stopped from chewing. "Wait, how many of your kind are out there?" Her hand gestured to the glass doors.

"About twenty thousand." He paused briefly, noting her rounded eyes. "My father's best friend, Doctor Daniel Holmes, invented a vaccine a few centuries ago." Theodor sipped from his coffee. "His genius discovery turned purebloods into hybrids."

"He sounds smart." She directed her butter knife at Theodor. "Or irresponsible, depending on the point of view."

"He literally revolutionized our kind's world. Very few vampires chose to stay purebloods, still sensitive to daylight." He placed his mug back on the table. "I also eat and drink normal food. I only need blood probably as much as you do, every few days."

Theodor bit from his own crunchy toast. *Okay, I admit, that was a cheap shot.* He purposely reminded her she belonged to the new species.

The way she lowered her gaze almost made him regret his small victory, earned too easy. "You shouldn't be ashamed of who you are."

A sad smile spread across her face. "You don't understand." She shook her head again. "GeMs are considered inferior, good for nothing, at the humans' mercy."

"That's wrong. GeMs are in fact the next step on the evolutionary scale." Theodor took a forkful from his omelet. "You're superior to humans. Most of your kind have incredible powers, abilities humans could never possess."

"That's not how they see it. Our need for blood pretty much turns us into slaves." The sadness in her tone bothered Theodor. She was wrong, and she didn't trust his words enough to believe him.

"Humans have feared vampires for over two thousand years. They've made up stories about us, hunted us. It's in the human's nature to fear and hate the unknown." Theodor sipped some more coffee, taking his time with the explanations. "We've learned throughout time to hide from them in plain sight, mix in, live among them, and let them believe in made-up myths."

"It's not the same for GeMs. Many humans refer to us as 'freaks' because of what our bodies need to survive."

He placed his hands on the table, his fists semi-closed. "I admit, in the old times, vampires fed on human blood, but that hasn't been the case for hundreds of years." He returned to his food and bit from a strip of crispy bacon. "I've never had human blood."

"Is it true that you're immortal? You don't age?"

Vivienne's curiosity won the fight against fear.

"It's true, but we're not impossible to kill."

"How old are you?"

"I'll turn five hundred in a few months."

"Are you serious?" Vivienne choked on her eggs and coughed a couple of times.

Theodor nodded and returned to his breakfast. At least for the moment, she seemed more comfortable with him, even if he wasn't her favorite person in the world.

"Wait a minute. If you are as old as you say, it means you lived through the Flood, in the Old World." Vivienne sipped again from her coffee. Pleasure covered her features instantly. "This coffee is so good."

"I only eat and drink conventional food, none of that synthetized stuff. As for the Old World and the Flood, yes, I did." He leaned against the backrest of his chair. For years he'd tried to forget those times. "I've seen the humans at their worst." Sadness circled around him every time he thought about the billions of dead he and his kind couldn't save.

"Tell me about it. I've read everything I could find, but there is so little information." Her eyes lit with excitement.

All her fear seemed to have succumbed to her desire to know more.

"I wouldn't know where to start. What do you want to know?"

"Everything."

Her answer made Theodor think of his sister. Both women shared the same thirst for knowledge. *They would get along just fine. Would they?*

"That would take a while, and before we venture down that path, I need some answers from you." Theodor smelled her fear resurfacing and hid his displeasure. "Today, I'm leaving. I'm going home." He stopped and waited for her reaction.

"This isn't your home?" Vivienne's hand froze in midair, holding a piece of bacon.

"This"—Theodor motioned around him-"is just one of my smaller properties. My home, my permanent residence, is south of Athens. I have an island where I live most of the time."

"You have an island?" She dropped the half-eaten strip of bacon on her plate.

It took all his control to stop himself from smiling. To be on the safe side, he covered his mouth with the napkin.

"Crete. I bought it after the Flood, while it was still under water." Theodor placed his dark-blue napkin on the table.

"What do you need an entire island for?"

"I hope to show you." Theodor rose to his feet and took a few slow steps. He stopped and whirled around, testing her again. "Come with me, you'll be safe."

"I can't." Vivienne hurried to shake her head. "I have to admit, I don't want to go back . . ." She hesitated for a couple of seconds, as if searching for her words. "Home. But I have no choice. If I don't return, Greg's going to turn me in." She lifted her gaze to him. "He has all my documents in a safe."

"Are you talking about the man who beat you almost to death?" He returned to his seat.

Vivienne nodded in silence. She wrapped her arms around her waist. Tears filled her eyes. In the daylight, her irises had turned golden.

After exploring her mind, he knew she had thought about leaving, running away, many times over the last year. When she finally did it, she hadn't counted on surviving the night.

The man who enslaved her kept her chained, starved, and weakened. He only gave her enough blood and food to keep her alive.

"I have to talk to you about something." He poured more coffee for both of them. "Healing is just one of my special abilities."

"What else can you do?" Curiosity sparked again.

"I can levitate people, objects, pretty much anything."

To demonstrate, Theodor motioned to his left and lifted one of the chairs from across the room.

"That's amazing," she whispered, her eyes rounded.

Theodor hid the amusement provoked by her reaction. The hard part of the conversation was still to come. He let the chair down slowly and turned his attention back to her.

"What else?"

"I can also control people's minds. I can hear anyone's

thoughts, see their memories, and influence their decisions."

"That sounds invasive." A deep crease appeared between her eyebrows. "And unethical," Vivienne added.

He sensed her fear spiking, surrounding her in a dark mist.

"Have you been inside my mind too?"

Theodor expected her question. She was a smart woman, a scientist.

"Yes. I have peeked into your most recent memories—"

"How much do you know?" It seemed patience wasn't her forte.

Mortals. They're always in a rush. Theodor heard the accelerated rhythm of her heart. "I don't abuse my power, and never have. I only wanted to know what happened to you, how you got in that alley, half-dead." He sipped more of his coffee, hoping his calm would find her, too. "I'm doing my best to keep out of your mind, but most times your thoughts are very loud, and as much as I'm trying to ignore them, they're just screaming at me."

"You said you can also control minds, influence what others think." The crease on her forehead smoothed. Her eyes narrowed to suspicious, golden slits.

Theodor noted the light tremor in her hand. She held the coffee cup halfway between her lips and the table.

"Correct. I didn't interfere with your decisions, if that's what you want to know." He placed his mug on the table. "Mind control is something I refrain from using unless I absolutely have to. I believe in everyone making their own choices"

Theodor breathed with relief when she accepted his explanations, even if they weren't what she wanted to hear.

"Is there anything else I should know?" She lifted the coffee mug to her lips.

"That's all that's different from other vampires. The rest is just basic, normal vampire stuff."

"Like?"

Theodor found her curiosity refreshing.

"Compared to humans, or what you are used to, there would be a significant difference when it comes to physical strength, speed, heightened senses." He nodded with each of the enumerated abilities. "I don't think I've missed anything. I've never talked about these things with anyone."

"How did you get me to sleep last night? Was that some sort of mind control?" Curiosity mixed with suspicion in her voice.

"No. It was another one of the basics, which I obviously omitted. It's called magnetism. In the old times, my kind used it on humans so they wouldn't suffer when the vampire fed on their blood." He leaned back again. "It places the subject into a controlled sleep, or in an almost hypnotic state."

"I see."

A few more seconds of silence floated between them, like a thick cloud, and Theodor walked away from the table.

At least she listened to what I had to say, and she's not running for the door. Not yet, anyway. His restlessness bothered him again. Her presence threw him off his usual calm.

"Since I know about your safety bag in the locker at Central Station, do you want me to send someone to retrieve it for you?" He had already admitted he'd been in her mind.

"It's all right. I don't want to be a bother."

"There's no bother. Jake, my assistant, would be more than willing to do it. You need some clothes"—he pointed to her feet— "and shoes."

At the mention of shoes, Theodor couldn't miss the way she curled her toes, as if she tried to hide them. *I'll give her the space to think about it.*

~ ~ ~

I want my bag, but he has already done so much for me. It's hard to believe he's real. A vampire . . . If he were a GeM, like me, I could have maybe—Oh, no. He might know what I'm thinking right now. She glanced toward him. The dark-navy, leather suit fit his body in a way that made her pulse accelerate.

Vivienne didn't expect miracles. They didn't exist. All she wanted was a normal life, or as close as possible to her idea of normality. Nothing would ever be the way she had dreamed. Everything was changed, forever.

Her fingers played with a button of the white shirt covering her. If he was in her mind, he didn't show any sign of it. Vivienne hoped he had better things to do than read her thoughts at all times.

"If you're sure it's not too much trouble."

"I'm positive." His flat answer sounded indifferent.

~ ~ ~

Theodor preferred to look away from her, not sure he could hide his smile. Her thoughts sent his blood on a trip to the heights of excitement. He only needed a few seconds to compose. As calm and calculated as always, he whirled around, facing her. He was on top of things again.

"Jake is on his way. When he gets back with your bag we can go."

"Wait. Did you send him before I agreed?"

"No, after. Just now. I can communicate with anyone I have a link with, no need for words. You want to try?" he asked, and Vivienne nodded.

"When he gets back, we can go to your place and get your documents, and everything else."

An excited smile appeared on her face. She wasn't afraid of him, at least for the moment, distracted by her fascination with his capabilities.

"I had never imagined all this was possible."

Theodor tilted his head. "Would you like more coffee?"

"Yes, thank you. About going to my place, I'm not sure it's a good idea."

"Why? You want your things, no?"

"Yes, but Greg might be there or come and . . ." Theodor sensed the claw of fear closing around her throat, stopping her from finishing her sentence. She jumped from one emotion to the next with a speed he found tiring.

"I'll come with you." Theodor clasped her wrist over the table. "I promise he won't touch you. He won't get past me."

"You don't know him. Even if he's human, Greg is the head of security at the research center." Vivienne withdrew her hand. "He's strong, always has a weapon. He's not—"

"He's human." Theodor interrupted her with determination. "You will be safe. I guarantee it." His chin jutted with confidence. "Do you know the combination for the safe?"

She just shook her head and took another sip from the hot coffee.

"Then we'll open it my way."

~ ~ ~

His words didn't fully register. Vivienne feared going home. Her hands trembled at the thought of the terrifying chains, and she almost dropped the coffee cup.

"How did you get infected? And why did this Greg guy hold so much power over you?"

Theodor's questions opened wide the gates holding back her memories.

"Over a year ago, Greg had asked me to marry him. We had already been living together for a couple of months. Maybe fate, or the fact I never loved him, stopped me from saying yes right away." Her voice fluctuated in spite of her efforts to sound steady. "I asked for a few days to think about it. Those few days . . ."

Vivienne shifted, uncomfortable in her chair under Theodor's scrutinizing gaze. Her mind traveled into the past, to the one night that changed everything.

"Only a couple of days after Greg's proposal, I stayed late at work, hoping to finish one of the tests. The results were slow."

"What kind of tests?"

"I was working with GeM blood samples, trying to isolate different genes." Vivienne felt more comfortable talking about her work than anything else.

"And, what happened?" Theodor leaned forward.

"I heard screams coming from a nearby building. The loud cries, and the pain behind them, reminded me of the rumors I heard before but never wanted to believe. Registered GeMs were subject to cruelty. Many had disappeared after visiting the center for blood donations." A deep sigh left her lips.

Theodor leaned back in his chair, he seemed comfortable.

"The second I decided to go and see with my own eyes if the rumors were true is still my biggest regret."

She fought back the tears, blinking a few times. A deep crease appeared between Theodor's brows, a sure sign he didn't liked what he'd heard.

"I'd never been in that building before, but my access card worked. Usually, one of my assistants went there and brought the genetic samples." Vivienne paused for a moment, then continued. "I walked through the labyrinth of barely illuminated, underground corridors, like those in a horror movie. From the room where they stored genetic samples, I peeked through the window into the next room. Every one of the rumors turned out to be terrifyingly true." Vivienne gasped for air.

"What did you see?" The tension in his voice expanded in his whole body. Muscles corded under the tanned skin.

"GeMs were chained and tortured." Guilt suffocated her. "All my work was based on those generous people willing to help science."

Hot and salty tears rolled down her face. She wiped them away in an attempt to control her emotions.

Theodor walked away from the table. After a few steps he turned to face her. A light twitch in his jaw traveled to his temple. *He really cares about others.*

More memories flashed in her mind, like lightning on a stormy summer night.

"Greg entered the containment area with a couple of his guards and hosed down a dozen or so GeMs with powerful jets of cold water. Clothes hung dirty and wet on skinny bodies. They all had bloodshot-red eyes." Vivienne paused for a few moments, her gaze fixated on the dark coffee. "After the water stopped, Greg and his two buddies started to kick and punch the poor people who lay crouched on the wet concrete floor." She could still hear their cries, and closed her eyes for a few moments.

Theodor returned to the table, pouring more coffee.

"If I ever met this guy, I'm going to kill him." An angry growl pushed through his clenched jaw.

Her hands clasped against each other. She squeezed them together so hard marks of her own fingernails imprinted into the pale skin.

"The sound of the explosion boomed in my ears, covering the desperate cries." Chills traveled her body. *It's just a memory. It's not real.* She wiped a few tears and sipped from the hot, black coffee.

"The genetic sample area, heavily insulated, had contained the blast to that one room." Vivienne lifted her gaze to Theodor. "I wasn't supposed to be there, blown against the thick wall with hundreds of shards from the broken vials darting my way." Her voice dwindled under the weight of her memories.

His hand covered hers, over the table. Comforting warmth radiated from his touch.

"I can still remember the exact moment I became infected. The physical pain had been nothing compared to the terrible knowledge that I had become a GeM."

"It was your destiny, accept it." Theodor gently squeezed her hand.

More tears made his image blurry.

Another sigh escaped her lips. "No," she whispered with sadness. "I became a slave that night."

Chapter 5

Serge hopped off the speeder on the private double landing. The penthouse his niece had in one of the skyscrapers came with this little luxury. After a few steps, he turned around to admire the view. The snow had slowed.

Paris. The new city didn't even resemble the old Paris he knew and loved. Where the Eiffel Tower used to dominate with its slick silhouette, a life-sized hologram flickered, a sorry attempt to match the once famous landmark. A bunch of ruins marked the place where Versailles once stood proud and majestic for centuries.

Serge let out a deep sigh, remembering the streets, the cafés, the art district, and the boats running up and down the Seine. It all belonged to a distant past, impossible to recreate. The City of Love, turned into a memory, had been replaced by just another sterile and gloomy settlement. *At least they kept the names.*

A gust of wind made his nose twitch. Aromas from a restaurant mixed with the smell of fresh fallen snow. The traffic lanes below continued to move in their endless humming.

Every time he visited his niece, memories haunted him.

For over eight hundred years, Serge had wandered Europe and lived many places, but Paris retained its special spot in his heart.

His twin brother had turned him there, after he accepted the invitation to become a vampire. Years later, in the same spot, they'd fought against each other and went their separate ways.

Almost two hundred years later, they met again, in a café. Green umbrellas had offered shade during torrid summer days and created intimacy in the crisp fall evenings. Scented flowers, in planters around the tables, had filled the animated streets with their sweet scent.

In Paris, he'd met the love of his life, Heather.

Serge shook his head and entered the golden, overly decorated living room. He sensed his niece's presence nearby. A bad vibe tingled the air.

One of the servants welcomed him and brought his favored green-colored tea. He was a regular, visiting at least once a month.

After the first sip, Serge let the memories continue to flow, bittersweet, like his tea.

Serge remembered his own shock when he'd found out he was an uncle. His brother never hid his disgust for humans, yet he had a daughter, Malvina. He kept her existence a secret. It turned out he had been wise to do so. At the time, Malvina had been twenty-nine, just turned, and in need of training.

"Uncle Serge, you're here already?"

They were supposed to go shopping for a special dress, and she wanted his opinion.

Malvina advanced into the room, interrupting his thoughts. Serge stood and turned to face her. Her red, fresh scar attracted his attention. She'd always been proud of her flawless skin.

"What happened?" His index finger pointed to her neck.

"Just a mishap." She waved her hand.

Serge sensed her anxiety. The earlier tingle intensified. Malvina had inherited her father's temper and character. For the last five hundred years, he feared that one day, in spite of his efforts, she would end up just like his brother.

"Come, sit. Have some tea and tell me about it."

She hesitated, and he grasped the severity of the situation. He knew her too well.

"It's not—"

"Don't tell me it's not important. If it wasn't, you wouldn't try to deny it."

In spite of hiding their blood ties, Serge remained the only person in the world who really knew her, trained her, and taught her everything she knew. He'd loved her unconditionally since the day they first met.

Malvina let her body sink into the soft cushions. The black leather couch rested on gold, curved legs Serge disliked. The sofa was too opulent for his simple taste.

"I see you had a tough night. I'm all ears."

With every word about her meeting with Prince Theodor, worry and disapproval grew inside him. Serge ran his hand through his dark, shoulder-length hair.

"Why am I finding out about all this just now?"

Serge took a few steps away from the couch. He stared absently somewhere outside. He couldn't see anything but old images flashing before his eyes. Distant times, fights between him and his brother.

"I was afraid you wouldn't approve. You always said that my father brought his death onto himself . . ." She lifted her gaze to him. "That he deserved to die."

"It's the truth." Serge turned around and faced her. "I've told you millions of times to stay away from their family." His hand waved toward the windows.

"I'll get my revenge. I promised myself I will and—"

"You don't get it, do you?" He took one step toward his niece. "All this will only get you killed." In a brief moment of fury, Serge hissed and whirled around again.

He needed to remain calm and convince her revenge wasn't worth the risk. His own reflection in the floor-to-ceiling glass stared back at him. Light hazel eyes filled with sadness.

"Uncle Serge, I need your help. We can get our revenge together."

Serge closed his eyes, hoping to stop the painful memories. It didn't work.

"What exactly do you think you will accomplish by convincing Prince Theodor De Croix to marry you?" He faced her again, afraid to hear her answer. "And don't tell me you love him. I know you better than that."

"As his wife, I can get close to him. I'll catch him with his guard down." She closed the distance between her and her uncle. "All I need is a couple of seconds, and I'm going to kill . . ." Malvina stopped, frozen her in place under her uncle's sharp gaze.

"You're not strong enough to kill him. Are you out of your mind?" His fangs glimmered in the bright light. "This is suicide."

"I can't best him in a direct fight. You are correct. I'm not sure anyone could for that matter. The bastard is impossible to take down that way." Malvina propped her hands on her hips. "But if he doesn't see my attack coming, he won't be prepared for it." Flames lit inside her eyes. "With his death, the rest of his family will be weakened. His snarky sister will follow him shortly." Malvina walked away from Serge, overtaken by excitement.

She's lost her mind. He followed her growing anticipation.

"With both the children dead, their parents might still be a challenge, but I will take them out, as well as the snobby Queen Emelia." She clasped her hands in front of her, as if holding the most precious thing in the Universe between them. "The Veres brothers will be the last ones. Killing Vlad's sons will bring me all the recognition I need."

Serge shook his head. He could see all the flaws in her plan. The death of one of the De Croix family would only serve to draw them closer together, harden their resolve.

But Malvina was stubborn, and all he could hope for was to dissuade her from the course of self-destruction she held so tight.

"You do realize, that once his family meets you, it'll be a matter of time before they'd know who you are, right?" He paused for a moment but didn't expect an answer. "Besides, Theodor can see your plans. He can get in your mind."

"Not if I keep my shield up at all times." With a spark of pride, she propped her hands on her waist.

"It would only make him more suspicious, have the reverse effect. Look at you, Malvina. You are alive only because he didn't want you dead."

Serge fought the impulse to yell at her, to shake her to reality, to try and make her understand.

"I'll have to move fast." She stood her ground.

"Yes, you should run," Serge agreed, "out of his way, out of his reach." He shoved his hands into his pockets, unable to stop them from trembling. "We should disappear for a while."

"No. This time we do it my way. I'm done running and hiding." Her chin jutted forward. "I'll kill Theodor and his blasted family." Resolve echoed in her voice. "I will unite the covens and claim leadership over all the vampires in the world." Her eyes glinted with a demonic light. "The pathetic humans won't stand a chance."

Serge had seen that glow before, in her father's eyes. That same demon lived inside her, too.

"So this is what you're after. You want power." He finally understood his niece's real motives. "Revenge for your father's death is just an insignificant part of it."

He stopped before anger could get the best of him and exited to the large terrace. His boots hit hard on the cold stone floors.

"Uncle Serge, I need your help, please," Malvina yelled, running after him. "He was your brother!"

"He was. All these years I've missed him dearly. Unlike you, I never used his death as a catalyst, or pretended I wanted revenge." Serge covered his chest with an opened hand. "I tried my best to keep you from following in his footsteps. The path you have chosen to walk leads to death." He moved his hand to her shoulder and lowered his voice. "I saw your father make mistakes, deadly ones. Now you are desperate to take the same road to destruction. I couldn't stop him. His thirst for power ended him. We can go away, leave all this behind." He had to try one more time to change her mind.

"I can't believe you are turning your back on me." Malvina stepped away from him.

"I won't help you get killed." Serge darted for his speeder.

"Uncle Serge!" she yelled behind him.

He glanced at her over his shoulder. "We'll keep in touch."

Serge took off on the recreational speeder he'd rented and dropped off the terrace, merging into one of the traffic lanes. He could barely see anything ahead of him.

Ivan . . . Brother . . . I have failed you. She has too much of you in her.

~ ~ ~

Jake returned with Vivienne's bag in only a few minutes. Theodor waited for her in the living room.

He measured her from her ponytail to the black tennis shoes she wore. "Not exactly winter wear."

His remark brought a pink blush to the tips of her delicate ears. Plain jeans, a hoodie over a thin shirt, and the comfy shoes were not great in snow.

"I wasn't thinking of winter. It's an emergency bag. It will have to do for now."

Theodor shook his head and opened a gateway.

They exited the portal about fifty yards from Greg's place. *At least she doesn't have to walk through the snow for long.*

The duplex welcomed them with a quiet calm. Theodor scanned around the clean, almost sterile home, and followed her upstairs to the bedroom.

Vivienne hurried to move the picture hiding the safe.

"Step back."

He punched it once, and the door caved in, crumpling like cardboard. Theodor pulled one of the edges and opened the safe, giving her access to the contents.

Vivienne grabbed a flat box and the envelope with her documents, ignoring everything else. After one quick glance, as if to make sure everything was inside, she threw them in her purse, and rushed to pack the rest of her things.

Theodor noticed the chains on the floor between the bedroom and the connected bathroom as soon as they entered. Old-fashioned, made from heavy, rusted metal, they were stained with blood.

Theodor sniffed it, and recognized it as belonging to Vivienne. He wished Greg would show up, so he could make him suffer.

As if answering his request, the entrance door opened and a couple of seconds later closed. Theodor sensed her fear spiking.

"It's him . . ." Vivienne whispered and froze, with clothes clutched tightly in her hands.

Theodor bolted to her side.

"Everything is going to be all right. Finish packing, and don't worry about him." He moved her hands toward the duffel bag where she had already thrown some clothes.

Vivienne shivered, and an empty stare settled in her eyes.

The rushed, heavy steps on the stairs made Theodor turn to face the door.

"I knew you would be back. I see you brought a friend. Are you also a freak?" Greg measured Theodor.

"If you mean nonhuman, then yes."

Theodor's response brought disgust and a grimace of superiority to Greg's face.

Only a couple of inches taller than Vivienne, Greg had a muscular build, making him appear stocky.

He pulled a gun from the back of his pants and pointed it toward Theodor, ready to fire.

"I'm going to tell you this only once." Theodor confronted him with a calm, deep voice. "Don't try to fight me. You can't win." His blood boiled inside with the force and intensity of a volcano.

"You need to learn your place, slave." A grin stretched Greg's thin lips over uneven, crooked teeth. One of the front ones was half-missing. "I won't fight you, I'll kill you." He aimed toward Theodor's forehead.

Before his finger even touched the trigger, Theodor had disarmed him and held him with one hand closed around his throat about a foot above the ground. Greg's legs dangled at first, then he tried to kick.

"No, you don't know *your* place," Theodor hissed, letting the other man see his fangs.

"An abomination with fangs. This is new."

In spite of Greg's apparent cool, reality set in. Theodor indulged in the familiar smell of fear.

"How many ribs did you have broken, Viv? Was it three?"

Theodor ignored Greg's kicks. The shorter man could barely touch him. His hands tried and failed to unclench the powerful grip around his throat.

Without waiting for an answer, Theodor hit the other man. His fist connected, and the sound of one broken rib filled his ears like a delightful symphony.

Greg's moan of pain didn't bother Theodor, and he started his count. "One."

"If you think a broken rib will stop me"—words exited Greg's mouth between gasps of air—"you don't know me."

"You're scum. I'm familiar with your kind." Theodor displayed a repulsed grin. His second punch landed, breaking another rib. "Two."

"I'll kill you." Greg couldn't even kick in Theodor's direction anymore. "Both of you," Greg yelled. White foam formed at the corner of his mouth.

"I don't think so." Theodor shook his head. "You are weak and inferior." For the third time, his fist impacted Greg's ribs. "Three."

Another groan revealed unbearable pain. The hate in the other man's eyes incited Theodor. He dropped him to the floor.

Greg couldn't stand. He tried to drag himself across the floor to the nearest wall. "If it wasn't for the broken ribs, I would kill you."

"Is that so?" Theodor arched his right brow with interest. "Let's test that theory. Shall we?"

Theodor dropped to one knee and placed his right hand on Greg's abdomen, healing the broken ribs. The mix of confusion and fear in his adversary's eyes stirred Theodor's inner beast, who surfaced and fed on it.

"What did you just do to me?"

"I healed you." He rose to his feet. "You want to fight me, go ahead." Theodor opened his arms in an invitation. "I might even let you touch me."

When he'd healed Greg, Theodor sensed Vivienne's fear reaching new heights. Her hands started to shake with the two shoe boxes she held.

Theodor glanced over his shoulder. His eyes met hers. *"Don't worry, keep packing."* He pushed his words into her mind, setting her in motion. She dropped the boxes beside the bag.

Greg launched himself. Theodor avoided him. His body blurred in circles around the other man. He knew how to scare humans with his speed.

"Coward. You keep running away from me." Frustration was evident in Greg's tone—he couldn't land one blow. "Are you afraid?"

"Fine. I'll let you hit me." Theodor pointed to his jaw.

Greg didn't wait for a second invitation. His fist shot forward to make the first contact. The sound of every bone in his right hand shattering mixed with his moans of excruciating pain.

"What the hell are you?" he asked, preparing to deliver another blow with the other hand.

Theodor reopened his arms wide with a condescending air, enticing Greg to take his best shot. The second hit, to his stomach, had no effect whatsoever on Theodor.

"I'm your death," Theodor hissed and indulged in the new wave of terror washing over the human in front of him. It wasn't a fair fight, but he didn't care.

"Now . . . Where were we?" Theodor asked with sarcasm as his fist broke one of Greg's ribs. "One."

"No. Not again." Greg anticipated the next hit. He took one step back in an attempt to reach the wall behind him.

"Two." Another rib snapped with a muffled sound.

Theodor continued his count, eliciting more fear. He wanted his opponent to foresee the next blow and the pain coming with it.

With two broken ribs, and his right hand useless, Greg hunched in pain.

"I should've chained you and beat you, like you did her." Theodor waved toward Vivienne. "How does it feel to be helpless in front of someone stronger than you? Three."

"Vivienne, make him stop," Greg begged, his voice just above a whisper. Talking with broken ribs hurt. "I love you."

"You have got to be kidding." Theodor's disgust hit the walls, the same walls that had witnessed Vivienne's tears, her suffering, her humiliation. *This sorry excuse for a man is trying to manipulate her.* Theodor glanced toward Vivienne.

She continued to pack with trembling hands, as if she didn't hear him.

"We were going to marry," Greg tried again.

Theodor circled around him, like a lion hunting his prey. "I bet. You're quite a charmer. The gifts you gave her every day were memorable."

Vivienne zipped closed the second bag containing her things. Theodor sensed her fear spiraling out of control. He closed his right hand around the other man's neck and lifted him off the ground, this time against the wall.

Greg's boots hit the plaster. He tried to use it as leverage to free himself.

Theodor tightened his hold on Vivienne's tormentor. He took his time, prolonging the agony.

Greg's heels marked the wall behind him. The scraped paint and small rubble dusted the dark hardwood flooring, the same surface that had held Vivienne's tears and spilled blood.

Theodor tilted his head to one side and stared in his adversary's eyes. Greg hung defeated, at his mercy, but Theodor wasn't in a merciful mood. "You are a disgrace to humans everywhere."

Theodor hissed between his fangs. He wanted to make sure the last image in Greg's memory would be a terrifying one. With one flick of his wrist, he broke Greg's neck and let his lifeless body hit the floor.

"You . . . You killed him." Vivienne whispered, blinking rapidly. She covered her mouth with her hands.

"Of course, I did. He deserved it." Theodor lifted his gaze to her. "Are you all right?"

He charged to her side. Color drained from her face, making him think she would faint.

"I doubt I'll ever be all right."

Theodor picked up her bags with ease and walked to the door, stepping over the body blocking his way. To his surprise, Vivienne pushed Greg's body with the tip of her shoe. The way she stared at him made Theodor fight an involuntary smile.

She didn't fear the man anymore.

Tears rolled from her eyes, and she continued to stare. Without any warning, she kicked him.

"You bastard." All of her suffering came out through anger. Every kick into the lifeless body brought her closer to getting her closure.

Theodor set the bags down just outside the room and approached Vivienne. He didn't interrupt her. She needed to close that chapter of her life, and she chose to do it with kicks.

This is a nice surprise. I didn't think she would have the courage. His gaze moved from Vivienne to the slumped body she hit and back. He held in an amused smile and made a call.

"I need you to make it look like a robbery gone bad," Theodor instructed Jake at the end of their brief conversation. He turned his attention back to Vivienne.

"Viv." About fifteen minutes later, he tried for the first time to stop her.

"He was a monster. He didn't deserve to live," she continued to yell and slam her foot into Greg's body.

"I know. That's why I killed him." He closed his hands on her shoulders. "You've kicked him enough. Let's go."

Theodor tried to remove her from the room, but she wouldn't go. She couldn't stop. He turned her to face him.

"That's enough, Viv. He's dead." His tone was low and serious, holding that much more weight. "He can't hurt you anymore. Let it go."

Vivienne cried in his arms, until Jake entered the room followed by a group of three men. Theodor nodded toward them and helped Vivienne to the door. Limping, she stopped in the doorway.

"It's all in the past." Theodor directed her away from her former prison. "He's a fleeting memory now."

Before taking another step, Vivienne turned her head again toward the man who had enslaved and tormented her.

"Rot in hell."

Chapter 6

Theodor dropped the bags and carried Vivienne to the couch for the second time in less than twenty-four hours. He helped her sit and kneeled.

This is becoming an occurrence I could do without. She's not strong enough to keep getting hurt like this. Even if he killed Greg, Theodor was still mad at him. *I wish I could kill him all over again, and again, and again.*

He took off his leather gloves with quick and short movements. At least he hadn't forgotten them this time.

"Let's see the damage."

Gently, he pulled off her wet shoe, letting it hit the floor with a muffled thud. Vivienne's moan of pain stopped him briefly, but he had to continue. She had two broken toes. Theodor nested her foot between his hands.

"It's going to be all right. You kicked him good."

He tried to lighten the mood, sensing her sudden discomfort. She started to shake in his hands, and he blamed it, as usual, on the cold. Her shoes, wet from the short walk in the snow, the only logical explanation.

The light reflected off his onyx ring, attracting Vivienne's attention.

"Interesting ring. Is it some sort of heirloom?" She couldn't hide her curiosity.

Theodor peeked at his right hand.

"Yes, all the men from my bloodline wear one. There are three of us."

"What do you mean?" she insisted.

Theodor decided it was as good of a time as any to tell her the truth.

"I am a direct descendent of Vlad Veres."

"The vampire?" Her eyes rounded.

"No, the commander of the southern stuffed bunnies." He paused waiting for at least a smile from her. It never came. "Of course, the vampire."

"You mean he's real?"

Theodor nodded. "He was. Vlad died about a thousand years ago. His sons, Mihai and Gabriel Veres, are my uncles, the other two wearing rings." Theodor glanced again to his. "They kept this one, which belonged to Vlad"—he wiggled his pinky— "locked away in a vault for centuries, hoping one day another man belonging to their bloodline would emerge."

"And that is you." Her eyes lingered on the black ring.

The two elaborate symbols resembling the letter 'V' faced each other, holding a multifaceted onyx between them.

"Yes."

"Is that why people call you *Your Majesty?*"

"No." Theodor shook his head. "My mother's side of the family is Veres. My father's is royalty." He opened his hands, releasing her foot. "My grandmother, Queen Emelia, was born a princess." His explanations left Vivienne speechless.

Theodor figured she needed some time to process everything.

With the pain gone and her foot healed, Vivienne avoided his gaze.

"Thank you for everything." The sadness in her whisper disappointed Theodor. *What the hell was I expecting?*

He rose to his feet and walked away from her.

"It was the least I could do. We are going to have some lunch."

"Huh?"

"Lunch, the meal in the middle of the day. Do you remember it?" He heard his own annoyed tone.

"For almost a year while I was Greg's prisoner, I didn't have any." Tears threatened, and her lower lip quivered.

Her sentence floated in the air for a while, until Theodor interrupted the uncomfortable silence.

"I need to take care of a few things. I'll only be a few minutes." He left the room, giving her some space.

~ ~ ~

Her eyes tracked his movements until he exited, and the door closed behind him. He'd worn another one of the navy-blue leather suits, without the long coat from the previous night. Every living cell in her body sang a tune she didn't recognize when he'd carried her in his arms, making her dizzy.

When he'd knelt in front of her, a black medallion slid on a matching chain from under his vest. It resembled a shield, with symbols on it. Leftover tears hadn't allowed her to see them well.

His deep-blue eyes intrigued her most. She could swear there were tiny wisps dancing in them at times. An accelerated pulse pounded in her temples, and she massaged them, closing her eyes.

Suddenly, reality struck her, and she opened her eyes. *No. This is not happening. I can't be attracted to him. He's a vampire, a descendent of the most powerful of them. And a prince. We belong to different worlds, different species.*

She wrapped her arms around her waist, trying to control the shiver coursing through her body. She failed.

The snow had stopped, and the sun tried to smile between gray clouds. Vivienne shook her head and ran to her bags. *I have to leave.*

~ ~ ~

Theodor had to regain his control. Vivienne threw him off his usual composed self. There was nothing to take care of. He needed a reason to put some distance between them. *What the hell am I doing? Why do I want her to come with me? Why do I care? Maybe she won't. If she decides to walk away, so be it. That should take care of destiny's mistake. She can't be the one.*

"She just can't," Theodor growled, pacing the hallway.

He'd stayed in her mind even if he had left the room. Her earlier reactions and thoughts resonated in his body. Theodor grew mad at himself.

She wasn't the first pretty girl attracted to him. There were hundreds of them, maybe more. Who could remember them all? He should do what he always did. Not care.

A servant carrying their lunches walked past him and into the living room. Theodor kept his distance, trying to figure out his next move.

Damn it. I have better things to do than sit here and try to find answers to questions I don't even know. With his decision made, he re-entered the room.

A sudden and unexpected wave of tenderness swept over him—a long forgotten feeling. Her left leg bent beneath her body, Vivienne sat on the soft rug, lacing up a boot on her right foot. A winter coat rested on top of the bags.

An invisible force guided his steps, and he approached her in silence. She barely made it up to his knee. His hands itched with a mix of empowerment and desire he had never experienced before.

"Looks like you're ready to go."

Startled, Vivienne lifted her face to him only for a second, returning her gaze to the tan-colored boots.

He noticed the spark of fear even if it vanished as quick as it appeared. Theodor held back a growl.

"Yes. I've caused enough commotion. I'll be out of here in a—"

"Are you in a hurry to get to Paris?" Theodor cut into her explanation with a tone as cold and sharp as an ice blade.

At his words, her hands froze on the long laces.

"I guess you know about Paris." Her answer infuriated Theodor.

"What is it there? Do you have friends or family waiting for you?" he asked without a trace of compassion.

"No. I don't have anyone."

"Everyone has somebody, some sort of family." Theodor suspected she hid something.

With shaking hands, she continued to lace her boot. She had to try to tie the ends a few times.

"I don't. My grandmother, Pearl, raised me." Her voice withered to a whisper. "She died four years ago."

Theodor crossed his arms over his chest. He regretted he hadn't investigated her mind deeper.

"Where are your parents?"

Vivienne pulled on the other boot and started to tighten the laces with slow movements, as if trying to keep busy, to buy time.

"I never met them. My mother died. I killed her—"

"What? How did you kill her?" Theodor's tone rose, a rare occurrence. *What kind of monster is she? How could she kill her own mother?*

"She died when she gave birth to me."

"That doesn't mean you killed her." Theodor let out a relieved breath.

"That's what my grandma used to say." She glanced in his direction, then returned her attention to her boots. "She told me my mother's own foolishness killed her, when she ran away with a man she knew nothing about."

Theodor waited for her to continue. Instead, silence stood between them like a barbed wire fence.

She finished with her laces and rose to her feet. Her

boots seemed light and the soft suede far from appropriate against the cold or snow.

"Was that man your father?"

Vivienne shrugged, keeping her eyes on the pattern of the thick rug. A few strands of hair slipped over her shoulders, hiding her face.

"I assume so. Grandma Pearl never told me his name or anything else about him." She straightened the hoodie she wore. "I'm not sure if she didn't know or didn't want me to."

Theodor uncrossed his arms. He had jumped to judge her, to call her a monster, and now guilt lingered around him.

"Come, let's eat. Lunch is getting cold."

She followed him to the table and sat in the chair he held out for her.

"If that's the case, why do you want to go to Paris? Why not any other city?"

He noted her hands folding on her lap, an obvious sign of discomfort. She crossed her ankles and her left foot tapped the air. *I make her nervous. Good, maybe she'll stop trying to hide things from me.*

"Paris has the highest concentration of GeMs, or so I remember from older statistics. I figured it would be easier to find a safe place and a job."

She finally gazed at him through the steam rising from the black glass bowls.

"I see." Theodor started to eat, hoping she would too.

He continued to monitor her thoughts, not wanting to miss anything. *At least she relaxed if nothing else.*

"This soup went straight to my soul. Thank you."

Theodor nodded and both of them finished their soup in silence.

"You said you are a biochemist, right?"

Vivienne took a sandwich from the plate he held in front of her. "Yes."

"Then it shouldn't be hard to find a job. Scientists are in high demand." Theodor examined her with curiosity.

She didn't react to his reassurance.

All right. I'm only going to try this once. If it works, fine. If it doesn't, it's maybe for the best.

"You could work at the research center on the island." Theodor stared at her. "You would of course have to sign a *silent agreement*, which is a non-disclosure contract, just like everyone else—"

"Are you offering me a job?" Vivienne narrowed her eyes. Suspicion thickened the air around them.

"I guess I am. You could live in one of the small villas. Everyone living on Crete is either a vampire or a human that knows about us." He took a bite from his sandwich. The smoked meat was one of his favorites. "No one from the outside world can step foot on the island without a special pass. It is, after all, private property." Theodor finished chewing, then swallowed. "The humans living on Crete are the most protected ones in the world. The security is tight, and there are rules, but I believe you would like it."

"What makes you think I would like to live on an isolated island full of vampires?"

Oh, yeah. There's that. Well, what better way to understand my kind?

A multitude of answers entered his mind, but after closer consideration, Theodor figured they were all too snarky, and she would probably misunderstand him. And why did he care?

"You want a safe place, where you can live without fear, without hiding who you are. On Crete, nobody is above anyone else." He picked up the rest of the sandwich off his plate. "Humans, vampires, GeMs, all have their strengths and their weaknesses. It would be the perfect place for you to learn the truth about us, knowing you're safe at all times.

I can guarantee you that." He closed his argument and took another mouthful.

Vivienne's mind raced a thousand miles per second and Theodor found it hard to keep up with all her thoughts.

~ ~ ~

His offer tempted her. If it wasn't for all those vampires, she would've accepted right away. All her life she'd followed her grandmother's advice and always thought of consequences before taking any action. She had never acted on an impulse.

Except one time, two years ago, when she got promoted to lead of a research team in Vienna. That same day she'd booked herself the most expensive trip she found. It remained the most daring thing she had ever done.

This time wasn't a vacation but a life-changing decision.

"I'll think about it."

"Good. You have about an hour."

Vivienne's sandwich dropped on the glassy surface of the plate in front of her. The slices of bread bounced and revealed the meat and cheese inside. He expected her to make such an important decision in an hour?

"You're joking, right?"

"Do I look like it?"

She hated when people answered with a question.

"I've told you earlier I'm going home today."

She lowered her gaze to the half-eaten grilled sandwich. *What a mess.* With the tips of her fingers, she pushed the tomato slice that had slid away into place.

Vivienne considered her chance to start fresh. She could still have at least a version of what she considered a normal life.

Old dreams, forgotten in the past year, worked their way back into her mind. Since she could remember, Vivienne worked hard toward becoming the world's most renowned scientist, finding a cure for GeMs.

Can I trust him? Vivienne glanced in Theodor's direction, only to see him walk away from the table. He pressed a couple of buttons on his bracer and all kinds of screens popped up. He seemed absorbed in reading them, and Vivienne continued to study him.

Good looking men are jerks. They know the power they have over women, and they don't hesitate to use it. Her grandmother's words echoed true in her mind. She already made that mistake. Twice.

Theodor had saved her life, and he didn't show any interest in her. He never smiled or gave her any reason to think he would try to get in her bed. *Maybe vampires don't smile?*

What if he was her guardian angel? Her great-great-grandmother had one, the beautiful woman dressed in white who saved her during the Flood sixteen generations ago. Maybe he was hers.

And all those vampires? Vivienne still thought they killed humans. She searched deep in his eyes, glancing over the multiple screens. They seemed empty and cold in spite of the deep, rich cobalt color.

~ ~ ~

I could say so many things to her right now, but I'm not going to. This is her decision. I can't believe I'm allowing someone else to make a choice for me. One of this importance. Should I influence her and get this done with? Damn it, I, myself, don't know what I want her decision to be.

Theodor closed the opened screens and returned to his seat. The chair squeaked under his weight.

Vivienne lifted her golden eyes to him.

"What do you want in exchange?" she asked.

"What do you mean?"

"You are giving me a safe place to stay, a job. Nothing is free in this world, so what do you want from me?" Her insistence bothered him.

"Nothing." Theodor stopped for a second. *Liar,* his conscience screamed from deep within. "Even if I am offering you a job, you still have to do it. The villa where you will live is not rent-free. The salary from your job is double what anyone else would pay." He stood and paced. "I want you to have a fair chance at a new life, discover who you are, what you want. I believe you've had enough suffering." Outside, the white snow sparkled under the sun's caress. "You're free to do anything you want, leave anytime you think you've had enough of Crete."

Theodor noticed her doubt. Vivienne had admitted to herself she lived on borrowed time. If he hadn't turned into that dark alley, the previous night would've been her last.

Theodor shook his head. He couldn't say anything without admitting he'd been in her mind nonstop. *Better keep quiet.*

"I'll come with you, on one condition."

He tensed, his jaw clenched, and he felt the muscles twitching under his skin. *What is it with all these women? What makes them think they can impose their terms on me? Does it say 'stupid' on my forehead?* He hid his anger and nodded to her.

"You will have to tell me everything about the Flood and the Old World." Her shy smile almost melted his heart. Almost.

Theodor exhaled, relieved. He could live with her terms. "Deal."

~ ~ ~

His home on Crete surpassed Vivienne's expectations. In addition to the numerous towers, the castle had breathtaking views. It reminded her of her luxury vacation. *That's twice in one hour.*

Outside, on the terrace, she inhaled loudly, giving Theodor some space with his people. He barked orders right and left. Shuffled, rushed steps resonated on the ivory stone floors.

At her right, white crested waves caressed the pink sand. On the left side, they crashed against rocks. She stood at what seemed to be a crossroads between different worlds. Vivienne lost herself in the moment. Her own life had reached the point of no return. Nothing would ever be the same.

With her transition into the GeM's world, her existence spiraled beyond her ability to control it. Theodor gave her the chance to take hold of her own life once again.

She took off the hoodie and tied the sleeves around her waist. The hot, humid air infused her body with warmth. *Hard to believe that only a few hours ago I almost froze to death.*

The beach went for miles and miles. Ribbons of pink and white sand intertwined in a hypnotic effect. On the other side, boulders were stacked in a majestic, impenetrable wall.

She closed her eyes for a few seconds, leaning against the banister, and imagined sitting there, admiring sunsets.

Theodor's deep breath, right beside her, startled her back to reality. He stood tall, with his hands clasped behind him.

"It's always good to be home."

He seemed happy. Who wouldn't be happy here?

"This is incredible," she whispered, turning her attention back to the spectacular blue sea.

"I'm glad you like it. I hope you won't regret your decision."

"Are you kidding me? This is paradise."

~ ~ ~

Vivienne opened her arms and twirled. Her eyes glistened, a perfect match with her wavy hair. Rivers of flowing honey, soft caramel silks billowing in the wind, and warm, tangerine sunsets came into Theodor's mind.

A warm breeze played in her hair, and a few strands danced around her face. Theodor fought the urge to touch them.

"Paradise. Do you believe in it?" he asked, curious.

Vivienne hesitated, delaying her answer.

Theodor's gaze turned to the ever-moving water. With her by his side, even the sea appeared different, calmer and more beautiful. When the universe rearranged for him the previous night, it revealed a better world.

"I'm not sure. If you would have asked me that question yesterday, I would have told you I believe in hell. I've lived in it."

The glow in her eyes vanished.

Chapter 7

Serge entered the greenhouse and inhaled the warm air in spite of the blizzard raging outside. About twenty years ago he'd built it and planted with his own hands all the varieties of heather bushes he could find. Various species bloomed at different times throughout the year. It was his sanctuary, her shrine.

The white frames formed a sizeable octagonal-shaped construction enclosed with double-pane glass panels. The golden tint made it seem sunny even during the most stubborn storm. Serge's dragging steps led him down a narrow pathway to the bench in the middle, right by the oval-shaped pond.

A deep sigh left his lips the moment he sat and pressed the tiny button on the side of the antique, wooden bench. A life-sized hologram came to life—a beautiful woman with golden-brown hair and lavender eyes smiled and twirled atop the heather bushes. Her laugh filled his heart.

"Heather, my love . . ."

Painful memories intertwined with the happiest ones in his mind, and a sad smile tugged at the corners of his lips. Thirty years later, he loved her as much as he did the day he made that recording.

He allowed himself to dwell in the lost world for a while. It had been a long time since hopes and plans for a happy future busied his mind. Hiding who and what he was from the woman he loved had proven to be the biggest mistake of his life.

Serge bent forward and held his head in his hands. He had lost Heather the moment the truth came out. The memory of her terror still sent shivers through his body. Revealing he was a vampire made her run. He figured she needed some time and space to deal with everything, accept him. He had never seen her again.

Worn by the strong emotions, Serge straightened, leaning on the backrest. The wood squeaked in protest under his weight. Every single day for two decades, he'd searched for the love of his life, rummaged every city in the world. He never found her, as if she had evaporated in thin air.

So many times, Serge wished to have been more like his brother. He should have stopped and turned her that night. Regrets didn't help. He wasn't like his brother. Perhaps being a vampire wasn't for him.

From a distance, he'd witnessed his parents ageing, brokenhearted after they'd lost both their sons. They died only days apart. The girl he'd thought he loved at the time moved on after his disappearance, married, lived her life, and withered slowly.

Next, he lost his twin brother, Ivan. Their physical appearance was almost identical except for the color of their eyes, light hazel versus deep brown. In all other aspects, they couldn't have been more contradictory.

Malvina, his niece, became the center of his life. He went to great lengths to keep both of them out of any entanglements that would've drawn attention. As Ivan's brother and daughter, their execution would've been certain and swift. The Veres and De Croix families led the New World, their influence and power unquestionable.

When Serge met Heather, for the first time in his long, lonely life, he learned the true meaning of the word *happy*. He had thought she was his chance to live the life he always wanted. It all summed up to six months shadowed by his lies. The hope to find her faded every passing day.

Left with nothing and no one, except Malvina, Serge couldn't afford to lose her too. He couldn't bear it.

"Foolish child." His muttered whisper had no witnesses.

The night had swallowed yet another day when Serge rose from the bench and turned off the hologram. Exhausted, he hauled himself into the house through the snowstorm. A warm, crackling fire welcomed him in the study.

The storm raged outside, and the wind sent long, sinister whistles into the darkness. With a glass of red wine in hand, he sat in the comfortable chair. The light from the fire danced with shadows. He needed a plan. That was his forte.

"I will find a way."

~ ~ ~

"Are you ready to see your new home?" Theodor's question ended the long silence.

"Yes, of course." Vivienne's pulse accelerated with anticipation. *A new beginning is always exciting.*

He motioned toward the door. Five minutes later, they left the palace grounds in a speeder.

The short ride gave her a chance to see a small part of the island. Guards patrolling everywhere made her uneasy, knowing already they were all, or mostly, vampires.

Theodor had told her he rebuilt the island almost one hundred years after the Flood, when it emerged from the water. Crete was a recreation of the Old World, a sanctuary for vampires from all over the world, regardless of their allegiance.

"What about the rest of the island?"

"Farmlands and wilderness. Most farmers are humans, providing fresh produce and animals." His gaze never left the busy road.

Her mind swirled with visions of magical lands she only read about in old books. It was hard to believe a place like that existed.

With only the one city, towered by Theodor's palace, the island was home to about fifty thousand people.

Vivienne took in every detail on their ride. *Magical indeed.*

Shops and restaurants, houses and real vegetation all around, gave the island a certain air, different from the rest of the world. There were no impersonal black skyscrapers or busy speeder air lanes. *I love it.*

~ ~ ~

The heat in the middle of the day and the strong sun brought a glow to her skin and shimmering gold back into her eyes. Theodor studied her with increased attention and amusement. She exuded excitement and animation. *It seems she likes Crete I wonder if she's ready for her next test.*

Theodor turned a sharp corner and entered a residential area. He stopped in front of one of the white houses situated all the way back into a cul-de-sac. Hand extended, Theodor jumped off the speeder first, helping Vivienne do the same.

"This is it."

He studied every one of her reactions. Vivienne's eyes rounded with surprise in front of the one-story home with mature flowering trees on either side.

A smile stretched her lips at the sight of the branches bent under the weight of thousands of tiny, hot-pink blossoms. Multicolored flowers filled the planters placed on lush, green grass. Sweet and fresh scents swirled all around.

He advanced with Vivienne by his side on the walkway and stopped at the entrance under the small overhang.

"Please place your hand on the screen." Theodor had programmed the access panel to respond to her palm print, making sure the system recognized her.

"Is this for security, or just instead of a key?"

"Both." Theodor pressed more buttons and entered a password. The panel flashed green.

He opened the door. "Welcome to your new home."

Timid steps carried her inside. Theodor followed and closed the door. A click assured him it was locked. *Good, she should be safe here.*

Immaculate white stone floors with a matte finish echoed under Vivienne's steps. *Humans make so much noise when they walk.*

A spacious living room, separated by two thick, round columns from the dining room, had little furniture, the basics. Two couches covered in a soft cream fabric faced each other with a low, glass-topped table nestled between them. The low arrangement of white roses sat in the middle of the table, in a bright red vase.

"The flowers are beautiful. Are they real?" Vivienne ran to them.

"Of course, they are. You're on Crete. Here, pretty much everything is real."

Her right knee rested on the soft rug, and she buried her nose in the scented flowers. She inhaled loudly, closing her eyes.

"They smell so good . . ."

Is this the first time she's seen flowers? Theodor continued to scrutinize her with interest. It seemed like she just discovered the world around her.

Allowing himself to see the surroundings through her eyes, he indulged in her excitement.

He continued to show her around, from room to room. The dining room contained a round table and chairs. A flat glass tray held an assortment of fruits.

The kitchen was clean and basic. The synthesizing unit took most of the back wall.

"Do you know how to cook? And I mean conventional food." Theodor pointed to the six burners stove.

Honey ringlets danced around her face when she shook her head. "No. But I'm a pro with a synthesizing unit."

"Here is your chance to learn, if you want. Farmers come every day to the market we passed by when we came." His thumb signaled over his shoulder. "The produce is always fresh and affordable, unlike in the big cities."

Theodor remained alert and carefully attentive to every one of her thoughts. He didn't want to miss anything. Her short vision of the two of them having dinner, in spite of the fact she had no idea how to cook, made him tilt his head with increased interest.

A long hallway led to the simple but spacious bedroom. On the way, Vivienne found the luxurious bathroom across the dressing room where her things waited to be unpacked.

Her excitement filled the small villa. He expected to see the roof blowing off.

Theodor saved the terrace for last. The sea view made Vivienne lean against the stone half wall with a happy giggle. He searched her thoughts and sniffed the air for her reactions but couldn't detect even a trace of fear.

A knock on the door interrupted him, and Theodor hurried across the living room. *Must be Jake. He's the only one that knows we are here.*

Vivienne followed him inside and saw when his assistant handed him a small box.

"Is everything taken care of?" Theodor asked, and Jake bowed respectfully.

"Yes, Your Majesty. Everything is the way you requested. Miss Vivienne." He left before she had a chance to respond.

Theodor closed the door and turned to Vivienne, curious to see how she would react.

He opened the box and took out the wide cuff bracelet.

"Welcome to your new life," he said and grabbed her left hand.

"What is this?" Vivienne retreated, taking a step back. A deep crease appeared between her brows.

He sensed her suspicion. "Your bracer."

His short answer made her take another step away from him. "I can't accept it."

Theodor reached for her arm a second time, placing the bracer around her delicate wrist. It locked with a beeping sound.

"It contains all your information, your comm system, banking, help, porting, everything."

"Oh. I'm sorry, I didn't know." She avoided his gaze.

Theodor moved behind her, encircling her with his arms. "Here, let me explain how it works."

Her wrist in the palm of his hand, Theodor pressed the first button. "This one is your new identification. You press it every time you are requested to prove who you are." She nodded, and he continued. "The second one is porting. The menu is self-explanatory." Theodor carried on with his explanations.

When they got to the banking section, Vivienne's wariness made a strong comeback.

"What do you mean my bank account? I don't have one."

"Earlier, Jake found a lot of credits in Greg's safe, close to a million, and—"

"What? Greg had all that money?" She turned toward him with rounded eyes.

"Yes. I figured they would be a good start for you." He pressed another couple of buttons. "We made it look like a robbery, so we couldn't just leave the credits in the safe."

"So, you're telling me that I have a bank account with close to a million credits in it?" Vivienne's voice went up an octave.

"Almost." His index finger pointed to the numbers on the screen. "The first month is rent-free, after that you can decide if you want to pay every month, or a few at a time."

Theodor monitored her thoughts and reactions, hiding his own. He followed each butterfly he made dance in her stomach. His heart skipped a beat every time hers accelerated.

It took all his self-control when their hands brushed against each other. The need to hug her close to him made every cell of his body scream with desire.

When he bent lower, and his breath fanned over her skin, her mind wandered away from his instructions.

She had surpassed his expectations.

Well, well, well. This is a nice surprise. He stepped away from her and gazed toward the sea.

"Thank you." Vivienne's whisper made him smile inside, but he kept same seriousness on the outside.

"You are welcome. Everyone living on the island has a bracer."

"This fancy?" She held her hand up.

From the corner of his eye, Theodor saw her admiration. The platinum and precious champagne gems glimmered, reflecting in her eyes.

"Maybe not as fancy. But . . . you're my friend." He tensed, waiting for her reaction.

"I am?" Her question sounded genuine, and Theodor figured he could push a little further.

"Unless you don't want to be."

Vivienne turned her attention away from him, toward the grand view of the sea.

"Of course. I'm not sure I will ever be able to repay you for everything you have done for me, show my gratitude."

Theodor took a few steps away from her.

"In that case, you should have dinner with me tonight. What do you say?"

"I . . . I don't know."

Her hesitation amused him. "Do you have other plans?"

"No. I just don't want to interfere with your life. You have already done so much."

"Dinner at seven o'clock, my place." He pressed a button on his bracer, opening a portal. His tone didn't leave any room for negotiations. "My address is already in the memory of your bracer. It's the third one, after home and work."

Vivienne nodded, and the next second Theodor disappeared in the purple swirl.

~ ~ ~

As soon as she glanced at the screen displaying the time, she realized she only had two and a half hours to get ready. Vivienne ran to the dressing room, trying to figure out what to wear.

Her gaze fell on her emergency bag. *Should I prepare it again?* Her grandma proved to be right. *'Never rely on a man. Listen to me, I know what I'm talking about. You should always have an emergency bag in a safe place with credits and a change of clothes. You never know.'*

She had dropped hers at the Central Station's locker the day before she moved in with Greg. That same day she sold some of her furniture and donated the rest. A sigh escaped her lips.

Images from the last year played before her eyes. Less than twenty-four hours ago she was still Greg's slave. A strong shiver coursed through her body and set her in motion. *No use dwelling in the past.*

She hurried to unpack the few things she had and organized her dressing room. Her favorite cream sundress reminded her of better times, before Greg. Vivienne decided to wear it that evening.

"I need a shower," she murmured and hid her safety bag inside one of the large travel bags nestled in a corner.

~ ~ ~

Vivienne stepped out of the gateway at seven, and Theodor welcomed her with a tilt of his head. *I'm curious how she will react to my parents' presence.*

Her erratic heart forced him to hide another smile.

Damn it. This girl keeps surprising me. She is the only one who has made me smile for no apparent reason. How silly.

As soon as they entered the living room, Vivienne stopped.

"Viv, these are my parents, Prince—"

"You're real . . . The angel." Vivienne trembled and stared at Princess Ana.

"I'm no angel." Theodor's mother smiled and shook her head.

"You are. I have the proof. You saved my great-great-grandmother during the Flood," Vivienne insisted, her hands pressing on her chest.

"What kind of proof?" Prince Andree intervened with a suspicious tone.

Her eyes moved to the man towering beside her angel. "A recording. It's in my box." Vivienne turned to Theodor. "I can go get it."

"I wouldn't mind seeing it," the princess encouraged her with a smile.

Vivienne nodded toward Theodor's mother and tried to open a portal. She was still learning how to use her new bracer. Theodor opened one for her and spared her fumbling with the buttons.

"Thank you. I'll be right back," she added and disappeared into the portal.

"What was all that about?" Prince Andree stared at his son with an expecting air.

"I'm not sure. She does have a small box, but I didn't look inside."

"We'll find out soon enough." Princess Ana smiled at her son. "She's very pretty, by the way."

Theodor focused on the view out the open glass doors. Without them noticing, he peeked at his parents.

The way they sat together, held hands, and gazed at each other made him acknowledge the emptiness deep inside him. Could Vivienne be the one to bring him what he missed? Would she ever look at him the way his mother gazed at his father even after five centuries together?

He tried to imagine a possible future. The memory of her fear got in the way. If she was the one destined to him, she still had a long way ahead of her.

Vivienne returned a couple of minutes later and showed them the small box. Slowly, she opened the lid. Heads gathered together, and they all looked inside.

"An iPhone?" Theodor was the first to react. "This thing is ancient."

"You know what it is?" Vivienne turned her attention to him. "I had no idea what it's called."

"Of course, we all had some of those in the Old World. May I?" Theodor waited for her approval before grabbing the phone and inspecting it. "The battery is dead."

Vivienne's bracer twisted on her thin wrist when she turned the box upside down. The hidden double bottom flipped opened and a memory stick fell in the palm of her hand.

"This recording was important to my family and every generation did their best to keep it up-to-date." She handed the stick to Theodor. "It should be compatible with most home systems." Golden sparks of pride lit her eyes.

Her excitement filled the room like a refreshing cool mist.

Vivienne had just started to recover after meeting his parents when her fear escalated. Before Theodor had a chance to calm her, she hid behind him.

"Are they . . .?"

His parents' unblinking eyes focused on her.

"Yes, we're also vampires, but we would never harm

you," Princess Ana said first. "I trust Theo told you that we protect humans," she continued, smiling at Vivienne.

Theodor's attention shifted from his mother to Vivienne and back.

"Please, come sit and tell me why you think I'm an angel." Princess Ana patted the cushion beside her, on the wide ivory couch. "Very few people today are even familiar with the concept."

Vivienne quivered, and Theodor gently covered her hands with his.

"They won't hurt you, Viv. I promise."

As much as it bothered him that she was afraid of them, he couldn't ignore her hands holding tight to his. His heart turned traitor and quickened.

She slowly let go of him. With timid steps, she advanced toward his mother. Her high heels touched the stone floors with hesitation.

Vivienne sat on the edge of the sofa, as if ready to run any moment. Even if she found the courage to smile back, her hands kept smoothing nonexistent creases on her dress.

"I'm the sixteenth generation in my family that exists only because you saved my great-great-grandmother." She clasped her hands together in an attempt to hide discomfort. "I call her that because there are too many *greats* to be said."

"I did?" Princess Ana arched a brow.

"She was about thirteen when the Flood happened four hundred years ago, and on that recording, you're saving her." Vivienne nodded toward the phone Theodor was still turning on all sides. "You lifted her in the air, above the water, and took her to safe, higher ground. She called you her *guardian angel.* We all did." Vivienne glanced at everyone gathered around her. "For sixteen generations, the recording has been passed down in my family as a reminder of why we exist. You made it possible."

"During the Flood we saved thousands. Not nearly as many as we would've wanted, but it was all we could do." A sigh pushed through Princess Ana's lips. "Has anyone else seen this recording?" Theodor's mother kept the same gentle smile in her eyes.

He sensed Vivienne's fear diminish. She didn't seem to be afraid of the woman responsible for her family's existence.

"No." She shook her head. "It's the secret our family has kept all this time. We know people don't believe in angels." Vivienne lowered her gaze. "We would've been categorized as crazy. I'm the only one still alive that knows about it."

Theodor motioned next to the round table set for four. "Let's have dinner before it gets cold. We can watch the recording after."

Chapter 8

The food looked delicious and smelled even better. Theodor continued his detailed observation. Vivienne was an endless source of emotions.

White frosted glass plates contrasted with the food. Grill lines on the steak and the mixed vegetables delighted Vivienne's senses with their different textures and colors.

Her reactions brought smiles around the table. With one exception: Theodor. He wasn't ready to let her into his heart. She had to prove herself before he would allow it, and he wasn't easy to impress.

Vivienne sat across from Princess Ana. Theodor and his father occupied the other two spots at the round table, facing each other. Her nervousness attracted his attention. Between bites, she kept glancing from the windows and to the door, as if she tried to formulate a getaway plan.

Theodor couldn't ignore her behavior. Vivienne's focus, divided between food and an eventual escape route, brought her yet another *failed* check mark on his mental list. Her lack of trust made him wonder if she would ever accept him.

"This is your chance to ask any questions you want about the Flood. We've all been through it." He had to try and bring her to more comfortable territory.

Vivienne turned her head in Theodor's direction, curiosity animating her eyes. He could see how, at least for the moment, she forgot she was having dinner with vampires.

"The Flood? What do you want to know about it?" Prince Andree's question caused her to redirect her attention to him.

"Everything. I read all I could find, but I want to know more. There's little information about the Old World and the Flood." Vivienne stopped when Theodor's parents smiled at each other. "Did I say something?" She turned her confused gaze back to Theodor.

"The way you answered makes us all think of Thora, my sister. She always wanted to know everything about anything."

Her quick movement made her long hair bounce around her face, and Theodor's earlier fury melted in ringlets of honey.

"You have a sister?"

"He does. They're twins."

Princess Ana's answer caused Vivienne's fear to spike again for no apparent reason. Theodor kept busy with his food, impaling a piece of potato way too hard, trying to ignore the waves of fear afflicting him, one after another.

"You should know I was human once, but I always wanted to be a vampire, even if at the time I didn't believe in their existence." Theodor's mother paused for a moment. "It had been a fantasy for me, an unrealistic dream, until I met Queen Emelia and especially Andree."

Princess Ana gazed at her husband with love glistening in her eyes. Her hand reached over the table and grabbed his, squeezing it lightly-a simple gesture overloaded with emotions. They both smiled at the exact same time.

That, right there is what I want. Theodor peeked at the woman that apparently destiny had reserved for him. Her fear was his answer.

"You were a human and wanted to be a vampire? Weren't you afraid?" Vivienne's voice fluctuated.

Theodor chewed his food harder than necessary after giving her another unfavorable check mark. *Yeah, this is a mistake. She can't be mine.*

"She never feared us, or me," Prince Andree answered. He lifted his wife's hand to his lips and kissed it gently.

A tiny smile bloomed on Vivienne's lips.

Theodor was used to his parents' shows of affection for each other.

A few images from earlier that day flashed through her mind, under Theodor's constant surveillance. Her memories of the two of them made his heart quicken its pace and brought a rosy hue to her cheeks.

She remembered who, and what, he was. Vivienne shook her head. *'I have absolutely no desire to be like them.'*

Theodor heard her resolution and his heart sank back into the dark pit where it had lived for the last few centuries.

"I admit, I don't know much about you, about vampires," Vivienne continued. "But I thought they"—she quickly corrected herself— "you couldn't have children."

"That is partially true. Vampire men can, while vampire women cannot," Theodor's father explained to her between two mouthfuls of food.

"Then how—?"

"As I said, I was human," Theodor's mother intervened again. "We married three days after we met, and I got pregnant on our honeymoon." She smiled at her husband again. "Andree turned me a couple of months later."

Vivienne stared at Princess Ana with curiosity and admiration.

Theodor's parents still held hands over the table. Their love surrounded them like a bright aura he'd seen many times before.

"You probably should also know that we all share the same special abilities." Princess Ana smiled at Vivienne.

"We know what you are and have been thinking." Prince Andree's words caused Vivienne's eyes to open wider. "In this family there are no secrets. Love and trust are given and accepted unconditionally."

Theodor found out the same instant as her that she wasn't ready to have her mind opened in front of all three of them.

He couldn't help but wonder if she ever would accept vampires in general, him in particular. She seemed to be too afraid to judge them fairly, to overcome the misconceptions about his kind. Somewhere deep inside he hoped her analytical mind would prevail. At least for the time being, it didn't. Another negative check mark.

A few seconds of uncomfortable silence floated around them like a dark cloud. Theodor scored accordingly Vivienne's every thought, every gesture, and reaction, acting as judge and executioner. He hid his disappointment well, and his tiny moments of hope even better.

Both his parents disapproved of his actions through their links with one another. He chose to play by his rules and ignored their objections.

"What do you want to know about the Flood?" Prince Andree's question brought Vivienne back to more familiar ground, where her desire for knowledge rose above anything else.

"From what I read, I understood that everything started with the alien ship that fell from the sky—"

"Didn't exactly fall." Prince Andree corrected her. "Collided would be a more appropriate term for what happened."

"What do you mean?"

"That ship crashed into Earth at full speed, even after our atmosphere might have slowed it. Given its sheer size, if it would have impacted on land instead of the ocean, the whole planet would have shattered."

"How big was it?" Vivienne's eyebrows went up, wrinkling her forehead.

"Perhaps half the size of Australia. It had multiple levels, and could have accommodated a few cities."

"And nobody saw it coming?" Vivienne's impatience interrupted him again.

"Our satellites detected it, but there was no time for any sort of advance warning to the oncoming threat. Even if there had been, the destruction was unavoidable."

Prince Andree stopped for a couple of seconds, placing his knife and fork down. It seemed he had lost his appetite.

"The powerful shock of the impact only marked the beginning. The initial wave, as high as the depths of the ocean, crushed everything in its way. In a matter of seconds, entire cities, countries, were wiped out." His voice resonated with dark memories in Theodor's mind.

That was a birthday from hell for Thora and me.

"The consecutive waves only made the situation worse, and just hours after the impact, only a few areas of land remained dry." Prince Andree glanced to his wife. "We were prepared, ready to do anything, but the destruction surpassed our expectations."

"Did you know what was going to happen? How?" Vivienne's voice sounded screechy with surprise.

"My best friend, Ella, can see into the future. She saw it the day Theo and Theodora were born. Her visions and the prophecies led the same way." Theodor's mother's voice lost volume. "A flood would happen in exactly one hundred years, on Theo and his sister's birthday. We didn't know what would cause it, but we knew the day." A sad smile tugged at the corner of Princess Ana's lips.

"And you didn't warn the humans?" Vivienne's voice rose with indignation.

"How could we have?" Theodor's tone softened. "There was no way to explain what we knew without admitting who we are. Can you imagine the panic? The humans would've killed each other before the Flood would have." He played with his peas, lining them up on the edge of his plate—a habit he'd picked up from his mother. "We had one hundred years to prepare for it. Most of everything you see in museums and libraries today we managed to salvage before that day."

Theodor's answer was laced with sadness. No matter how much he tried to convince himself that he'd done everything he could, the memories of those times always made him feel he should've done more.

"We warned the humans that knew about us and helped them take their families to safety, but we could only do so much." He lowered his gaze, guilt still lingered in his mind. "We organized camps for the survivors, transportation, and supplies."

More of the uncomfortable silence. Theodor rose to his feet, placing his napkin on the table. "Let's see that recording."

One by one, they all moved to the living room and stood in front of the translucent screen.

"Make yourselves comfortable." Theodor gestured to the couches, but everyone ignored him.

From the first seconds, Princess Ana let out a small yelp and covered her mouth with her right hand.

Her husband's arm went around her waist. Theodor watched the images, his mind back in time. His arm rested on Vivienne's lower back by reflex. He sensed instantly the comfort his touch brought her, and how it didn't fail at elevating her pulse. The same instant, he regretted his gesture, considered it a moment of weakness. This time was a wash for her score.

~ ~ ~

The images played in front of her eyes, mixed with vivid memories. Princess Ana saw herself standing in the distance on the top of some ruins.

She levitated people, saving them from ledges, balconies, or rooftops where they were stranded. After setting them down, somewhere behind her, others rushed them to helicopters taking them to safety.

Some of the buildings barely stood. Debris, vehicles, and bodies belonging to humans and animals mixed with the muddy waters. It moved like a wave of death, swallowing every bit of life in its way.

Gas lines, ignited by broken high voltage cables, erupted in terrifying explosions. She'd hoped she would never see those images again, but there they were playing before her.

The dark sky appeared gray, covered in low and heavy clouds. In spite of the pouring rain, columns of smoke rose everywhere. Screams and cries for help mingled with the sound of concrete and steel grinding together. The ground shook, and the explosions seemed like they would never stop.

A large part of a wrecked train, swept along with the flood waters. The still connected cars shifted back and forth, leveling everything in their path.

On the screen, the ground shook beneath her feet. Princess Ana ran, and the instant her soiled white boots left the edge of the partial building, an explosion collapsed the rest. With one quick, high jump she landed on a nearby unstable rooftop.

Almost four hundred years later, she could still hear the terrifying sounds and smell the death all around. Her breath quickened, and she grabbed Andree's hand, in need of his strength and support.

The princess remembered the argument they'd had before determining their roles in the rescue missions. He'd wanted her safe. Only her smaller frame and the fact she was faster than him won that battle of wills. One of many throughout five centuries.

Nobody else would have made it out from that explosion. The power of it had propelled her through the air, helping her jump farther.

Andree squeezed her hand. She could only imagine what he felt when that happened, all those years ago.

In the middle of the remaining parts of structures still above the water, she had glanced around. With the train approaching, time had run short. Removing as many people from harm's way as she could had been her priority.

One older couple had held onto one another in a desperate embrace. Their eyes opened wide with terror under gray, wet hair hanging around their age-marked faces.

She tighten her hold on her husband's hand. That couple had haunted her for centuries, and now she was seeing them die all over again. *Once was more than enough.*

Princess Ana saw herself gazing straight into the camera. She remembered the exact instant she'd discovered, behind her, the young girl holding a phone and crying with silent sobs. *If she would've cried louder, I would've heard her earlier. Maybe I could've saved them all.*

A wind gust came out of nowhere. Her long, white cape billowed out and up, resembling bright, heavenly wings against the foreboding sky. *That's why Vivienne and her family thought I was an angel.* Even the morbid sounds had stopped for that one sole instant.

She'd turned her head to the older couple. Their lips moved soundlessly. It seemed they prayed, staring into each other's eyes, not wanting to see what was coming. They knew. She had to choose: the couple or the little girl. There wasn't enough time to save them all.

In order to levitate them, she needed to have a straight line of sight. She couldn't see them all at the same time. They were on opposite sides of her.

A heaviness pressed on her chest. *I didn't have enough time. I couldn't save them all no matter how I look at it.*

Her black, wet hair had whipped across her face when she turned from the little girl to the couple and back. She closed her eyes for a fraction of a second and murmured something.

"I hope I'm doing the right thing," she remembered.

With a deep breath, she lifted the young girl, moving her to safety. The older couple disappeared into the abyssal muddy waters. Their building collapsed and sucked them within. They hadn't even screamed, just continued to hold onto one another.

Princess Ana jumped to safety the last second before her rooftop, the last one still standing, collapsed next.

The recording ended just before she touched the ground. A void filled the room.

"That little girl is your great-great-great . . ." Princess Ana stared at Vivienne.

Vivienne nodded, tears filling her eyes, reminding Ana when she'd last cried—centuries ago.

"Thank you." Princess Ana hugged her.

~ ~ ~

To Theodor's surprise, Vivienne wasn't scared. Guilt literally suffocated her. It counted as a good reaction in his book and added it to her unstable score.

"I didn't mean to bring back bad memories," Vivienne whispered.

"No." Princess Ana took Vivienne's hands into hers and sat on the couch. "You brought me closure."

Theodor let out a relieved breath. His hand didn't touch her anymore, but now he missed her. *Damn it. What the hell is wrong with me?*

"Closure?" Vivienne sat beside Theodor's mother.

"Yes. That, what you all just saw, was the first time I'd had to choose between one life and another. One of many in those days of rescue. All these years, I've carried around the weight of my choices, wondering if I saved the right person."

Princess Ana stopped for a few seconds. Her husband's hand squeezed her shoulder, and she glanced at him. Theodor sensed the energy between them, flowing strong and intense.

His gaze moved in Vivienne's direction. He hoped to feel something from her, an emotion directed toward him. Even a trace would've been something. Nothing.

"You, being here today, sixteen generations later, brought me the peace of mind I longed for." Ana squeezed Vivienne's hands. "I saved that little girl, and a whole family came into existence because of it. You're the proof I made the right choice." Princess Ana smiled and hugged Vivienne one more time.

Theodor heard Vivienne's steady pulse. Her show of no fear brought her another favorable check mark.

"I didn't even clear her memory. It didn't seem right. She was just a kid," Theodor's mother continued after a few seconds of silence, calmer and composed. "Nobody would have believed her anyway."

"Clear her memory? What do you mean?"

"Just as we can influence someone's decisions, we can also clear parts of memory, replace them, or alter them." Vivienne gazed at Theodor in a visible effort to understand his explanation. *I hope she won't freak out now.*

"All the people we rescued . . ." Prince Andree sat beside his wife. His arm wrapped around her shoulders. "We erased from their memory the way they were saved. When they regained consciousness, they were all told that rescue teams found them and brought them to the shelters." A sad smile tugged at his lips. "We could not afford them knowing what had really happened, how we saved them, who we are."

"It's not fair." Vivienne objected. "You should've at least received recognition for the lives you saved."

Theodor turned around to hide a slight smile. She finally saw them in a more accurate light, started to understand they weren't the enemy. *That deserves a good check mark. Hell, I'll give her two.*

"We couldn't, not without revealing our existence," Princess Ana answered with the same kind smile as before.

It had been a good idea to have Vivienne meet his parents. *My mother has a calming effect on her.* Around her, Vivienne's fear dissipated.

"You saved so many and still lost thirty percent of the population."

"Wherever you got that information from, it is wrong. Thirty percent of the initial population survived." Prince Andree attention swung from his wife to Vivienne.

Her surprise brought sad smiles to Theodor's parents' faces.

"It was a great loss. We didn't lose just humans. We also lost animals, entire species gone." Theodor's father snapped his fingers to show how long it took for them to disappear. "The earth had shifted a few degrees off the orbit under the impact with the ship. It was not enough to throw the planet off course and make it uninhabitable, but it did change the climate, the environment." He let out a sigh. "All those years of evolution wiped out in one day."

Vivienne's curiosity to know more stirred Theodor's interest, and he focused on her mind.

She seemed to understand the guilt his kind had carried for hundreds of years. They weren't monsters anymore, but guardians.

Hope bloomed again in Theodor's heart even if she only thought so about him and his family. *She still fears us as a whole.* He started pacing.

"How did the survivors continue to live on after all that?" Vivienne asked after a while.

"After the first shock, when humans understood what had happened, they tried to find other survivors. Unfortunately, days after the impact, there were no more stranded survivors, only more bodies." Theodor inhaled and exhaled loudly. "The reality that so very few survived made them come to one conclusion, probably the smartest thing human kind ever did. They decided to unite."

He sat in one of the comfortable chairs across from the couch.

"They realized that the energy and resources put into one government for each country would be of better use in rebuilding, in progress. Now they knew there were others, out there." He pointed his index finger to the sky. "The ship that almost ended life on Earth came from somewhere. The first planetary council formed shortly after." Theodor picked up his glass and tilted it from side to side. "From that day on, there were no borders, no more countries, just one planet with ruins of what used to be civilization. They understood that divided, none of them had any chance at rebuilding. Everyone made genuine efforts to adapt to a new world still in its infancy."

Theodor stopped and glanced at Vivienne. Her eyes sparkled with desire to know more. She had listened to his every word, absorbing every bit of information. Her fascination was real.

"Those *countries*, why did they need them? I never quite understood that part." Her curiosity pushed the conversation in a new direction.

He finally took a sip and set the glass back on the side table. "I'm not sure if *need* is the right word. It was the way the Old World had been structured." He leaned forward and rested his forearms on his knees. "For instance, in Europe there were about fifty countries and over twenty languages spoken. Each of those countries wanted their independence, their own laws, government—"

"So, every few hundred kilometers there was a different country, a different language spoken, a border?" Vivienne appeared to have a hard time imagining it all.

"Pretty much. Each country had their culture. It was quite interesting." Theodor remembered how he visited them all with his sister before the Flood.

"Were people allowed to go everywhere, like now?"

"No. You would've needed a *visa*, like a temporary permit given to you by the authorities of the country you wanted to enter," Theodor's father volunteered. "The more advanced a country was, the harder it would've been to obtain those permissions. Countries wanted to protect themselves and what they had."

Vivienne turned her attention to Prince Andree, confusion still present in her eyes. "Let me get this right. If someone was born in a less advanced country, they would be forced to live there?"

"Yes." He nodded. "They could try and immigrate to other countries with an elevated level of socioeconomic opportunity, but it was hard and discouraged many."

"I'm glad I didn't live in those times." Her whisper brought smiles all around.

Theodor covered the lower half of his face with his hand. His eyes traveled to the thick rug covering the light-cream stone floor.

"It was different. At the time, there were no portals, no food processing units, no speeders." Theodor's father pointed to her iPhone. "That is what they used for communication. Nothing was like you know today."

Through his link with his father, Theodor recommended they keep for a later discussion the times when they traveled on horses, or when handwritten letters were the main way of communication. Theodor snickered inside, trying to guess what her reaction to those things might be.

"It must've taken forever to go anywhere." Vivienne's words rang true and funny at the same time.

"Just another way of life." Theodor's answer floated about the silent room.

Chapter 9

Vivienne controlled her urge to bolt for the door. Under Theodor's scrutiny, she became more uncomfortable. Nervousness made her tuck a few imaginary hairs behind her ear and clasp her hands together on her lap. She even bit her lip, one of her many quirks.

"How did we get where we are today?" she asked, breaking the silence.

"The ship that almost ended our world held everything you see today. All the technology we have learned, we found in the wreckage," Theodor's father clarified for her with patience, as if she were a child. "Well, the ship seemed intact, just a few dents. That is also where you came from." Prince Andree stared at her.

"Me? Were GeMs on the ship?" Vivienne almost jumped off the couch.

"No. There was not one living soul when we opened it." Theodor's father seemed amused. "Later, we learned that there was what would best be described as a virus, which got released into our atmosphere. It must have been part of the air composition from Vamphora, the planet from where the ship originated."

"Vamphora? I've never heard of it." Vivienne tried to remember if she ever came across that name. Nope.

"And you probably will not either. I am not sure if it still exists."

Prince Andree continued to explain to her about the first expedition of the people from Vamphora, the reason for vampire's existence. They had experimented with humans on Earth, trying to find a new home for their own kind.

Theodor had been right. When he told her that everything she knew about vampires wasn't true, he wasn't joking. She definitely didn't expect them to be half-alien.

Touched by whatever it was those vamphorians had in their stored life-support, she was infected, too. Humans, GeMs, and vampires were connected at a deeper level than she would've imagined, or liked for that matter.

"Wait a minute. Did you find the source of the mutations?" Vivienne rose to her feet. "Do you know what exactly altered the humans' DNA?"

"No. We have scientists working on it, and you will join some of them." Theodor remained calm. "We're calling it a *smart virus*. The first infected were all young, healthy adults, as if this virus knew what to look for, choosing its hosts."

Theodor sipped from the wine glass he held. For a couple of seconds, her gaze followed the deep red liquid swishing around in the globe-like crystal glass.

His calm contrasted with Vivienne's sudden agitation. *How can they all be this composed? This is important. It could change so much. If I knew about all this before, when I tried to find a pattern, I might've advanced my research.*

She took a few steps. Ideas she had dismissed in the past resurfaced in her scientist mind.

"It makes sense," she whispered. "I've tried to infect GeMs with all kinds of viruses, known diseases, but they got purged every time. I thought it was something wrong with my testing."

"You infected people?" Princes Ana's horror caused Vivienne to twirl on her heels.

"No, only genetic material, blood samples." Her voice squeaked.

"Interesting. Do you have those notes?" Theodor kept his same unnatural calmness.

"No. I didn't really stick around to retrieve any material after the accident." Vivienne lowered her head. "But I remember everything."

A violent tremor coursed through her body, and she wrapped her arms around her waist. The memory of that night always brought chills and sadness.

"Knowing what I know now, I could try a different approach. I may have a chance to isolate the virus and find a cure for GeMs," she continued, thinking out loud.

Her personal life, pain, everything not related to her research took a back seat. Her true scientist nature came through. New plans and old hopes blended in her mind with the speed of light.

"A cure? GeMs are not sick." Prince Andree's objection brought her back to reality.

"Reverse the alterations," Vivienne corrected herself.

"Over twenty-five percent of the existing population today are GeMs." Prince Andree waved toward the windows. "What makes you think they want to devolve and become humans?" Theodor's father rose to his feet.

Vivienne stared at him. She hadn't expected such a strong reaction. *I guess I touched a nerve. He isn't happy with me right about now.*

"These people are superior to humans. Some have incredible abilities that insure them high paying jobs." Prince Andree paced the living room. "Most have been born GeMs for generations. Their powers have combined, evolved."

Every one of his steps punctuated his words. Vivienne didn't need any special abilities to know he was furious. She could see it, especially in the tight fists held by his sides.

"I am truly sorry that your experience has been a bad one. That heartless bastard deserved to die, and if Theo had not killed him, I would have." Theodor's father clenched his jaw. "Most GeMs are happy with the way they are. Maybe you should get to know and understand them before rushing to *cure* them."

Prince Andree's words echoed in Vivienne's mind. She had entered a whole new world. Maybe he was right, and she should understand GeMs more before passing judgement. The analytical part of her brain kicked in, setting aside her mixed feelings for a while.

~ ~ ~

Theodor monitored all of her thoughts and kept mostly quiet while his parents carried on the conversation.

Under the excuse she had an early meeting the next day, the interview Theodor arranged for her at the research center, Vivienne left close to midnight.

A few moments of silence followed after she disappeared into the swirls of the portal.

Princess Ana rose to her feet, approaching her son.

"Theo, I have no doubt now. This girl is your destiny."

"Why is that?" He stared at his mother, only to see her warm, loving smile.

Her hand squeezed his arm. "Don't you see the connection? I saved that little girl all those years ago so you and Vivienne could come to pass." She gestured to the direction where the portal closed. "Your destiny sealed the second I chose to save her great-great-grandmother instead of the old couple."

His mother's explanation didn't satisfy him. All he could sense from Vivienne was her fear, sometimes sheer terror, other times attraction, hot desire. He grew more confused than before the dinner.

"I have to go. I promised Ella we would shop today for our dresses. The New Year's ball is nearing," Princess Ana said, reminding him about the fast-approaching deadline.

Great, another one. I'll have even less time left until my birthday, the day I could lose my coven.

His parents hugged, and Theodor witnessed again the special connection they had with one another. *Vivienne will never hug me like that.*

Theodor's mother opened a portal.

"See you later." His father winked at her.

"See you." She smiled and shifted her attention to Theodor. "Before I go . . ." His mother hesitated. "Are you going to invite Vivienne to the ball?"

Theodor shook his head. "I'm not sure she would want to go. I don't think so."

"If you won't, I will." A smile spread across her lips. "She won't say no to me."

His mother's words still resonated in his mind after she stepped into the portal. Theodor ran both his hands through his hair. "She can't be the one," he whispered.

An all-knowing smile tugged at the corner of his father's lips. "I have seen this stubborn look on your face before. You have had it since you were about two feet tall." His hand lowered to show the height. "And in the mirror, long before that."

Theodor straightened his frame. At six foot four inches, he was about an inch taller than his father.

"I prefer to call it perseverance."

"You may call it what you will. But just because you choose to fight your destiny does not mean it will change." He sipped from his glass of wine. "You should know that much by now."

Theodor paced in the vast living room, one of the many habits inherited from his father.

"Why her? Why couldn't destiny reward me with a strong woman who won't fear me?" His questions materialized out loud for the first time, finally out of his mind. "I had hoped the one destined to me would be someone who trusts me, gazes at me the way Mom looks at you. I think I deserve that much."

"Theo, just because your mother and I fell in love with each other the second we met, does not mean it will work the same way for you." His eyes took a faraway stare, as if he looked back in time. "Even so, I still had to prove myself. It took time for her to accept me as a whole." A smile lifted the corners of his lips. "And do not kid yourself, Vivienne is a strong woman." Prince Andree waved in the general direction of where the portal had swallowed her earlier.

Theodor stopped in his tracks. "Are you serious? Do we speak of the same woman?"

"She is human, well GeM, but you know what I mean. You cannot expect her to be as strong as you. Your mother was the same way before I turned her—"

"At least she wasn't afraid of you." Theodor cut the air in front of him with his hand.

"So? Make her trust you." Prince Andree walked toward his son. "You are both attracted to each other. And do not bother trying to deny it." He lifted his right hand at the first sign of opposition. "Anyone can see it. There is a lot of tension between you two. Why exactly do you reject her?"

Theodor gazed outside through the glass doors. The perfectly round moon resembling a silver coin hung high in the dark sky, shining over the calm waters of the sea. It appeared tranquil.

Inside him, a storm raged. He took a deep breath, trying to control the lightning behind his eyes reflected in the shiny surface, and the thunder deep inside his mind. The white shirt stretched over his chest. His gaze fell on the extra hard-working buttons trying to hold it together and exhaled. *Maybe I should order new, larger ones.*

"I can't see myself with someone like her." Theodor adjusted his shirt. "She doesn't trust me, and she's too afraid of what we are." His voice dropped in volume, muffled by sadness. "You've met her, you must've seen beyond the brave face she put up."

"Theo, let her see you." His father's hand momentarily closed on his shoulder. "And I mean the real you. Not this cold, calculated, ready to kill at any moment man who everyone knows and fears." He retrieved his hand. "I am certain that if you let her in, she—"

"No." Theodor opposed the idea without a second thought. "She has to earn it." He stood his ground.

"That is why you are keeping score, totaling her passes and failures?"

Theodor gazed to his father. He stood beside him, mirroring his posture.

An image from childhood flashed in his mind. At about fourteen he started to measure up to his father. Barely reaching to his shoulder, Theodor promised himself that one day, he would be just like him. By the time he stopped aging, they resembled two statues taken from the same mold.

"You are not being fair, Theo." His father's words yanked him back to the present.

"Fair?" Theodor's brow arched. "Do you really want to broach that topic with me? Nothing's been fair for me." He struggled to control his temper. "There was no other choice but become what I am," he pointed to his own chest. "It's not fair that I had to fight all my life for everything I've ever accomplished. The prophecy wasn't fair. Destiny, it isn't fair."

"There is always a choice." His father's calm voice did nothing to diminish Theodor's fury. "Yours, up to this point, was to follow ambition. But things change, evolve, and so should you."

Theodor's frustration against his own existence had bubbled inside for hundreds of years. Yes, being the most powerful vampire was satisfying, and he relished it. What he didn't enjoy was the struggle.

"You know what I mean. I united our people. That didn't come without sacrifices." Theodor let out a sigh. "I didn't ask to be the one to do it."

"So, you are punishing Vivienne for it," his father replied. His gaze caressed the ever-moving water.

"Why should I let her in? I'm not even sure I want her." Theodor's sad whisper was laced with disappointment.

"It would not kill you if you smiled once in a while." Prince Andree continued after a few moments of silence.

"What does my smiling have to do with anything?"

"You would be surprised. Try it. Look, I am not going to tell you how to live your life." Prince Andree faced his son. "You are old enough to know what you want. Just remember, destiny calls only once. It is your choice to accept or decline. But if she is the one, and you let her go"—he pointed again to the spot where the portal had been swirling— "you will not have another chance."

"Maybe it's for the best. This almighty fate already graced me with a half-dead GeM that's afraid of me." Theodor had a hard time controlling his frustration. "What can be worse, a completely dead one?"

Prince Andree walked away from his son. "Theo, being a vampire has equal advantages and disadvantages. If you find the one destined to you, you could literally live the proverbial *ever after*." A spark of happiness lit his father's eyes. His parents' relationship was the perfect example of that fairy tale. "If you lose her, you may be miserable for just as long. In our case, that is a very, very long time to be unhappy. You could, in theory, find someone else, but it will not be the same."

A heavy silence settled between them. Prince Andree returned to the couch.

"Perhaps it's not an entirely bad idea to marry Malvina after all." Theodor's words broke the silence.

"Pfff, Malvina?" His father waved, as if dismissing the other woman. "I thought you wanted to kill her."

"I do, just not before I have her people, if they even exist."

Theodor sat across from his father.

"You would honestly consider sacrificing your beliefs for this goal of yours?" He leaned forward resting his elbows on his knees. "I knew that contract you signed was a bad idea." His father shook his head. "Malvina is a distraction. Whether you end her or not will not affect your fate. She is clearly not part of it. Vivienne is." There was conviction in his tone.

"Maybe, maybe not." Theodor relaxed in his chair. "You know, you are right about one thing. There is a lot of tension between us." He nodded slowly. "I should just get it out of my system by sleeping with her. That'll prove she's not the one."

Theodor took another sip of his wine and placed the glass on the side table to his right. The crystal clinked against the marble top.

A smirk crossed over his father's face. "Or bring you the confirmation of what your mother and I believe. Perhaps even break your 'no more than once' rule."

Theodor's laughter filled the room. He heard himself, how forced and fake it sounded, and stopped. His lips drained the remaining wine in his glass.

"Theo, there is no other man in this world prouder of his son than me. Your accomplishments have surpassed all my expectations." A smile traveled from his lips to his eyes. "You have become the most powerful of our kind. It pains me to see the price you paid for it. You have lost yourself in the process."

Theodor rested his right ankle over his left knee. "I did not. Nothing is lost, just locked away, safe from everything."

"Well, I hope you did not throw that key away. You will need it." His father nodded, as if it made him more convincing. "If you want to have a chance at being happy, now is the time. It seems there is one more fight for you."

"Talk about fairness, huh? I'm growing tired of all this." Theodor massaged his temples. "I hoped there will be something that I won't have to go through hell and back to get."

Prince Andree rose to his feet and approached his son. His right hand clasped on Theodor's shoulder, and they stared at each other.

"This is the only battle that really matters. Everything until now only prepared you for the hardest of all: the fight against yourself."

Theodor didn't answer, just watched his father open a portal and disappear inside. Another deep sigh left his lips.

Viv, you're making quite a mess of my life. This has to stop. I have to do something. He pushed himself up. The chair creaked, relieved of his body's weight.

Only minutes later, Theodor opened his own portal and stepped through.

The door to her bedroom stood wide open, and one of the windows was left ajar to allow in the warm breeze. The long, white chiffon sheers brushed against the floor in the faint moonlight. *She needs protective screens for all the windows and the door to the terrace.*

As soon as he entered the room, Theodor froze.

Where the hell is she? The question formed in his mind at the sight of the empty bed. He sensed her presence. A tiny cry attracted his attention. It came from within the room, and he advanced with caution.

The second he saw her, Theodor tilted his head to one side.

What is she doing sleeping on the floor?

Carefully, he hid behind the heavy drapery right beside her, just in case she woke up.

Vivienne crouched on one side, within the folded comforter she'd pulled from the bed. She used half of it to sleep on, covering herself with the other.

Theodor stared at her without blinking.

She hugged the pillow against her body. The moonlight revealed tears glistening on her face.

His first impulse was to take her in his arms and lay her back in the bed, to wake her up from what he guessed was a nightmare and tell her everything would be all right. The same moment, he stopped himself. He had no explanation for being in her bedroom to start with. How would he justify it? *The old 'I was in the neighborhood' excuse isn't going to cut it. She can't know I'm here.*

Curiosity got the best of him, and he checked in her mind. He had to know what she dreamed about. A nightmare, images from the last year haunted her. Theodor's anger rose. Killing the monster who tortured her hadn't sufficed. He should have kept him alive and made him suffer longer.

Her dream helped him figure out why she slept beside the bed. After a year spent chained to the floor, the bed was too soft. It suffocated her.

"No!" A sudden yelp kicked Theodor out of her mind.

The nightmare ended. Her tears soaked the pillow.

She's so damaged. Sorry sweetheart, but in spite of everything, I'm not the one to fix it all. I can't. I'm just as broken.

Chapter 10

Malvina's day escalated from bad to terrible. After making it out alive from the meeting with Theodor, she hoped that Uncle Serge would be on her side. *Well, that idea crashed and burned.*

She shook off the gloomy cloud floating over her head, and went in search of the dress of her dreams. Almost seven hours of shopping later, she still hadn't found it. *At least I have the address of a great designer and a meeting with him set for tomorrow. I'll make sure he makes a stunning evening gown for me.* She hissed and unclenched her fists when she stepped over the threshold into the living room.

Back in her apartment, Malvina paced furiously on the cold floor. It was imperative to make it to this year's Grand Ball hosted by Queen Emelia. And she didn't have a dress, or an invitation to go. Yet.

Malvina needed to be seen in public with Theodor. Rumors still had weight in their world. Whispering the correct words into the right ears could force his hand, and maybe find her some allies.

The night spread its wings over the city, and the falling rain washed away the remaining snow. Vertical streams ran along the glass doors and floor-to-ceiling windows.

The sound of a speeder landing outside attracted her attention. Malvina rushed to open the glass doors, hoping her uncle had come back to tell her he would help. It wasn't him, but Victor. Almost as good.

She watched him grab a body wrapped in a blanket from

the back seat of his rented speeder. Malvina ran to him, her high-heeled boots splashing through the small puddles.

"Vic."

"Hey, beautiful. I thought you would need a *pick-me-up* to brighten this gloomy day."

Victor's secret weapon, his voice. It made her knees soft. Most vampires were immune to their own kind's tricks, but he'd perfected his skill to the point where nobody could resist him. His smooth, melodious voice reverberated all the way inside her bones. Victor could seduce any woman he desired only by speaking.

He opened the blanket and showed her the unconscious body of a human wrapped in filthy rags. Droplets of rain bounced off the woman's shaved head.

"You really are the best." Excitement replaced all the worries from only minutes ago. "Is she safe?"

"Of course. I found her wondering in some back alley." Victor motioned with his head somewhere behind him, toward the city. "It seems she recently sold her hair for whatever drugs she took. She's high as a kite."

Malvina lifted one of the woman's eyelids.

"It's only *spark*, that cheap hallucinogen for humans. We're good. Damn, she stinks." She crinkled her nose.

Victor carried, then placed the human in a corner of the large terrace.

Malvina leaned over the body at the same time with him. She drew Victor closer, and after a passionate kiss, both their fangs descended. Hisses saturated the air with viciousness, and desire.

The rain and cold didn't bother her, nor Victor. As for the human, she couldn't care less.

Big, heavy drops soaked Malvina's dress in seconds. The round beads kept falling in a symphony of sound on the terrace, against the walls and glass, covering the noise from the speeder lanes below.

Her fangs tore the flesh on the victim's neck with famine and need. The blood escaping her hungry lips, diluted by rain, stained the pale skin. Even if unconscious, the body convulsed for a few seconds. Victor sat across from her, mirroring her actions on the other side of the human.

Precious ruby, life-giving fluid satisfied her thirst. Malvina's eyes rolled back in ecstasy. It was forbidden to kill humans for their blood, but both she and Victor loved the thrill of it. They shared the secret. Only minutes later, the human lay drained, lifeless, under the pouring rain.

Malvina wiped her lips with the back of her hand.

"I needed this."

"I'm glad I could be of service." Desire sparked in his eyes.

"Let me dispose of this." Malvina grinned, pointing to the inert body at their feet. She picked it up with ease and threw it over the edge of the terrace.

They both leaned over and watched the body fall the fifty-nine floors. First, it hit one of the fluorescent oversized signs mounted on the side of the building. Limbs flew in different directions. The torso cracked open, and the skull split. The fall continued for the dismembered parts, hitting more signs on the way down. It wasn't much that made it to the ground.

"Won't her remains raise suspicion?" Victor couldn't hide the worried tone in his mesmerizing voice.

"Do you remember all those *accidents* so many humans seemed to have with their speeders, and their bodies got smashed against the ground?" A smile bloomed over Malvina's lips, like a cat that just swallowed the canary. "Damn, I broke a nail in those rags she wore." She admired her otherwise perfect fake black nails.

"Yes, what does that have to do with . . . ? Oh." Revelation sparkled in his dark eyes.

Most of those incidents weren't accidents. They were bodies thrown from high enough to be unrecognizable splattered all over the pavement. Malvina's smile widened at his apprehension.

"The authorities figured the only explanation for the massive damage to the bodies had to be a fall from about the height of the speeder lanes." Malvina pointed toward the traffic lanes, about fifteen levels below her terrace.

With uncontrollable desire, Malvina jumped into his arms. She forgot about the lost nail and wrapped herself around him. Rain continued to wash over their heated bodies.

"We should go inside."

She approved his suggestion with another moan of pleasure and let him take both of them inside her penthouse. With one fluid move, Victor removed the black minidress she wore. The stretchy fabric fell on the floor with a swoosh.

A couple of hours later, they lay in the bed. Victor turned his gaze to her.

"You want to talk about this?" He traced a line with his finger along her scar.

His voice drove her insane with renewed desire, as much as his touch.

"There's nothing to talk about. It was a mishap." She displayed an irresistible smile.

They weren't best friends or confidantes. They used each other for purely physical pleasure.

"I have to admit, it's sexy." Victor kissed the red, still-healing line that stopped above her heart.

Malvina hissed and closed her eyes with delight. His melodious voice, the low tone, almost hypnotized her.

"Before I forget, I have something for you." Victor turned and searched for his clothes on the floor right by the bed.

She ran her fingers in sensual lines on his back. The previous night flashed in her mind again. Malvina remembered how her fingertips tingled over Theodor's muscles. Prince Theofrost was immune to her charm.

A second later, Victor held a black envelope the size of a business card between his index and middle finger, flaunting it before her eyes.

"What is it?" Malvina sat.

She grabbed it from his hand but didn't open it right away, waiting for an answer. The back of his hand moved down, skimming along the side of her neck.

"Do you remember what you told me a while ago? That you have never attended the New Year's Ball?"

A happy squeak escaped her lips, and she opened the envelope. Inside, a black plastic card had gold letters engraved on it. It was an invitation.

"Are you going to be there?" She saw her own reflection in the mirror behind him, her sparkling, fiery green eyes.

"No. I have different plans." He kissed her hand. "You can have it. As the director of the Research Institute on Crete, I always get one."

His answer pleased her even more. She could go ahead with her plan without having to lose him in the crowd. Her mind wandered for a second to the dress she would have made for the occasion. *That designer better come through, or he's going to dive off my terrace.*

Everything seemed to fall in place. Finally, her day turned better, and things started to look up. She placed the invitation on her night table and turned back to the man that made it possible.

"Thank you. Time to show you my gratitude," Malvina whispered. Her first kiss, on his chest, was followed by another, and another. Moans and whispers filled her bedroom surrounded by clouds.

~ ~ ~

Vivienne couldn't wait for her meeting. She had two hours to spare. In the last year, she missed her work. The idea of picking up where she left off made her nervous and excited.

Prince Andree had a point. She doubted her work from the past years would be of any help. It seemed like discovering a cure nobody wanted wasn't exactly something to be proud of. *I needed to think things through.*

A short glance in the full-length mirror made her stop for a few seconds— clothes hung loose on her body from all the weight loss.

Her hands glided over the silky cream blouse, one of her favorites. It made her eyes appear brighter. Vivienne continued to run open palms over her hips. The black pencil skirt was at least one size too large. Vivienne turned around, unsuccessfully trying to see her back.

At least the high-heeled shoes fit perfectly. Shrugging her shoulders, she walked away from the mirror. Perhaps she should try and eat more since her life seemed to be settling in a good, comfortable place thanks to Theodor.

"Theo." The soft whisper flew from her lips and into the silent room.

Why couldn't he be some old, disgusting looking vampire so I could only feel gratitude? Why did he have to be so impossibly perfect? Aware of the attraction, Vivienne let out a deep sigh.

A bunch of butterflies danced in her stomach at the memory of his touch. *Maybe some breakfast would make me feel better.*

She stopped in front of the synthesizer unit in the kitchen. The button marked *coffee* revived images from the previous morning. *Best one I ever tasted. And the company* . . . Vivienne still tried to find the word her conscience wouldn't reject. '*Species are different for a reason. You never mix them.'* Her grandmother's words always found fertile ground in her mind. *Well, she'd never met Theodor either.*

His deep-blue eyes had something that drew her in, a mix of power and calmness. Sometimes dark shadows passed through them. Was that the reason he never smiled? At first, she thought vampires didn't do that, but his parents did. What had happened to him? What killed his smile?

No. He's all kinds of wrong. She shook her head. The low bun she had gathered her hair into that morning didn't even move.

She had always been attracted to the wrong men. First Destin, he seemed like the perfect guy. Until he left her after the one night together, convinced she wasn't worthy of his interest. He was the one that broke her confidence.

Then Greg. A strong shiver shook her body. How had she failed to see him for what he was? It took her a year and the accident to discover the monster lurking inside him. Greg broke her body.

A knock startled Vivienne from her thoughts.

"It's me, Viv." Theodor's voice traveled through the massive wood door.

She hurried to open up. "Theo. What are you doing here?"

"Good morning. I thought we could have breakfast." He gestured over his shoulder.

Vivienne peaked behind him at the two servants beside a floating table loaded with breakfast. She stepped aside, and let all of them in.

"Where would you like this, Your Majesty?" One of the two women scanned her surroundings.

"Outside."

"I was about to synthesize something." Vivienne closed the door with a slight frown. Not that she minded, but she was trying to get him out of her mind, not into her home.

"This is better." He waved his hand, dismissing her idea of synthesized food.

After a few steps, Theodor stopped and turned to face her. "How did you sleep?"

"Good, thanks. Why?" Vivienne asked, quickly fearing that somehow, he knew she'd slept on the floor.

"Just curious. I know humans in general have trouble sleeping in a new, unfamiliar place." He gestured around them. "It was your first night here."

"Oh. I love this place, and I slept great. Thanks again."

Phew. He is only being polite. Vivienne relaxed and watched the servants bow, then leave. Breakfast waited on the terrace. The aroma of the coffee tickled her nostrils.

"I'm not sure if I told you yesterday, but your bed is adjustable." His gaze hid something she couldn't identify. "Right now, it's most likely on the default setting, but you can make it as soft or hard as you like."

"Really? I do tend to like it a bit harder." Vivienne avoided his gaze. *That came out in all shades of wrong.*

"Come, I'll show you." He closed his hand on her wrist, gently dragging her to the bedroom.

It's so weird to have him here, adjusting my bed. Vivienne's ears burned, her pulse accelerated, and her hands turned cold and clammy. He revealed the controller for the bed hidden in the corner of her night table. His lips moved, a sure sign he talked, but she couldn't hear a word.

A few times he glanced at her, then back at the control, until she suddenly heard him.

"Hop on and see how it is."

What? Did he just ask me to get on the bed?

"It's fine. I'll make any extra adjustments tonight." She wiped her hands against her black skirt and took a step toward the door.

"Very well." His flat tone contrasted with the vertical line marking his forehead..

Is it possible he knows how I feel? He can read minds. I have to stop this. I have to keep my distance, I have to—

"Today, I'll have security screens installed on all your windows and the terrace door." His words plucked her from the thoughts running and colliding with each other in a never-ending chaos.

She stared at him, trying to understand what he'd just said. "Okay."

"Are you all right?" Theodor tilted his head to the side.

She could swear tiny blue wisps danced in his eyes.

"Yeah, I'm fine. I guess I'm nervous about the meeting." She had to say something, and it wasn't entirely a lie. "How about that breakfast?" Anything to get him out of her bedroom.

"You look . . ."—Theodor seemed to search for the right word—"professional." Back on the terrace, he held the chair for her to sit.

Vivienne knew that sometimes she came across as too rigid. "Thank you."

The crashing waves covered her whisper. An unnerving silence settled between them for a short while. *At least the toast is crunchy.*

"When you're finished with the meeting, call me. I need you in the *Sanctum* today to sign your pact of secrecy."

"*Sanctum?*" Vivienne swallowed her food.

"Yes, it's where we meet, where ceremonies are held, that sort of thing."

"And me signing the document, is that much of a big deal?" A ball of bad sat like a knot in her stomach, fighting the food.

"Yes. Every single contract is important. There are two copies that you will have to sign." Theodor sipped from his coffee. "The electronic one is pretty straightforward, but the traditional one is the most important. At least for us."

"Which *us?*" Vivienne narrowed her eyes. She suspected he wasn't telling her everything.

"Us, vampires. The traditional agreement is paper, and you will sign it with a drop of your blood."

"What?" Vivienne's fear reached new heights. *Why do I have to sign in blood?* She almost jumped off her seat. *Is this agreement more than he's letting me know?* She completely forgot about the food in front of her.

"Relax, it's safe. Everyone before you signed it and survived." Theodor placed his cup on the table. "Nobody will attack you. You have to stop thinking that everyone wants to hurt you, Viv." He squeezed her hand over the table. "It's only going to be the two of us."

She understood he was trying to make her feel better. Being alone with him anywhere started to worry her. He could break the last intact piece of her being, her heart. Vivienne withdrew her hand and moved it to her lap.

Without the comfort and warmth of his touch, she felt cold, lonely, but at least her heart was safe.

"Are you married?" The words came out of nowhere and flew off her lips without her consent.

"No. Why?"

"Just curious. Do you have a girlfriend?" she pressed instead of dropping the subject. *Just shut up. What's wrong with me?*

"No. Are you offering?" Theodor's question startled her.

"No. That isn't why I asked, I—"

"Why are you asking then?" Theodor took another sip of his coffee after placing his napkin on top of his empty plate. His gaze cut through her. It burned her inside, and she expected to see smoke rising.

"You said we're friends. I know very little about you." She gasped at the first excuse crossing her mind. "I'm trying to figure out why you're single, why you never smile."

The chair screeched against the floor when Theodor stood. His boots didn't make a sound over the large stone tiles.

"I never met the right girl." It seemed like every single one of the waves caressing the sand became important, capturing all his attention, as if it was a matter of life and death.

"In five hundred years?" Vivienne's left eyebrow arched and Theodor turned to face her.

"Precisely. You see, the older I get, the more I know, the more I expect." He puffed his chest, causing his leather vest to stretch to its limit. "Finding someone to meet the criteria is not easy."

The tiny lights returned in his eyes. Too bad every one of them sheltered a shadow.

"I'm sorry, I didn't mean to intrude." She sipped from her coffee.

"I'll expect your call. Have a good day." He rushed out of her villa, leaving her alone on the terrace.

Vivienne blinked a few times after he disappeared. The waves continued their song in the warm morning.

I'll sign your stupid agreement, and that's it. I'm going to avoid him like the plague. I have to stay away from him. Things will only get worse. It's all wrong. He is the wrong type of man. The wrong species.

Chapter 11

Vivienne exited the portal in the Research Center. A couple dozen more gateways lined up in the lengthy room. Luminescent globes glided on designated paths, their light reflecting off the shiny black floors.

A dark-haired man held a sign with her name on it. His midnight eyes measured her from the top of her head to the tip of her shoes.

"Hello, I'm Vivienne Ferre." She flashed the best smile in her arsenal. A good first impression was a must.

"I'm Doctor Karr, Victor Karr. Please call me Victor."

"Oh, you're the director of this facility?" Vivienne's genuine surprise brought a smile to his angular face. She knew exactly who he was. His name, associated with major research work, had guided her through the years.

"Yes I am."

"And are you . . .?" She hesitated, not knowing if it would be appropriate to ask him directly which species he belonged to.

"Vampire. I understand you are a GeM, right?"

Damn. His voice is incredible. And what do these people eat? Are all vampires this good looking? Theo, this guy . . . Theo. I have to stop thinking of him.

"That's correct."

"It's a pleasure to meet you and an honor to welcome you aboard our team. Please scan your bracer here. It'll give you the clearance you need to move through the facility, and access out database."

Vivienne followed his instructions. The kiosk mounted on the far wall lit up and read the information. She had to touch the screen a few times. In less than two minutes, she obtained her clearance, second to highest.

Motion activated sliding doors opened before them to an impressive lobby. All exterior walls, made of glass, revealed the crisp view of the mountains. A few speeders, parked outside, shone under the sunlight.

Lush green forests for as far as she could see made Vivienne wonder if they were real or projections.

A few people stopped to exchange a couple of words with their director.

"About two years ago, your paper on genetic mutations fascinated me. You were the newest rising star of the Vienna Centre." He massaged his chin with a far-off stare. "Being a team leader at such young age is an accomplishment." His attention refocused on her. "I haven't heard anything about your work in over a year."

Vivienne turned her gaze to the shining floors with an unusual mix of embarrassment and pride. "About a year ago I had an accident and took some time off. I got infected . . ." A shiver coursed through her body. "Now I'm back."

Victor nodded. "Please follow me to your future lab."

"As a student in the Academy of Bioengineering, I read every single one of your publications." She stepped into the elevator with Victor. "Your infant vaccination program made me choose to work in research. Those vaccines saved so many lives. I wanted to make a difference just like you did." Vivienne displayed another shy smile.

"I'm sure you will. Don't forget, I worked on that project about two hundred years," he added in a whisper.

He's so easy to talk to. She wasn't afraid of him. Theodor, his parents, and now Victor made her question her inexplicable fear of vampires.

Out of the elevator, she followed Victor on the wide corridor, all the way to the end and around the corner.

After another few steps, they stopped in front of a laboratory. A simple white plaque with her name engraved in black letters hung on the door.

"Here we are. This is all yours." Victor unlocked the sliding glass panels for her, and Vivienne walked in.

The contents of the well-organized lab made her feel like a kid who had just discovered Candy Land.

Everything around her defined the absolute dream of any scientist. All the equipment was new, the latest, top-of-the-line models.

A glass exterior wall offered the same mountain view that had stolen her breath earlier. On the far side, a small office waited for her.

"When do you need me to start?" Vivienne whirled around and caught Victor staring at her. The tips of her ears burned, and she knew they must've turned bright pink.

"You may start as early as tomorrow, or as late as you need."

"I can start tomorrow." Her enthusiasm brought a smile to Victor lips. *I made a good impression.*

"Great. Unlike other places, here you don't have a set schedule. You may come in or leave anytime you want. There are no minimum hours required." Victor gestured to his surroundings. "All you have to do is report your work to me once a month. For the first three months, you don't have to since you're just starting. That should give you enough time to settle in."

"I can work as late as I want? There's no closing time?" From her past experiences, there was always a time when they locked the doors at night.

"No. You can also work from home if you'd like. I figured you might want some time to adjust to this place."

Victor stared at her, with increased attention. "I understand you moved to Crete recently. How do you like it?"

"Yesterday. I love it, and I'll adjust as I go."

"If you ever need anything, please let me know. When, and if, an assistant or more are necessary, give me a few days' notice, and I'll take care of it." His hand rested on her shoulder for a couple of seconds. "I'm usually pretty good about finding the right people, but as I said, I'll need a little time."

"Of course. I'm used to working alone, but if I need help, I'll let you know." Vivienne backed away from him, more out of habit.

He smiled again and tilted his head. Even with all the excitement, she noticed the tiny step he took closer to her. Vivienne didn't like when her personal space was invaded. Unless it was someone she wanted that close. A pair of cobalt eyes sparked in a corner of her mind.

"I've been living on this island for years, so if you need a guide, I'm all yours." He covered his chest with his right hand.

Vivienne appreciated his offer. She had made mistakes in the past, but Victor seemed straightforward, charming.

"Thank you. I'll keep that in mind." Vivienne smiled, already planning to ask him some questions in the next few days. First, she had to find out where the nearest blood bank was located.

"Oh, your desk unit is connected to the system." Victor nodded to the translucent screen on her desk. "You can research in any of the other centers in the world, including our closed network." He leaned in, as if he was about to share a secret. "So, if you want to learn more about us, vampires, feel free to use it."

Vivienne found everything overwhelming. Her laboratory, the job, and she had to admit, her boss wasn't bad either. *What's wrong with me? Why do I always notice the ones I should stay away from?*

"Please take your time. You may stay for as long as you'd like. Unfortunately, I have to go." Already walking toward the door, Victor waved his hand to the left side of the wide corridor. "If you ever need to see me, my office is at the end of the hallway. We passed it when we came in." He shoved both his hands into the pockets of his jacket. "My comm should already be in the memory of your bracer. It automatically downloaded when you scanned it for clearance."

"Okay. Thank you for everything, and I'm looking forward to working here together."

Victor smiled and after another one of his intense stares, left her lab, leaving Vivienne alone.

~ ~ ~

As soon as he entered his office, Victor closed the blinds, immersing the whole room in darkness. He let himself sink into the chair. The second he closed his eyes, his fangs descended.

I want her, and she's going to be mine. Her blood, her body, all mine. It was so hard to control myself, and not take her in my arms. The connection is strong, and I almost made a fool of myself trying to find something else to do with my hands. My Vivienne.

Plans started to shape in his mind, and a low hiss filled his office.

First, he needed to gain her trust. Second, he would make sure she knew how interested he was in her. Her acceptance would make everything so much better. And he absolutely needed to know where she lived.

Memories assaulted his mind. Another human had attracted his attention before. She'd captured his heart too, Sasha. One mistake, and he'd lost her. One second, his control had slipped away from him, and he'd killed her.

The pain of the loss left him numb. For six hundred years, he'd had no compassion, no remorse, nothing. He'd existed through six centuries like an empty shell. Until now. Vivienne had an effect on him. Her scent awakened in him feelings he never thought he would experience again. This time around, he would be careful. He wasn't going to make another mistake.

"It won't happen again."

~ ~ ~

"How was your meeting?" Theodor asked Vivienne as soon as she stepped out of the portal at his place.

He didn't need to, judging by her still sparkling eyes.

"Great. I can't wait to start tomorrow. Thank you again for everything."

He nodded and walked with her, side by side, on their way to the *Sanctum*. Theodor had spent his morning and part of that afternoon doing his regular work. A few too many times he'd had to interrupt, distracted by their earlier conversation.

Vivienne had lied to him, again, when she'd said she'd slept great. Her questions from breakfast followed him all day. The remark about him not smiling bothered him most. She didn't understand him. She never could. Not as long as she feared him.

His home stood completely separated from the imposing palace. A glass-enclosed bridge, following the rocky shore, connected the two. Guards at both ends of the passage ensured his privacy.

Inside the palace, silence filled the vast rooms. Vivienne's high heels resonated on shiny floors. Columns, at least three stories high, supported vaulted ceilings.

Theodor followed her gaze, lifted to the paintings above. He couldn't ignore the admiration filling her eyes. Huge illuminating spheres hung in midair, waiting for the darkness to start their preprogrammed glide.

With one motion of his right arm, Theodor opened the double doors a few steps ahead of them. The way she barely touched the floors with her heels, walking more on her toes, assured him he had managed to throw her out of her comfort zone. *She's nervous. This is going to bring me some answers.*

"What do those represent?" Vivienne stopped in front of two banners bearing symbols. "I've seen them before."

Theodor remembered the exact instant she had noticed his medallion sliding on the black chain around his neck.

"It's my family's crest. The shield with crossed daggers, or swords, is the symbol for guardian," he explained, stopping beside her and pointing to the banners. "We are eternal guardians"—Theodor indicated the sun and moon on the top and the bottom of the shield—"of life and love."

Vivienne focused on the remaining two symbols, the tree and the heart. "Interesting. Does this code of arms come from your mother's side of the family?"

"My father's." Theodor extended his right hand before them. "Welcome to the *Sanctum*."

Nerves tensed to their maximum, Vivienne stumbled after the first step and grabbed Theodor's arm.

"Is this an amphitheater?" Her words echoed, confirming it before he did.

"Yes, it is. I'm surprised you're familiar with the concept."

"I've read about it."

"Each of the five covens has one. Before the Flood we used to call it a meeting room, or a ceremony chamber. Everyone had a different name." He figured he would volunteer more information. "After the devastating events, we all agreed on *Sanctum*. It is, after all, our most sacred place."

"Five covens?" Vivienne gazed at him. "Can you tell me about them?" Her hands still held onto his arm.

Her touch sent a river of lava through his body, an empowering heat.

"All of them, including their respective territories belong to a member of my family. The First Coven covers the northern part of what used to be North America and belongs to Mihai Veres, the oldest of Vlad's sons."

"You said he's your uncle, right?"

"Yes, and so is Gabriel Veres, his brother. Only a couple of years younger, he leads The Second Coven, which is spread through the central part of North America." Theodor slightly lifted his arm offering her better support. "The Third Coven is officially lead by my grandmother, Queen Emelia De Croix. In reality, my parents are doing the heavy lifting. Their territory expands over South and Central America, including the most southern states from North America."

"That's a large area," Vivienne whispered.

"It is, but it also used to have the lowest numbers. That changed, of course." He paused before mentioning his own coven. Pride filled his heart. "Then, you have The Old Coven, which belongs to me. It expands over former Europe and the western part of Asia." Her hands felt cold on his arm. "Last one, The New Coven, belongs to my sister and occupies former Africa and the reminder of Asia."

"Your family leads all the vampires in the world?" She showed interest in learning about him and his kind.

Theodor felt the heat from earlier dissipating to a warmth he wasn't accustom to.

"We only lead those who belong to covens. Most are independents who don't want to answer to anyone for their actions." Theodor waved his hand toward a random direction. "They want to be their own boss. It's really a matter of personal preference. The independents also don't have the protection a coven offers."

Step after step, they descended to the lowest level, and Vivienne glanced back at the benches in the amphitheater. Theodor followed her gaze. Navy-blue pillows covered the white stone seats. She shivered, and her fear spiked.

"I figured you would be uncomfortable having witnesses. As I already told you, it's only us. You can relax."

He stopped in front of a low, long table also carved in stone. Vivienne finally let go of his arm. *Hmm. I was getting used to her holding onto me.*

The smooth surface of the white slab glistened in the light. A single datapad waited beside a roll of paper resembling a scroll, and a narrow, black box.

He picked up the datapad and tapped the screen a few times until the desired document appeared.

"Here. Read it, and sign in the box." Theodor indicated to the bottom of the text.

Vivienne grabbed the tablet-like device. One more glance in his direction, and she picked up the stylus attached to the side, starting to read.

Only a couple of steps away from her, Theodor crossed his arms over his chest.

The datapad shook in her hands. She shifted her weight from one foot to the other. Theodor noticed her biting her lower lip in an effort to focus on the agreement. He smiled slightly and leaned against the table behind him, crossing his ankles with a relaxed attitude. *Watching her is fun.*

After a couple of minutes, Vivienne interrupted him from his admiration. "Please correct me if I'm mistaken, but if I break the agreement and talk to anyone outside your society about you, I lose everything, including my life?"

"You agree to surrender any goods you might have accumulated during your contract." He uncrossed his ankles and straightened. "Your life would be in the hands of the Local Council."

"What is this Local Council?" she asked.

"Since you are in my territory, the Council is formed by the three highest ranked members of my coven."

"That includes you?"

Theodor considered a nod would suffice for an answer.

"It says here"—she pointed the stylus to a certain paragraph—"that if a conclusion cannot be reached by the Local Council, the case would be deferred to the High Council?"

"That's correct. The High Council is formed by the five leaders of the five covens. And yes, it includes me," he added.

"I have nothing to worry about. You saved my life. I'm not going to betray you." Vivienne signed and handed him the datapad.

Theodor saved the document and turned it off, placing it back on the table. He tried to find any trace of hesitation in her. To his surprise, for a change, there wasn't any. Next, he handed her the paper roll.

"This is the same thing, printed on paper. Please read it."

Vivienne read quickly and nodded at him.

'The sooner I finish here, the better. I can't wait to go home and avoid him for the rest of my life.' Theodor heard her loud thoughts.

Every second spent in each other's proximity made the attraction stronger, for both of them.

With slow, calculated moves, he flipped open the lid of the black box and seized the ceremonial dagger. The thin, sharp blade sent visible shivers throughout her body.

Vivienne extended her hand in front of him.

Precious stones, imbedded in the handle, glimmered in a multitude of lights reflected in the whole room. Theodor held her hand into his and gazed into her eyes.

"Do you promise to keep the secret you have been entrusted with for the rest of your life?"

Vivienne nodded. Her hand trembled in his. "Yes."

Theodor acknowledged her whisper with a slight smile, the first one he'd let her see.

Her heart beat faster, and the reaction widened his smile.

He slid the cold blade against the palm of her hand. One drop of blood glided over her skin and splattered against the white paper. Vivienne had taken a life oath.

Theodor placed the dagger back in the box and the document on the table, still holding her bleeding hand in his.

Her adrenaline rushed, the mix of desire and confusion washing over him in a warm sensation. The chemistry between them charged the air with an electricity he had never experienced before. Judging by her light tremors, the battle with herself was on the losing side, control slipping away.

His pulse accelerated when he lifted her hand to his lips, and witnessed Vivienne's heart somersaulting in her chest.

"Theo, what . . .?"

His fangs descended. Theodor expected her to flip out any second. There wasn't any sign of fear. That instant, he felt her trust, and hope for a possible future overtook his mind.

Vivienne opened her mouth as if to say something. No sound came out. Theodor's fangs grazed her skin.

The sweet smell and the taste of her blood on his tongue exploded inside him, beckoning his inner beast. He surfaced only to kneel in front of the powerful bond established between him and Vivienne.

Theodor accepted her as the one destined to him. The whole world shifted and rearranged again, like a couple of nights ago. *She's indeed the one I've waited for all my life. Is she ready to be mine? Not by far, but there's hope.*

~ ~ ~

"Theo." She finally found the strength to articulate a word.

"Thank you." Theodor's whisper ravaged her soul.

She knew, no matter how much she ran from him, she would never be the same. Something had changed deep inside her. Forever.

Vivienne couldn't stop thinking he must've used mind control on her somehow.

His smile melted her bones. Two deep dimples marked his cheeks, knocking all air out of her lungs and wiping all thought from her mind. Vivienne's legs trembled in an effort to support her. Both his hands closed around hers. He healed the small cut instantly and released her.

She lowered her gaze. *I need to get out of here.*

Theodor tilted her head backward. "I appreciate your trust and loyalty. You are free to go."

Vivienne stepped back fumbling with the buttons on her bracer. Her hands shook, her whole body quivered, and her heart beat out of control.

"See you." Vivienne entered the opened portal.

Chapter 12

"What the hell did I witness?"

Theodor turned around to see his friend, George, stepping forward from behind one of the columns. He hadn't seen or heard him enter the room. *He must've been here when we came in.*

"She signed her pact of secrecy." Theodor's answer was intended to be serious and flat but failed. An impish smirk bloomed on his lips.

"Really? Is that how we do it now?" George waved his hand in the direction of the closed portal. "And who is this girl?"

Theodor tried to hide his smile but instead, he started to laugh.

"Her name is Vivienne."

"At least you know her name. That's great, since you almost . . . half . . . married her there." George stopped a couple of steps away from Theodor.

They grabbed each other's forearms and touched shoulders in a quick embrace.

"Welcome back, my friend." Theodor remembered his manners.

"How long was I gone?" A joyful glimmer sparked in George's eyes. "I thought it had been five days, but here I am back, and you're smiling, laughing even."

"Let's get out of here. We need to talk. A lot has happened in the last few days." Theodor clasped his hand on his friend's shoulder.

"No kidding. It's great to see you smile again. I haven't seen you laugh like this since before the Flood. If this Vivienne is responsible for it, she's a keeper."

From Theodor's living room, his friend followed him to the terrace. After a few light jumps, they both sat on the rocks overlooking the sea.

George kept quiet the whole time Theodor told him how he'd met Vivienne, without holding back any details.

"At first, I rejected her, doubted her, but now I know she is the one." Theodor's shoulders slumped. "When I tasted her blood in the *Sanctum*, something happened, clicked into place like a missing piece. It's hard to explain."

Another sundown set the waters ablaze. The tangerine sky reflected on the ever-moving surface, the sea taking all possible shades of gold. It resembled liquid fire.

"Are you prepared to be rejected?"

Waves crashed against the bottom of the rocks, splashing around in millions of droplets. Theodor knew now, Vivienne could break his heart in just as many pieces.

"No. I won't give her the chance to do it."

A sad smile traveled through centuries and brought a glimmer to George's eyes. "I thought so too once, a long time ago." One, lonely deep sigh escaped into the humid air. "It didn't go as planned."

His friend, once happily married, lost the woman he loved. Theodor respected George's privacy and never asked.

"From what you've told me, I understand she's afraid of us, of our kind, even if she trusts you. Am I right?"

Theodor nodded in silence.

~ ~ ~

"When I met Clara, I knew she was the one from the beginning." George's voice covered the sound of the waves. "At the time, as a pureblood, I made sure she loved me, too, before telling her truth."

He paused for a few seconds. The pain accumulated throughout years made it hard to breathe. He focused on the round orange sun. It still hurt to talk about her, to say her name out loud.

"I begged Clara to let me turn her, explained to her we could be together literally forever." George dug from under his jacket a chain. Two wedding rings, the smaller one nested inside the larger, glimmered in the soft light. "She rejected my offer, convinced we are monsters, cursed souls . . . I had to make an impossible choice: her happiness or mine."

"What do you mean?" Theodor's interruption yanked George to the present. He knew how stubborn his friend could be, strict and unwilling to compromise. *I'm worried he's going to have his heart broken, or do something stupid.*

"She gave me the choice of accepting her as a human, or never seeing her again. I couldn't bear the thought." His shoulders slumped . . . "I accepted her terms. We married and spent the rest of her life together. As a mortal, Clara aged, withered away, and I couldn't do anything to stop it—"

"You should've turned her."

George turned to his friend. "Against her wishes?"

A few moments of silence floated between them. The waves seemed to have gotten stronger. A few of the droplets reached his boots.

"After fifty blissful yet painful years, she died in my arms. I stole a last kiss and with it, her last breath." George lowered his head. The sight of the wedding rings always brought him better-sweet memories. "I swore to never fall in love again and honored my promise for over one thousand years." He lifted his gaze to the horizon.

Violet clouds passed by the setting sun, dissipating in the proximity of the fiery globe. Slight traces of mauve mixed in the sky and faded away.

"I'll never ever let Viv go. She's been destined to me for a reason. I will turn her."

The determination in his voice made George smile. Once again, the fighter from within his prince surfaced. He didn't doubt him.

~ ~ ~

"How was your trip?" Theodor broke the silence after the sea swallowed half of the sun. "Anything to confirm our suspicions?"

"Well, I have good news and bad news."

"Start with the good."

"You were right. Your instincts proved again to be over the top."

"If that's the good, what's the bad?" Theodor rested his elbows on his knees.

"You were right"—George stared at his friend—"not all those human deaths are accidents. The authorities don't suspect anything. Our guys are keeping an eye on things."

"Someone is hunting in my territory and it's not okay." Theodor cut the air in front of him with is right hand. "Sooner or later, whoever it is will make a mistake. There has to be a way to connect all the victims."

"Those fake accidents have happened all over Europe. So far, we can't figure out who might be behind them. I've noticed one thing some of them have in common, beside the lack of blood, the severe mutilation." George paused, and Theodor tensed in anticipation. "The less damaged ones have deep cuts on their necks and parts of flesh missing."

"They're cutting off the marks of the bite, making sure there is no traceable DNA. Smart."

"We'll continue collecting evidence and stay alert. Our people know to do everything in their power to keep the authorities from suspecting anything. I'll receive more reports in the coming days."

"Good. Keep me up-to-date."

"Will you have time for this with everything else happening?"

"I'll make time for it. This is my coven"—his finger pointed down between them—"my territory, and I won't let anyone mock us."

Theodor's decision coincided with the whole sun sinking into the water. The sky turned to bright fuchsia, and a few peach clouds danced in the distance.

Whoever is doing this, is either incredibly smart, or really stupid. Whichever it is, he's messing with the wrong person.

~ ~ ~

"Uncle Serge." Malvina's happy voice brought her uncle back to reality inside the greenhouse.

He had turned off the hologram in anticipation of her visit.

"Malvina. Please sit." He patted the bench on the spot beside him. "We need to talk."

His serious tone brought a few wrinkles to her forehead. The second she sat, he rose to his feet.

"I've decided not to help you kill anyone." He lifted his hand, stopping her objection. "But I'll help you stay alive for as long as possible. You can still stop this crazy plan of yours. We could still disappear."

"No. I know the risks, but I won't stop until I have control over all the covens."

His deep, loud sigh filled the warm air in the greenhouse, mixing with the sweet aroma. Almost half of the heather bushes were in full bloom. He clasped his hands behind his back and started to pace.

"First, we need some damage control. Theodor is expecting you to introduce him to those twenty-some people. Correct?"

"Yes." Malvina rushed to nod. "I told him our group has twenty-three members. Sooner or later he will have to meet everyone."

"Make it sooner and reduce the number by one." He massaged his chin. "I can't be seen. If he gets into my mind, your plan, your life, is over."

"How am I going to justify your absence?"

"Tell him you lost one of your people. You had a strong disagreement on something, and he walked away. It's not unheard of."

"That might work."

Serge observed his niece. She seemed to be considering the idea. *A promising start.*

"You need to score some points with him. I'd suggest you call and volunteer to have him meet the group." Serge popped one of his favorite mints, offering one to Malvina as well. She declined it, and he slid the package back into his pocket. "The offering will tilt the balance in your favor."

"I can gather everyone and arrange the meeting. You're right. He doubted I have these people."

"His trust is hard to earn, and your shield isn't helping." Serge resumed his pacing.

"I can't let him see inside my mind. It would be the end." Malvina's disquiet almost amused her uncle.

"You can justify the shield as something you can't control. Make him believe you aren't shielding on purpose."

"Uncle Serge, you're the best." Malvina jumped up from the bench and hugged him.

His advice, his clever thinking, always kept them both out of trouble. This time he hoped to keep them alive. *Let's hope it works.*

"We'll have to come up with some cover story, something that won't raise any suspicions." He continued to think out loud. "It won't take them long to figure out who you are, but we can try." Serge changed his direction again. "Probably

Mihai will be the hardest to trick. He's spent time with Ivan, so he would notice your father's residual presence in you first."

A few moments of silence mixed with the warm air in the greenhouse.

"I've finally gotten an invitation to Queen Emelia's ball."

"That's a bad idea." Serge whirled on his heels to face his niece. "You shouldn't go."

He doubted she would listen to him. Her eyes already sparkled with excitement.

"It'll be good for me to be seen in public with Theodor. I've done my homework, and I know for a fact that he goes with his family every year." Malvina jumped up and down a couple of times. "I've never been to one of these parties. I can't wait." She twirled with her arms opened. "I've heard stories about them, about all the luxury and glamour. I have to go."

Serge had kept her away from it all. He'd always focused on their safety and ignored her desire to be a part of that world.

"I found the perfect dress too. It's being made for me. I need some jewelry." Malvina grabbed his arm, pleading, "Would you come with me? I need your help."

Serge nodded silently, defeated by her insistence. Malvina always attracted the wrong attention with her flashy style. He needed to make sure this time she exuded class, or at least her jewelry would. She had waited five hundred years to go to her first royal family ball, and guilt gnawed at him. *No matter the outcome, her first ball should be memorable. I'll make sure of it.*

~ ~ ~

As soon as she entered her lab the next morning, Vivienne noticed the flowers on the desk.

The most amazing orchid plant she'd ever seen had a card attached. Delicate green flowers displayed bright purple centers and hung heavy on a delicate stem. She had to touch it to make sure it was real.

With a smile on her face, Vivienne read the short note: *Welcome, and looking forward to working together.* Victor's flowery signature at the bottom occupied a whole line.

Her attention shifted to the black, elegant vase hosting one dozen white roses with bright red tips. Their scent filled the room. Vivienne knew who they were from. Theo.

Her smile melted away as soon as she read the stylish black card attached: *To your new beginning.*

Her mind travelled to the previous day. She could still sense the tingle caused by the touch of his lips, the light graze of his fangs on the palm of her hand. Her pulse accelerated in the back of her throat, and she wiped both her hands nervously on her beige skirt.

Before more memories would shake her decision to avoid him at all costs, Vivienne buttoned her lab coat.

The roses had started to open. Delicate, soft petals slightly curled outward. She skimmed her fingertips over the velvety flowers and buried her nose in them, inhaling loudly.

His deep-blue eyes glittering with dancing flames flashed into her mind again. Staying away from Theodor would be a challenge. *Why am I so attracted to him? I know better.* With a deep sigh, she turned her attention to work and started her computer.

Vivienne needed to use all her determination in order to focus. Late in the afternoon, she politely thanked Theodor for the flowers and declined his invitation to dinner. She had to suppress her own desire to see him.

The short call interrupted her, and she found it impossible to resume her work. Instead, she immersed herself in reading everything she could find about vampires. *Maybe I should learn about them after all. It can't hurt.*

In the following few days, Vivienne used every single excuse she could think of to stay away from him, including not answering his calls. She dedicated a couple of days to shopping, and a new wardrobe filled her dressing room.

When she wasn't in her lab, Vivienne read the information she had transferred to her datapad. Her thirst for knowledge pushed her forward.

The warm weather, inviting sun, and gorgeous beach drew her outside. After a few good hours spent on the fine sand, she obtained a healthy glow, a sun-kissed color.

As much as she avoided Theodor, Vivienne accepted Victor's presence. He seemed to be everywhere. When she lost all account of time, he would be the one dragging her into the break room for lunch or for walks outside.

~ ~ ~

A week after she started to work for him, Victor stopped by to remind her of the late hour. Vivienne stared at her screen with tight fists, as if she was ready to punch it. Her eyebrows scrunched with frustration under the light projected from the single luminescent globe floating about eight feet in the air.

"Looks like you're having trouble. Can I help with anything?" He walked behind her desk.

"I was trying to get this information downloaded"—she touched the screen—"but it won't work."

"Allow me," Victor whispered in her ear. His arms encircled Vivienne and took over the keyboard. Using his own password, he tried to access the data she wanted downloaded from the closed network. "It's not a matter of clearance, just a poor connection and slow response from the source."

Victor took advantage of her distraction with the slow downloading file, and lowered his head, close to hers, their cheeks almost touching.

Vivienne's scent, fresh and sweet, made his blood rush. The touch of her back against his chest forced him to fight against his body's reactions. His fangs started their descent. The need to taste her skin became impossible to resist. He licked his lips.

The sound of the opening sliding doors made him lift his gaze.

"Theo." Vivienne finally abandoned her screen.

"Prince Theodor." Victor straightened up. His fangs receded.

"Am I interrupting?"

Damn right, you are. What the hell is he here for? He's the last person I expected to see. Hands in his pockets, Victor stepped away from the woman stirring his senses. *She's irresistible.*

"Not at all. Vivienne had some trouble accessing some information, and I helped." He adopted a calm and indifferent tone. *At least my fangs aren't giving away my thoughts.*

Theodor advanced, staring at Victor. "Would you mind giving us a moment?"

He didn't want to, but it was probably the smart thing to do. "I'll be in my office if you need me."

~ ~ ~

After one more glance toward the closing door, Theodor turned all his attention to Vivienne.

Her hands clasped nervously on her lap. Her ankles crossed under the desk. *She's wearing her favorite blue shoes.*

"I apologize for disturbing you at work." He tilted his head. "My parents asked me to invite you to their place for dinner, this coming Friday night."

"I'm working. Sorry." Vivienne declined too quick. "What are you doing?" she hurried to ask when he opened his bracer.

"My mother said to call her if you said no." Theodor dialed his parents' frequency and the translucent screen opened above his wrist.

Vivienne let out a sigh and rolled her eyes. *She's cute when she does that.*

Distracted, Theodor didn't pay any attention to the ongoing conversation. He kept glancing toward the door. Victor's behavior unsettled him. *I have to talk to him.*

"I'm looking forward to it." Vivienne returned a smile to his mother.

"I'll pick you up Friday night at seven," Theodor offered as soon as he terminated the short call.

"Okay. I'm going home." Vivienne rose to her feet. "It's been a long day."

Another lame excuse to avoid him, but Theodor had a surprise planned for the next day. "Of course. Have a good night."

With the shortest nod, Theodor left her lab. He had one more stop.

Chapter 13

A wave of dark, powerful energy carried Theodor into Victor's office. With each step anger built up inside him, accelerating his pulse.

The other man stood in front of one of the closed windows, hands stuck in the pockets of his black, tailored pants.

"Prince Theodor, what can I do for you?"

Theodor measured Victor, his attempt at calmness. The tension filling the air told him otherwise. *He's nervous, just as he should be.*

Similar in height, Victor was slender with an athletic build. *He would have the advantage of being faster, in theory at least.* A straight, almost pointy nose, fit with the high cheekbones and thin lips, giving him an aristocratic appearance.

Theodor knew his massive build provided a great deal of physical strength. The inheritance from his father served him well. He clenched his jaw. Tension caused his muscles to tighten like sprung coils, ready to snap.

"Stay away from her," Theodor growled. His index finger almost touched Victor's chest.

"What are you talking about?" The innocent air Victor adopted didn't suit him and infuriated Theodor.

"You know damn well what I'm talking about. Don't play with me, Victor."

"I have no idea—"

Theodor's hand tightened around Victor's throat with the speed of light. "I'm only going to tell you this one more time. Stay away from Vivienne." Theodor accentuated every word, pausing after each one. He released him but continued the staring contest.

In return, Victor held Theodor's gaze for a couple of seconds. He walked away a few steps, and Theodor beamed with satisfaction. *Ha. I won that one.*

"I didn't know you were interested. The one-night stand champion of the world interested in one of my favorite girls . . ." Victor didn't finish his phrase, as if taunting him.

Theodor's fists tightened, and his fangs descended. "That is none of your business. This is my territory"—he pointed to the floor—"and if anything, she's mine. And off limits. Just because she works for you, doesn't make her one of your girls." Theodor crossed his arms over his chest, intentionally showing off his corded muscles. "Your reputation isn't much better either. Leave her alone."

Victor swallowed hard, and lowered his head.

And that's two wins. I've got this. Theodor held back a satisfied smile. He needed to get his point across and make sure Victor knew he was about to cross a dangerous line.

"Oh, but living in your territory makes her yours?" A new spark of black hope gleamed in Victor's eyes. "Look, I'm going to be a good sport here." Without any sign of intimidation, he tilted his head to the side. "What do you say we share?"

Theodor smelled the adrenaline rushing through the other man's body, the thrill of the hunt. Victor played with fire.

"Is this what she is to you? A game?" Theodor growled and stepped closer to Victor. "You're toying with her life." His fists rose slightly, ready to hit him.

"It's not like I'm going to kill her." A sleazy smile spread across Victor's face. "Just have some fun. I'll even make sure she enjoys it."

Theodor reached his limit and saw in the window's reflection the flames light up his eyes. *Perhaps I counted my small victories too soon.* Another threatening hiss made Victor retreat before Theodor's fury.

"You're going to stay away from her." Again, he pointed an index finger, this time in the other man's face. "Do you understand me?"

"Should I remind you, I don't take orders from you?" His chin jotted up. "I'm independent, not one of your lackeys. You can't tell me what to do."

Victor displayed his fangs, just as long and deadly as Theodor's.

Does he really think he can scare me? What a joke. Theodor relaxed his shoulders and puffed his chest.

"You don't need to take orders from me. I'll grace you with a warning." Theodor's voice turned to steel and ice. "If you touch Vivienne, I will kill you." He whirled around and started toward the door.

"What about letting her choose?" Victor's words made Theodor stop and half turn his head, glancing over his shoulder.

This guy is either stupid or knows something I don't. Theodor turned his back to Victor without another word. It was in everyone's best interest to walk away.

"Are you afraid she would choose me?" Victor taunted him and Theodor was tempted to fight his new adversary.

His inner beast stirred. Considering his volatile nature, he had controlled himself admirably up until then. Close to losing his calm, Theodor fought his impulse to kill the other man right then and there.

"I warned you. You touch one hair on her, and I'll turn you to ashes."

Theodor exited Victor's office and let his threat float behind him in the dark room.

He went straight home, furious. Victor wasn't going to back down, and he knew it. *Now is his choice to live, or die.*

~ ~ ~

Victor sat in his chair. His eyes still lingered on the closed door. The surprising turn of events found him unprepared.

How the hell do I fight against someone like Prince Theodor? He was alive only because Theodor didn't want him dead. Yet. Theofrost, the beast, lived up to his reputation. Victor had seen the temptation in his rival's savage eyes.

A chill crept up his spine. The whole situation proved to be more complicated.

He needed to revise his plans. He'd had competition before, but never someone as powerful as Prince Theodor.

His mind wandered to the sensations that had overloaded his senses. Vivienne was worth any risk and effort. She would be his with or without her consent.

Victor rushed out of his office. *I have work to do.*

~ ~ ~

Vivienne skipped dinner and went straight to bed. The tiredness and dizziness from the past few days intensified with each passing minute. Refusing to accept what she had become was definitely not the way to go about. *I'll leave early tomorrow morning and get some blood. There's a kiosk at the corner of my street and the main boulevard. A ten-minute walk won't kill me.*

After the year spent on just enough blood to stay alive, her body had adapted to ignore the signs of needing to feed. Now, she paid the price. *I shouldn't have waited until this late. If only I had bought a few vials and kept them in the fridge.*

She fell asleep quickly but woke up in pain. She ran a high fever, and the thirst became unbearable.

In and out of consciousness, Vivienne had a hard time differentiating the hallucinations from reality. *I'm going to die all alone. Nobody will miss me, or even know I'm in trouble, until the stench of my decomposing corpse alerts someone.*

Her whole body shook, cold and heat taking turns every few seconds. Terrifying monsters crept forward from the corners of her frightened mind. She tried to scream but no sound registered in her years. Her hands fought the suffocating covers. The sheet twisted around her feet like vines dragging her away from her world, and she kicked it.

There are no monsters. There are no monsters. There are no monsters. She blinked a few times, making sure she was awake.

After a couple attempts, Vivienne managed to slide out of bed, only to collapse right beside it. Climbing back in, surpassed her limit. *My bracer. If I can call for help, I can make it. Who do I even call?*

A quick glance out the window revealed the darkness, and she lost the concept of time. It might as well have been an eternity.

With all the strength she could muster, she grabbed her bracer from the night table. Her vision played tricks, and a funnel swallowed her, everything started to swirl around.

Vivienne managed to open the screen, but the effort to remain awake wore her out. Her fingertips pressed another button, and the list of names displayed. *Theo. Maybe I shouldn't have avoided him.* If she could only press the button one more time. Just once.

The sweet, deep nothing engulfed her, dark and welcoming.

~ ~ ~

Theodor knew her schedule, and at seven o'clock sharp knocked at her door. He waited for an answer, listened for the slightest noise inside. Nothing. The second knock echoed in the fresh morning. A cold chill of danger crawled up his spine. *Something's not right.*

Overriding the access panel, in only seconds, he entered her home. There was no movement.

The two servants followed him with breakfast and closed the door behind them. Their steps echoed on the stone tiles, mixing with the rustle of the long skirts they wore as uniforms.

Through his heightened senses, Theodor detected Vivienne in the bedroom and ran to her.

The second he saw her on the floor, his heart stopped. "Viv." Gently, Theodor lifted her in his arms and sat on the edge of the bed. *She's burning with fever.*

"Viv, answer me." He shook her lightly, searching for a response. Nothing, not a sound, no movement, not one muscle reacted. He found only a barely detectable pulse.

Theodor checked under her eyelids. Completely red, bloodshot eyes, worse than the night he found her in the dark alley, prodded him into action.

"Blood. She needs blood." He raised his voice, glancing at the two helpers petrified in the doorway.

One of them, the taller of the two, ran to the fridge.

"She doesn't have any," the woman yelled, panicked, running back.

"Go home and get some. Hurry."

With trembling hands, she opened a portal and disappeared inside.

"Say something." Theodor rocked Vivienne's unconscious body back and forth.

Long strands of wet hair plastered to her face, and he brushed them away, one by one. Her body convulsed under his touch.

She needs blood. Now. I can't afford to wait.

Without any hesitation, Theodor bit into his left wrist. Blood started to trickle, and he forced it between her lips.

Why didn't I see it last night? How could I be so blind? I let anger cloud everything. Should've known better.

He remembered how pale she'd been, and her fragile balance. *I've been too busy being furious at Victor.* His pulse raced the same way it did the moment he'd seen the other man so close behind her.

A hiss escaped between his fangs. Victor had infuriated him enough to distract him from what was important—Vivienne's safety and well-being.

Theodor opened and closed his fist a couple of times to make the blood flow quicker and pressed his wrist against her lips. A few drops made it inside her mouth.

Images from the previous night flooded his mind uninvited. Victor's arms around her, his hands *accidentally* grazing her skin, their heads almost touching. He closed his eyes.

"Please drink." His whisper didn't seem to have any effect.

Theodor tightened his hold on her and buried his face in her hair. It smelled like the ocean. The invisible claw of fear squeezed his throat.

He indulged in other's fear, but never his own. The suffocating sensation forced him to inhale deeply and reopen his eyes.

"Don't do this to me."

His blood could save her life. But as a mortal, she could have an adverse reaction to vampire blood. A few drops were all she needed to stay alive. Anything more than a couple mouthfuls, would've killed her.

"What's taking so damn long? Where's that blood?" he yelled at the other servant.

The short, older woman shrugged, avoiding eye contact.

A low, weak moan attracted Theodor's attention back to Vivienne. Her parched lips moved, and he pressed his wrist against them again.

"Viv, drink my blood. Please, you have to."

"Theo."

Her whisper made his heart pick up the pace even if she lay still unconscious. *She called my name.* A feel-good sensation swelled inside him.

"Take my blood. Drink, damn it."

Theodor forced her mouth open. With his left fist closed, a few more drops dripped, and he directed them straight to her throat, forcing her to swallow.

She coughed. Her eyes fluttered open, revealing two ruby globes.

"Theo. I can't see . . ." Her panic hurt him. Her hands grabbed onto his arms.

"I'm right here. Please drink a few more drops. Everything's going to be okay," Theodor whispered.

She was scared, and all he could do was hold her, keep her alive. An unfamiliar sensation of guilt and helplessness cracked open one of the icy layers protecting his heart. He could swear he heard it breaking.

Her lips closed around his wound, and she swallowed a mouthful of blood.

At least she's not shaking anymore. He exhaled, and his head fell back. The sensation of her lips on his wrist drinking his blood made him lose control for a short second. A hiss pushed through.

Every drop of the precious, life-giving fluid leaving his body intensified his senses. Instead of weakening, his power spiked to new heights.

After another mouthful, Theodor withdrew his hand.

"That's enough. Drinking more will make you sick."

The same instant, the servant came running into the room with the blood, followed by Jake.

Theodor grabbed the mug from her unsteady hands and passed it to Vivienne. By the time she started to drink, he had healed himself.

She'll be all right. He glanced to her night stand. It had been less than ten minutes since he'd entered the room. Beside the clock, the black vase still held the roses he'd sent her.

Vivienne almost finished drinking when her body started to shake again. Her tiny hands held the mug over his, causing the remaining blood to spill over them and the cream-colored sheets.

Theodor sensed her body heating up again. She was reacting to his blood.

Damn it. I thought she didn't have enough to cause this.

"Start the shower. Cold." He placed the mug on the night table and rose to his feet with Vivienne in his arms.

"Change the bed and make sure her fridge is stocked with blood. Jake, cancel any plans I had for today. I won't be available for anyone. Oh, and replace those flowers with fresh ones."

Theodor barked instructions on his way to the shower. He had to lower her temperature. She could die from excessive internal heat.

"Theo, what's going . . . ?"

Vivienne lost consciousness in the middle of her sentence. He held her tight in his arms.

"Stay with me," he whispered.

The freezing water ran over both their bodies. He couldn't feel the cold, and it seemed neither could she.

Theodor leaned against the wall and pressed his lips to her burning forehead—his favorite way to check her temperature. Her skin tasted just as sweet as he imagined it would.

His gaze stopped for a second on the bottles of soaps and

shampoo. They were different shades of turquoise-blue, and their scent written in gold letters—ocean breeze.

She had bought them on her two-day shopping spree. Theodor had followed her, without her knowing, from store to store. He studied her every move, every reaction, and discovered more of her tiny quirks he found amusing and cute.

She always bit her lip when thinking or trying to focus on something. Playing with a string of hair, twisting it, was a tell of her indecision. He had to hold back a laugh when she rolled her eyes, a sure sign of annoyance. *I think that one is my favorite.*

Her reaction to smells she didn't like made him smile. He remembered her sniffing a few other fragrances of soaps and crinkling her nose.

After a while, her temperature finally lowered. He had no idea how long they stood under the freezing-cold running water. Her skin turned translucent, and her lips a dark shade of purple.

The two women rushed her into the dressing room and dried her with towels, after which they dressed her in a clean nightie. Jake had already returned and held a clean leather suit for Theodor.

"Did you take care of everything?" He stopped before stepping into her dressing room to change his own wet clothes.

"Yes, Your Majesty." Jake bowed and waited for the next instructions.

Back in her bedroom, Theodor checked on Vivienne. She seemed to be out of danger. Her body felt cold under his touch, and he climbed into the bed with her, under the covers. With a short wave of his hand, he sent the servants and Jake away.

Theodor propped a few pillows against the headboard,

holding Vivienne on top of him. His body heat would help her gradually warm up.

He glanced again to the clock on her night stand. Three hours had elapsed since he'd found her on the floor. The fresh roses brought a cheerful spot of color to the room, and their sweet scent filled the air.

Vivienne's heart beat at a normal rate, her pulse strong and steady. Even breaths escaped her lips and brushed over his chest. Theodor closed his eyes.

His discussion with George resurfaced in his mind. The unbearable thought of losing her suffocated him. He had to convince her to let him turn her. *I'll find a way.*

Chapter 14

The screams mixed with bone chatter elevated her pulse out of control. Hands over her ears, Vivienne squeezed her eyes shut. Heat surrounded her, penetrated all the way to her core, burning her. Reopening her eyes, she stared at the flames erupting from inside her body, through her skin. She checked her hands—full of blood.

Her heart pounded in the back of her throat sending pulses to her temples.

A whirlwind whistled all around. Vivienne couldn't see the ground. Suspended in the air, she heard more voices whispering words she couldn't understand.

Tresses of hair fell wet on her face, drenched in blood. She didn't recognize the dirty, stained, cream dress shredded on her body.

The flames burned hotter. Vivienne dared a glance around. In the cyclone of blood spinning around her, bones mixed with body parts in various stages of decay. She wanted to scream, but no sound came out. Her mouth dried with agonizing thirst.

A bleeding wrist materialized in front of her, and a familiar voice kept telling her to drink.

She did. The blood slid down her throat and eased her agony. From somewhere near, a whisper echoed in her ears and a recognizable smell invaded her nose.

"Don't do this to me." A man's voice, deep and soothing, caused her to blink her eyes open. Blurry vision made it impossible to identify him.

Expensive cologne tickled her senses. Instead of eyes, blue flames burned with a cold glow. Vivienne found comfort in them against the heat.

"You need to stop," the voice continued, but she couldn't. She needed the blood to quench her thirst. Her hands held tight onto the wrist.

His skin turned grey, the blue flames faded. Flesh shrank, revealing bones.

"Viv." Another whisper made her gaze at his face.

"Theo!" Vivienne screamed and opened her eyes.

Strong arms closed around her quivering body.

"I'm right here. It's just a bad dream. Viv . . ."

His voice became distant, and her eyes closed, heavy with grogginess.

She still held onto his arm when he started to disintegrate. Chunks of flesh detached from his body, sucked into the whirlwind. Repeating his name over and over again didn't stop the process, nor slow it down.

Everything around her quaked, even if there was no solid ground. The air became unstable. In the free fall, the air brushed upward against her body. She struggled to catch onto something.

Darkness and freezing cold surrounded her. The arm she held onto disintegrated from her hands slowly, piece by piece. Her teeth chattered.

"Stay with me." She screamed again, as loud as she could. Still no sound. A cold, dark place surrounded her. Ice pellets hit her body from all directions. A sweet, flowery aroma touched like a balm on her senses. She could barely distinguish the blue flames, now far away.

"No!" Vivienne sat, eyes wide open, not sure where she was.

"Everything's all right, Viv. You're safe."

She stared at him, trying to control her fast beating heart and rushed, shallow breaths.

"Theo."

"Yes, it's me. You had a bad dream. It's over now."

Vivienne glanced around, recognizing her bedroom. The roses on her nightstand, spreading a sweet scent, were fresh, not wilted as she remembered them. Sunlight flooded the room, filtering through the cream draperies in a soft glow.

"Breathe. You're okay." He stroked her back in a slow motion, up and down, infusing her with comfort. "I'm right here."

She acknowledged his voice and gazed at the blue wisps dancing inside his eyes. Her stare followed the contour of his straight nose, and dipped to his lips, slightly curved upwards. The dimples in his cheeks begged her to touch them.

Her hand rose to the side of his face. Light stubble grazed her fingertips. *He's real.* It wasn't another dream.

"You're really here." Vivienne finally gained control over her racing senses. "I didn't kill you."

"Of course not." His reassurance rumbled out of his chest, and his hand pressed her head against him.

Reality hit her. The nightmare ended. She was awake and aware. Heat raced through her body in contact with his, as hot as in her dream. *Why am I on top of him?*

The question formed in her mind from a multitude of scrambled pieces, like a puzzle on master difficulty. His heart drummed in her ear, and his breath caused both of them to rise and fall in a slow, relaxing rhythm.

Vivienne lifted her gaze to him.

"What are you doing in my bed?"

"Keeping you warm."

His smile alone could ignite blazes inside her body.

"I'm not cold."

"You don't remember?"

At his question, Vivienne searched her still jumbled mind. More pieces of the puzzle jumped from hidden corners. Everything blurred, and confusion settled in. She couldn't tell reality from dream. And she wasn't going to make any progress as long as he held her.

"Not much . . . Did you make me drink your blood?" Vivienne pushed up, trying to distance herself from him. Her judgment became seriously impaired in his proximity.

Theodor's arms tightened, and he set her back on top of him. "I did. It was that or let you die."

Vivienne indulged in the mind and body-melting sensations for the next few minutes, listening to him tell her how he found her unconscious, and everything that happened after. Her body molded against his.

"So, you saved my life again."

Theodor gently tipped her face to him, and she dove in the depths of the bottomless, mesmerizing blue.

"Don't you ever do this again." A slight line marked the middle of his forehead. "When was the last time you had blood?"

She turned her gaze away. "The night you found me."

"That was ten days ago." His voice rose a little, as if he couldn't believe her words. "Do you have a death wish? You should have blood every four, five days at most in order to prevent the slightest hint of thirst." He gently released her chin and brushed away a strand of her hair. "Why would you wait so long?" His tone softened again, like a warm cloud. "What were you thinking?"

Vivienne swallowed the sudden lump in her throat and avoided his piercing eyes.

"Since I got infected, Greg had been the one bringing me blood. After all that time spent without knowing what day it was due to frequent blackouts, I'm still trying to adjust, to learn about all this."

Theodor relaxed and exhaled.

"He always gave me very little blood, leaving me thirsty for more, not a full mug like you did. I've become accustomed to ignoring the signs."

Her voice quieted, and Theodor hugged her closer to him.

"Jake stocked your fridge with blood." She swore his lips touched the top of her head. Heat flew freely through her body like a river of fire. "Please drink one full vial every four, five days. I don't want to go through this again."

The obvious care in his tone touched something inside her, hit a switch and initiated the slow, sweet process of liquefying her bones. She nodded silently and tried to put some distance between them.

"Where do you think you're going?"

"To get dressed. I'm late—"

"I'm not letting you out of my sight today." His interruption didn't leave room for any negotiations. "Spend the day with me. Please?"

Staying in his arms, in her bed, with barely any clothes on, wasn't a good idea. One question screamed in her mind, hitting every corner of her consciousness.

"Why were you here to start with?" She gazed at him. "How did you get in?" The blue magical wisps in his eyes performed a mesmerizing ritual.

"I wanted to surprise you with breakfast since you have been avoiding me for a whole week." A new smile bloomed on his lips. "When you didn't answer the door, I overrode the entry panel."

Vivienne hurried to say the first thing that crossed her mind. "I haven't been avoiding you."

Theodor's laugh filled the quiet room and flooded her heart. She found herself torn between being mad at him for catching her lying and the desire to kiss him.

Those full lips had tempted her before, appearing in her dreams a few times during the past week. Now they stretched over strong, white teeth, somehow reminding her of a predator. He was one. Vampires were at the top of the hunting pyramid.

"You're a terrible liar."

Tension charged the air between them.

"Maybe. A little. May I go dress now?" She raised her voice slightly, infuriated for getting caught so easy.

"Maybe? A little?" He repeated her exact words, as if he wanted to make sure she could hear her own lie. "You have deliberately avoided seeing me more than once a day for a week straight."

He confronted her with darkened eyes.

Vivienne had little choice but to admit the truth. "Fine, I avoided you. Happy?" she snapped at him. "Now, I need to get dressed."

"No, I'm not happy." He settled more comfortably on top of the pillows and held her firmly against his body. "And you can go dress right after you answer one question. Why?"

Vivienne lost her resolve and, for a short while, got lost in the never-ending blue pools. A trace of sanity returned, and she started to squirm, trying to get away from him.

"I'd rather talk with clothes on."

Theodor let out a low growl, and with a quick movement, he rolled her over, trapping her body under his, holding her wrists in his hands.

"Why?"

Vivienne couldn't control the tinge of fear touching her. *After saving my life twice he wouldn't hurt me. Would he? I can't give him the answer he wants. No.*

"Let me go." Vivienne tried again to escape him. She would've had better luck moving a concrete wall with her bare hands.

"Answer my question. Why?"

Determination settled in his eyes. He wasn't going to let it go. She tried to control her panic.

"I'll tell you after I get dressed."

Her answer made his brows furrow, and a half smile curled his lips with superiority.

"I would've never taken you for the stubborn kind. You should know, I can be more headstrong than a pack of mules." His warning, calm and cold, left no doubt in her mind. "You aren't going anywhere until you answer me. And I'm pretty comfortable." He wiggled on top of her.

The deep-blue vortex in his eyes lured her in, an enticing world of unlimited possibilities.

"I didn't want to see you." She turned her head toward the window.

"What kind of lame excuse is that? Stop running in a circle, Viv." His annoyance was quickly replaced with the softest tone. "Look at me."

Tears pooled in her eyes when she stared at him. He wasn't leaving her any way out.

"Why?"

"You seem to like asking this question a lot," Vivienne snapped again.

"And you seem to like avoiding it just as much."

There was steel and ice mixed in his voice. She was backed into a corner, and the only way out was through him. *Or maybe around him?*

"The truth. And don't forget, I'll know if you try to lie to me again."

Tears started to run on her cheeks, reaching the corners of her mouth. Theodor released her, cupping her face. With his thumbs, he wiped away the hot and salty, tiny droplets.

"Would it help if I told you I feel the same way?"

"What?" she barely found the strength to ask.

Vivienne didn't trust her ears. His admission couldn't be real, was just her imagination, her mind played tricks on her. *This is not the first time I've heard things. It can't be true.*

"I'm attracted to you as much as you are to me, Viv."

She opened her mouth to say something, but his thumb brushed lightly against her lower lip, erasing all thought.

His head dipped, and hot air fanned over her face, setting it ablaze. Breath caught in her chest, and she blinked a few times. When his eyes lowered to her lips, Vivienne regained her sharpness.

"You . . . You knew?"

His smile sent lava through her veins, melting everything in its way. She couldn't move even if she wanted to.

"What do you think?"

"But it's wrong."

She tried again to push him away. Panic overtook her.

"It's not wrong. It's destiny."

~ ~ ~

"Destiny? We belong to different species. You're a vampire," she almost yelled at him.

"Viv." Theodor held her tight in spite of her escalating fear. Her old terror was back, hurting him.

"Please, let me go."

Theodor let out a deep, loud sigh and rolled over, freeing her.

"We'll spend the day at my place." He pulled on his boots and listened to her bare feet running over the stone tiles.

Theodor glanced over his shoulder and saw her slamming the dressing room door. He ran and stopped by it, wanting to take it down, go in, and hold her in his arms again. Instead, he let his forehead touch the hard surface.

He heard her leaning against the other side of the door and slowly sliding down to the floor, between sobs.

I'm such an idiot . . . He balled his hands into fists and closed his eyes.

It wasn't the less than two inches of solid wood that kept him from her. Theodor could've gone through the damn door as if it wasn't there. Her fear raised the invisible barrier holding him back. She remained untouchable for as long as she feared him.

Her steps echoed in the dressing room, farther and farther away from him. Soft sounds of clothes being shuffled around followed shortly, and he leaned against the wall.

I can't even blame her. I rejected her too. I thought we were wrong for each other. He inhaled deeply a few times, trying to control his urges to kiss her, to taste her lips.

He walked a thin line. The short confrontation with Victor flashed in his mind. Victor's suggestion to let Vivienne chose between them made him growl between fully extended fangs.

Would she prefer him? No. She's attracted to me. And she's completely wrong thinking that Victor is a friend.

He wasn't going to lose her. Not to Victor, not to anyone else.

"She's mine," Theodor muttered under his breath and crossed his arms over his chest. *I'll fight anyone for her. This is one thing I know how to do. Unfortunately.* Fangs retracted and he exhaled, relaxing.

Vivienne came out wrapped in a long robe, clutching to her chest the clothes she had chosen for the day.

"That's original," he teased her.

"I need to take a shower."

Theodor moved with the high-speed characteristic to all vampires and opened the bathroom door for her.

Vivienne stepped over the threshold and turned to him.

"And stop moving fast like that." With one quick movement, before he had a chance to say anything, she slammed the door in his face. The second time in only a few minutes.

A smile bloomed on his lips. He took her actions as a challenge, and he'd never backed down from one before.

Theodor walked to the living room and stood tall in front

of the glass sliding doors. He clasped his hands at the small of his back and stared at the agitated waters.

The wind pushed the waves into high peaks with white, feathered tips. One after another, they crashed against the sand in an explosion of droplets.

So, the war of wills starts now. I know I can win this one. The sound of the running shower interrupted his thoughts. One memory crept up in his mind—her unconscious, convulsing body burning in his arms under the cold water.

He could have lost her forever.

~ ~ ~

Only steps away from him, Vivienne let the warm water run over her body. She needed to find her calm. Theodor proved impossible to fool. Her plan to avoid him had blown up in her face. He knew her secret, and she couldn't do anything to change the facts.

A new idea arose in her mind. Maybe she should accept spending time with him. The undeniable fact that they belonged to different species should have been enough to make both of them keep their distance.

I have to drink blood every four to five days. I didn't know it was so often. The small vials Greg used to bring her appeared clear in her mind. It would have taken five or six of them to fill one of the mugs Theodor had given her. *Theo . . .*

Vivienne remembered his eyes, his lips, his hot breath tickling her skin, and closed her eyes. Kissing a vampire was surely not on her list of things to do. Kissing Theo, the man who saved her life, twice, was a whole different story.

Memories are waterproof. The scent of the shampoo relaxed her for a while and helped her sort her chaotic thoughts.

The expression in Theodor's eyes from earlier made her let out a sigh and prop her hands on the shower wall. Water rinsed the foamy shampoo from her hair. It mixed with tears, glided along her body, and pooled at her feet, swirling around the drain. *I hurt him . . . He saved my life, and I called him a vampire. But he is one. And I'm a GeM, but I don't enjoy being called on it.*

Vivienne could only hope that their differences would be enough to keep her safe. Safe from him, and mostly, safe from her own instincts.

Chapter 15

A couple of hours later, after lunch, Vivienne lounged on his inviting terrace. She'd been reading the information she had transferred the previous day, hoping to keep Theodor away from her. Her plan worked, for a whole whopping five minutes.

Theodor's insistent stare made her drop her datapad. *Ugh. He's going to drill a hole in the side of my head.*

"What?"

"I didn't say a word."

"Then stop staring at me like I've grown an extra head or something."

A gust of wind twirled around them and wafted the light-blue beach dress around her crossed legs. Vivienne scrambled to hold it in place. The sudden movement caused her hair to escape from the loose bun. Still wet, it spread the scent of her shampoo, mixing in the salty air.

"You are beautiful."

Vivienne rolled her eyes and turned her gaze away from him. She had mirrors and used them—nothing special. He was obviously trying to engage her in a conversation. Her hands ran through her wet hair with the intention of gathering it again.

"You should keep it down. It'll dry faster."

Vivienne glanced at him again. He watched the waves breaking and splashing against the shore. In spite of the wind, the hot afternoon had lured them outside. She loved the comfortable lounge chairs with white pillows. *I should get one of these for my terrace.*

The sight of his profile sent a slight tremor through her body. She blamed it on her still wet hair and picked up her datapad.

"I see you've been reading about vampires." Theodor nodded to her device. "May I ask you why?"

Vivienne preferred to keep her eyes on the screen in front of her. She tried her hardest to keep the conversation to a minimum. It appeared he had different plans.

"You really have a soft spot for that question." She tried to get away with not answering.

A man walked through the opened doors to the terrace, saving her. *Thank you, whoever you are.*

The breeze teased his dark auburn hair, and he ran his hand through it, trying to keep the long strands out of his face.

His black leather suit assured Vivienne he was a vampire. It seemed it was their clothing of choice. His long coat brushed against one of the large stone urns decorating the terrace. Pretty red flowers bowed their heads under the leather's caress.

"Theo. I've been looking for you. New information on . . ." He froze when he noticed Vivienne on the lounge chair, hidden behind Theodor. "I apologize, I didn't realize you weren't alone."

"Viv, I would like you to meet George, my best friend, and second in command. George, this is Vivienne, the scientist I told you about."

Vivienne nodded, and George sat on a chair he pulled close to both of them.

"It's an honor to meet you, Miss Vivienne. I've heard so much about you."

"Please call me Vivienne." For some mysterious reason, she felt instantly comfortable in his presence. "Oh, and don't believe everything you hear."

George smiled and ventured into a light-hearted conversation. The tension between her and Theodor evaporated in the breeze.

"You said you have some new information. On what?" Theodor asked a few minutes later, interrupting the discussion about everything and nothing.

"Are you sure you want to talk business now?" George hesitated again.

Vivienne saw Theodor's nod. Her gaze moved between the two men.

"Okay, a couple more mutilated bodies appeared last week in Paris and Milan."

"Do we have any more clues?" Theodor's question sounded cold and professional.

Vivienne was curious to see him in action. She'd been wondering since she met him what a prince's job could possibly entail. *What about the bodies?* Curiosity got the best of her.

George pressed a few buttons on his bracer, and a display appeared, complete with pictures. The decomposing remains attracted her attention. The scientist in her surfaced.

"The body in Paris is the one worth mentioning. Here are the pictures. They found traces of *spark*. The victim was high when she died." He pointed to a couple fragments of her crushed skull. "This woman had a freshly shaved head, and the rags she'd worn for clothes leads us to believe she was homeless." George stared at Theodor. "It's possible she'd sold her hair for the drugs."

"So, what would she possibly be doing on a speeder?" Theodor glanced from the pictures to his friend. The next instant, a new picture attracted his attention. "There, what is that?" He indicated to a certain spot. "Can you zoom in?"

"I already know what that is"—George zoomed in—"a broken fingernail."

She observed the black, broken fingernail, a possible DNA source. Vivienne was about to tell them to check it when she saw the deep crease marking Theodor's forehead.

"Malvina," he whispered.

"Are we talking about the same Malvina pressuring you to marry her?"

Vivienne's eyebrows shot up in surprise at George's question. Luckily for her, another wind gust messed her hair, covering most of her face. By the time she tucked it back behind her ears, she'd regained control over her expressions.

She thought Theodor didn't have a girlfriend. He was engaged, about to get married?

When exactly had he lied to her? When he'd told her he was attracted to her, or when he'd said he didn't have a girlfriend? Both times? Vivienne noted his glance and kept an indifferent air. *I shouldn't care either way.*

"The one and only." Theodor shifted his attention back to the picture.

"Let's not jump to conclusions. The fake fingernail could belong to anyone. Do you have any idea how many women wear that sort of manicure?" George glanced at Vivienne's hands. Covered in a layer of beige nail polish, her nails weren't fake.

"I'm sure there are many, but how many of them would have the means and the opportunity to kill this woman?"

"What if the nail got there by accident, and has nothing to do with the way she died?" George continued to reason things out.

"It seems it was caught in her clothes, not lying on top of them. I think it broke when she threw the body." Theodor tapped the screen. "Oh, I so want her to have something to do with this. It would be the extra drop to motivate me to kill her."

For a second time, Vivienne stared at Theodor. His fangs descended, and his hiss sent chills down her back. She didn't want to be in that woman's shoes, whomever she might've been. What kind of monster was he? Did he really want to kill the woman he would marry?

"If she is behind this, she's covering her tracks well. There was no DNA found on that broken fake nail."

Well, there goes my suggestion. Vivienne crossed her arms over her chest.

"Hmm. Paris. Another body with less than normal blood levels, thrown from a speeder, or higher . . ." Theodor stopped thinking out loud. He and George glanced at each other.

"Higher." They both said at the same instant and rose to their feet. "Penthouse height." For the second time they spoke as one.

Vivienne knew she didn't have all the information, but she could read between lines. She understood they were after someone killing humans after drinking the victims' blood. Perhaps a thirsty vampire on the loose?

If their assumptions were correct, could it be the woman Theodor intended to marry? *I'm happy I didn't go to Paris after all. Dodged that one.*

"Have your men send us a list of penthouse owners. I doubt she would have it under her name, but I hope something will jump out at us."

"You want the list for Paris, or for all the cities in your territory?"

"All the cities where those accidents occurred. But start with Paris," Theodor decided after a short hesitation. "I have a feeling it's where we'll find answers."

Vivienne raised an eyebrow, impressed by how quickly he made connections that many would've missed. He didn't shy away from making spontaneous decisions and planning accordingly.

Theodor proved to be a born leader, and a fine-tuned strategist. It seemed nothing would stand in his way. She definitely didn't want to be on his bad side.

A tiny red light flashed on Theodor's bracer, and he checked it.

"Speaking of the devil, Malvina. I apologize, but I have to take this. I won't be long." He rushed inside, leaving Vivienne with George.

After a few moments of silence, Vivienne figured it would be impolite to return to her reading. George seemed nice, and she didn't need to ignore him, only his friend.

"How long have you known Theo?" she asked with genuine curiosity.

"Since the day he was born, almost five centuries."

The conversation floated light and effortless between laughs. George was indeed easy to talk to.

~ ~ ~

Inside, Theodor stood with his arms crossed over his chest in front of the large screen where he'd transferred the videocall.

"Malvina. I thought I made myself clear when I told you I would contact you. Did I stutter?"

His harsh tone demanded an apology, but Malvina wasn't the one to admit she was ever wrong.

"Theo, darling. I have good news, and I couldn't wait to share." She stopped for a second, waiting for his approval to continue.

Theodor waved his right hand in front of him as an invitation.

"I've managed to convince all of my people to meet you this coming weekend. Let me know when it's convenient for you." She bowed her head. Her top slid but failed to entice him.

Theodor's eyes followed the movement, glided over the porcelain skin. The scar he'd given her had healed nicely.

"I could probably do it Saturday night. It's the only time I can carve out about an hour for you."

"Wonderful. My place?" Malvina clapped her hands in excitement.

Theodor checked her nails. They were indeed fake, long, and black, but unfortunately, none missing. *Too bad.* One memory flashed in his mind, the night they last met. She had traced thin lines on his skin. A chill of disgust travelled through his body.

"No. Let me know when you're all ready, and I'll open a portal to my *Sanctum*." He hated the rundown, old house and would never step foot in that place again. "You'll all be sent back when the meeting is over."

"Are we going to be safe?" Malvina hesitated to accept his terms.

"You have my word. And you know it's good, unlike others." Theodor had to slip in a jab. He didn't trust her, and it wasn't a secret.

"I don't understand why you think I'm being dishonest."

"Drop your shield and prove me wrong," Theodor dared her, his eyes narrowed.

"I'm sorry I gave you the wrong impression. My shield is permanent." Her opened hands pointed to her temples. "I can't lower it or raise it as I wish."

Theodor searched for a sign, one muscle twitch that would give away her lie. *Either she speaks the truth, or she's a master liar. I am inclined to go with the latter.*

"If that's the case why haven't you said so from the beginning?" He studied her with suspicion, still hunting for a clue.

"I didn't want you to think I'm weak. You deserve the best princess by your side." Malvina lowered her head again. Theodor sensed how untrue her words were. He just couldn't prove it.

If she thought she was the one to stand by his side, she was in for a big surprise. Her annoying voice hurt his ears, and the words laced with lies infuriated him. His volatile temper was ready to erupt.

"I think I do too. Call me Saturday night at midnight when you have your people gathered."

"Theo. Is there any chance after the meeting for us to spend some time together?"

The languorous gaze made goosebumps of disgust rise on Theodor's skin.

"I told you I can barely take an hour for the meeting. My time is limited. And so is my patience," he added and glanced outside. Vivienne's laugh soothed his soul. She never seemed that relaxed with him.

"I didn't realize I'm interrupting." It was the closest Malvina had ever come to an apology. He had to hold back a satisfied smirk.

"Did you think I sit around and wait for your calls?"

The sarcasm in his voice brought a smile to Malvina's bright red lips. *She has thick skin. Too bad none was left on that fingernail fragment.*

"I wanted to give you the good news. I trust you won't try to mind control my people."

"I won't. Have a good day."

Theodor disconnected the call, cutting their conversation short. He wanted to go back outside on the terrace with Vivienne and his friend. Before rejoining them, he needed a few moments.

Malvina's offer surprised him. He'd suspected she didn't have those people in her group, but it turned out she did after all.

Vivienne laughed again, attracting his attention. She was nothing like Malvina, or anyone else.

A wave of sudden understanding swept over him. She proved to be the only one capable of awakening the man he was once, before he encased himself in frozen stone, before he let the beast within take over, before he descended in the black abyss of power.

Her simple presence made him smile. One glance at her, and passion lived again. *She brought life back into my existence.*

He might have saved her life, but she saved his soul. Vivienne lifted him from the bottomless, dark pit he blindingly lurked in for all this time.

Another layer of ice melted around his heart.

As soon as he returned to the terrace, George excused himself and left.

Vivienne grabbed her datapad with the clear intention to refocus on her reading. Theodor seized it from her hands.

"Let's go for a walk. Unless it's too windy for you, and you would prefer to go inside."

He held his hand in front of her. After a couple of seconds spent hesitating, she placed her hand into his and rose to her feet. The touch sent tingles through both their bodies at the same time.

"Those lights in your eyes . . ." Vivienne gestured toward him. "Do all vampires have them, or you're a special case?"

"It's rather a family trait." He couldn't help smiling. "My grandmother and my father were the first ones to have them, in silver. You've met my mother—hers are gold." He stared at Vivienne. "My sister Thora and I are the only ones that have them in blue."

She walked by his side, down the stone stairs leading to the beach.

The wind calmed the lower they descended. Not another soul on the beach for as far as he could see.

Already late afternoon, the sun offered another memorable show. The sky changed hues every second. From golds to tangerines and hot pinks, they bled into one another. The sea joined in, reflecting all the breathtaking colors.

After the last step, Vivienne stopped and tried to withdraw her hand from Theodor's.

With one quick move, he wrapped his arms around her body, drawing her close to him. Her heart instantly accelerated, and his joined in the rush. She might've tried to keep her distance from him, but he had different plans.

"If you let me turn you, your lights would probably be gold."

"What?" She quickly retreated from his embrace. Her eyes widened with terror, her lips trembled, and her breath became shallow.

"Viv—"

"Is this why you brought me here, to turn me into . . . one of you?"

Theodor reached out to her, trying to hug her close to him, but she continued to back away. Her fear spiked. He'd hoped she wouldn't be afraid of him anymore after he'd saved her life twice. *I guess I was wrong.*

"It's not why I brought you here."

I blamed her for trying to lie to me, and what do I do? I'm such a hypocrite.

"Stay away from me," Vivienne yelled, and tears pooled in her eyes.

"Viv, I would never hurt you."

Finally, he caught her and cradled her body against his. Gently, he tilted her face to him and wiped her tears. *I hate seeing her cry.*

"Please don't turn me."

Her whisper hurt him. He knew she would break his heart.

"I won't."

"Promise me."

Vivienne's demand saddened him more. He didn't want to lose her. "I promise I won't turn you against your wish."

Her fear filled his heart with pain. Without another word, he pressed her head to his chest and closed his eyes.

I have to find a way. I can't lose her. Not now, not ever. Controlling her mind or altering her decision is out of the question. I couldn't live the rest of my life wondering if she accepted me because she loved me enough to do so or because of my doing.

Two elongated shadows, desperately clinging to each other, darkened the sand behind them. The wind had stopped, but the storm inside him raged.

Theodor lifted her face to him again. Her long lashes fluttered opened, and her light-hazel eyes gazed at him.

Slowly, his head dipped. She opened her mouth as if trying to say something, but no sound came out.

His lips lightly touched hers, and Vivienne closed her eyes, forcing the tears down her cheeks. Theodor tasted her lips, sweeter than he expected. He backed a couple of inches to look in her eyes. Long lashes flew open.

Their first kiss hurt him. The salty droplets running down her face and to his lips turned what supposed to be a happy moment into a sad one. Guilt suffocated him. *I made her cry.*

"Viv . . ." His heartbroken whisper flew in the evening breeze.

"I want to go home."

"We need to talk." Theodor tried to keep her close to him.

She shook her head taking a couple of steps away from him. "I can't do it. Not right now. Please."

Defeated, Theodor let his arms fall to his sides. "This is not over." He noticed her trembling hands opening a portal.

"I know." Vivienne wiped more tears and stepped into the swirling gateway.

She's right. I can't say much right now either.

Chapter 16

Serge paced in front of the glass windows in his niece's penthouse. Malvina turned off her communication system and beamed at him.

"It went surprisingly well. You were right."

"I don't think he bought it. He obviously doubted your shield explanation." Serge massaged his chin with an absent air.

"I'll insist on the matter more next time." Malvina sank into the soft cushions on the couch.

Serge stood silent for a while. The fog covered most of the city, and he appreciated the obstructed view. It kept the memories at bay.

"You should start thinking about moving. You've lived here way too long." Serge's gaze followed the small floating sphere gliding by. Nothing more than a security camera doing its regular rounds, it passed the one-way windows every couple of hours.

His place, isolated in the middle of nowhere, only left him to worry about the paperwork. Every thirty years or so he filed a new sale document under different names. Like all the vampires in the world, he too, changed identities.

After his parents died, he bought their old home with a little land around it. Throughout the years, he'd added to it, buying the surrounding properties.

The Flood had covered the area completely, but at the first signs of the water receding, Serge expanded the property line again. Now he had over two hundred acres of wooded land. The house, built shortly after, had served as his residence for the last three hundred years.

He had hoped he would share it with the woman he loved. Instead, he'd spent the last quarter of a century with a hologram.

"Nobody really sees me. If everything goes as I hope, I'll move soon to Crete." His niece yanked him back to reality. "But I've thought about changing my eye color. I'm starting to get bored with these green contacts."

Malvina admired her perfect manicure, one of the two things she refused to change in her appearance.

"You should do something about the hair too." Serge turned to face her. "It attracts too much attention."

"Nope. The hair stays. I love it."

Serge shook his head in disapproval and went to sit on the other couch, facing her. "Have you practiced the background story?"

"Yes, so much that I'm starting to believe it myself." Malvina's loud laugh hit the walls of her living room.

"Good. The more you believe it, the less doubts it will raise. Don't forget who you have to convince."

"My dress will be ready next week."

Malvina's change of subject caused Serge to lift his gaze to her again.

"I can't wait." Her happy squeal reminded him of the danger ahead.

Serge hid the guilt gnawing at him nonstop. He'd kept her safe for centuries.

"After I see you in the dress, we'll go to Milan for some jewelry. I've already made a couple of calls."

Malvina jumped off the couch and hugged him. "Thank you. You have no idea how exciting this is."

"Please promise me that you'll be careful. I would never forgive myself if anything happened to you." Serge held her hands in his. "I promised your father to keep you safe."

His voice failed him, and his shoulders slumped.

"Everything is going to be fine." Malvina withdrew her hands. "I'm sorry you can't come see me at the ball with your own eyes." She twirled a couple of times.

"My presence there would kill us both."

~ ~ ~

Vivienne still struggled with accepting the facts. In theory, a year after she became a GeM, she should've known who she was, or at least how to manage her blood thirst.

After work and a frugal dinner consisting of fruits and cheese, she sat on her small terrace. She huddled in the corner of the cozy outdoor sofa, knees gathered to her chest. Memories from the past year swamped her mind, tears pooled, and her lower lip trembled.

After the accident, she'd been unconscious for a while. Vivienne still didn't know for how long. She'd woken up chained to the hard floor in excruciating pain.

Tears started to run down her cheeks. Her body hurt just as it had a year ago.

Greg had decided to make her suffer and didn't pull the glass shards out of her back. Some of them caused infections. She'd removed as many as she could reach.

He'd enjoyed pushing her against the wall. The remaining sharp glass pieces had dug into her flesh, causing her unbearable pain. Vivienne could still see the wall smeared with her blood.

Greg only took the remaining shards out and cleaned her cuts days later when the infections became so serious she'd started to hallucinate and run a high fever.

The memory of the disinfectant stabbing her wounds made Vivienne shiver. He'd wanted to keep her alive so he could torture her. The man had proved to be a master at it.

A deep sigh escaped her lips between sobs, and she

wiped the tears with the back of her hands. More tears came. She couldn't stop.

The chains had given her some leeway, allowing her to use part of the bathroom when she'd been alone. As soon as Greg returned home, he'd hang the chains off the floor on a hook he had mounted high on the wall.

Vivienne's hands touched a couple of spots on her neck. She could still feel the shocks from the torturous collar jolting through her body, smell the heated flesh and the burned skin.

Even if Theodor had healed her body that night, she remained damaged. The memories would always be there, her wounds deeper than skin.

For a year, she'd endured humiliation. Greg had demanded she beg for food and water, or just to use the bathroom.

He'd watched her when she showered. The memory of the freezing showers shook her body. Some other days he would eat in front of her without giving her any food.

The blackouts, when she would lose consciousness, had made it impossible for her to keep track of time. They were an escape, and she'd welcome them. No pain, no humiliation, just blissful nothing.

Night spread its wings over the beach and covered everything in darkness. The waves brushed against the sand and sent their song through the humid air.

First time she'd drank blood she threw up, a common reaction. Making a mess also served as a reason to get a beating from Greg. He'd called her a *disgusting freak.*

She'd paid with her dignity for every drop of blood that had kept her alive. *I'm still not convinced it was worth it.*

A violent shiver made her jump off the couch. Her arms closed around her waist. Vivienne ran to the kitchen and drank some water. Her hands shook and she spilled half of it on herself.

Vivienne didn't want to remember, but she couldn't escape. *I'll be a prisoner to my memories for the rest of my life.*

Theodor wanted to turn her, make her a vampire. All her life she'd been human. She thought like one. Her struggle to accept she had become a GeM was hard enough. *I can't see myself being a vampire. I don't want to.*

"No. Never."

That night, Vivienne cried herself to sleep. Next day, she decided to learn who she had become. She set aside everything else and focused her efforts on learning everything she could about the species she belonged to. On that same day, she officially registered changing her species from *human* to GeM in all of her official documents.

Leaning on the backrest of her chair, she stared at the screen with her new information. *My new life starts now. I didn't ask for it. Why did it had to be this way?*

She took a few steps toward the windows. The stunning view of the mountains calmed her every time. *Why do I always get what I don't want, but never receive what I wish for?*

~ ~ ~

A few minutes past seven in the evening, Theodor stepped out of the portal. *I wonder if she forgot, or she's just avoiding me again.*

He stopped in front of the glass doors and watched her for a while in her lab.

The last four days had been torture. He'd had to use all his will not to call her. Theodor figured she needed some space but visited her every night. For hours, he sat in her bedroom and resisted the temptation of searching her mind.

She had a couple of nightmares, and Theodor fought his instinct to come out of hiding. Her tears glistened in the moonlight like a plea to be touched. He wanted to kiss them away and tell her everything would be all right. Just as many times he stopped himself. *Myself, I'm not sure about the future.*

She made slow but steady progress in her journey to accept her GeM status. Baby steps, every day, proved it. He couldn't help but smile when she'd set an alarm on her bracer. Every fifth day, at intervals of six hours, a reminder to drink blood would vibrate on her wrist.

The more he learned about her, the more Theodor wanted to turn her. If she was going to adapt to a new life she might as well do it as a vampire. But she'd made him promise. And never in his life had he broken his word.

Theodor quietly observed Vivienne reading something on her datapad. One luminescent orb provided light above her head and dissipated the darkness in the lab. She leaned over the long counter and occasionally glanced to her right. A pile of open, old-fashioned books covered the cold stone and served as references.

Her back to the door, Vivienne faced the glass exterior wall. In the distance, the top of the mountains stood darker than the sky, true silent guardians.

Like always, she wore her white lab coat, that day, unbuttoned. Theodor's gaze traveled to the nude-colored high-heeled shoes.

Vivienne stood, keeping her weight on her left foot, the right one barely touching the ground. The tip of her shoe balanced her. At regular intervals of time, she moved her heel sideways. Another one of her quirks, a sign she was in deep thought.

I bet she's biting her lip. I'd like to help with that. He chuckled to himself. Almost right away Theodor shook his head. *I'm five hundred years old and acting like a horny teenager.*

"This is ridiculous," he muttered under his breath and stood in front of the motion sensor.

To his surprise, the doors didn't slide open, and he knocked. Why did she lock herself in? Was she afraid of something, or someone? If that door kept Victor out as well, he was okay with it. *That a girl.*

~ ~ ~

Vivienne heard the knock and turned, ready to say she was busy when she saw Theodor. *At least it's not Victor.* The man had unsuccessfully tried to talk to her for two days.

She missed seeing Theodor and absorbed every detail of his appearance on her way to open the door for him. The last time she'd seen him, when he'd kissed her on the beach, tears had obstructed her vision. That kiss had haunted her ever since.

He wore his leather pants, loosely fit over the dark-navy-colored boots. His hand ran through his midnight-black hair, and a couple of stubborn strands fell onto his forehead.

Vivienne wanted to touch them, and she wiped her hands over her hips, trying to control the urge.

The cobalt-blue button-up shirt, replacing his usual vest, made his eyes seem deeper and brighter than ever. Her pulse accelerated.

"Theo."

"Why did you lock the doors?" He proceeded into her lab, scanning every corner. "Something wrong?"

The sharp scent of his cologne whirled around her, and Vivienne inhaled it. *Damn it, I missed him.*

"I'm busy, and I don't like interruptions. What are you doing here?"

A half-smile tugged at the corners of his lips when he turned to face her. "I thought I'd find you here."

His smile softened her bones. Her heart backflipped in her chest. "Were you looking for me?"

Theodor arched his right brow in amusement. "I waited for you at your place for about a half hour."

"Why?"

"We were supposed to have dinner with my family. Remember?"

"That's tomorrow night." She returned to her books.

"It's today, Friday night."

Vivienne glanced over her shoulder, trying to figure out if he was joking. He seemed serious.

"Wait. I thought today was Thursday." She faced him, tempted to ask him for proof.

A wide smile stretched over his face, and Theodor advanced closer. "You lost a day somewhere. You're not really good at keeping time, are you?"

Vivienne glanced at the clock. She hated to be late. Especially when she knew his family expected them.

"I'm so sorry." Her words came out rushed. She peeled off her coat, throwing it on the counter. Her fingers quickly wrapped around the edge of her datapad. "We can go, so I can change."

"No time for that. We were supposed to be there already."

The tight, black pencil skirt she wore forced her to take small steps. Her high heels clicked rapidly on the concrete floor.

~ ~ ~

Theodor watched her, amused, with his head tilted to one side. When she leaned over the desk to grab her purse on the other side, he felt the smirk on his face vanishing.

His hands ached to touch her body stretched in front of him. He closed the distance between them before she straightened.

Vivienne left her purse on the desk beside her datapad. She brushed off a nonexistent crease on her skirt, a clear sign of anxiety. "In that case, how do I look?"

Only inches away, Theodor stared at her with intensity, listening to her loud thoughts. Her blood heated.

Theodor circled around her with slow, calculated steps, close enough for her to sense the heat radiating from him. Teasing inches stood between them, charged with desire.

He granted himself permission to immerse into the tiny pools of golden, decadent honey in her irises.

"You might want to lose that pen." He pointed to her hair, haphazardly gathered on top of her head. "It clashes with the rest of your outfit."

Vivienne lifted her hands quickly, but his reflexes were faster. He caught her wrists midair and gently forced her arms down.

"Allow me," Theodor whispered.

With his right hand, he removed the pen and placed it on the desk, on top of the datapad.

An avalanche of silky waves fell around her face and down her back. Theodor couldn't resist the temptation any longer. His left hand brushed the side of her neck, and his fingers ran through her golden ringlets.

"Theo."

Her whisper flew from her lips without her permission. He knew she intended to stop him. Instead, it sounded like an invitation, a call Theodor didn't delay to answer.

His head dipped, and he stared straight into her soul. The whole world around them came to a sudden halt.

Theodor claimed her lips. His left hand tightened under her hair, cupping her head, and his right arm wrapped around her waist.

Vivienne placed her hands on his chest and closed her eyes. *'If I lived in hell for a year, I'm in heaven now.'* Theodor heard her thoughts and rushed to answer, pushing his words in her mind. *"Not yet, beautiful, but I can take you there."*

Unlike the last time, passion overtook him. Theodor closed his eyes, and a deep moan rolled from his chest. Desire charged his body, a want he refused to fight back.

The explosion of sensations intoxicated him, and he hugged her body against his.

A sudden presence made Theodor open his eyes and glance behind Vivienne toward the door.

Victor. He was watching them, with his hands stuck in his pockets and a deep crease between the brows. His eyes darkened with threat, like the depths of hell itself.

Theodor stared back at him. The silent confrontation only lasted a couple of seconds. Victor left without a sound, and Theodor returned his attention to the woman in his arms.

~ ~ ~

His gaze traveled from her lips to her eyes.

"Viv."

Nobody had ever said her name like that. She'd never kissed a vampire before either. Reality sparked back to life in her mind, and she took a step back.

"You said we were late."

Theodor tilted her face to him, holding her chin in his hand. "We are, and we'll continue this after dinner."

The promise in his eyes sent a million tiny tingles through her body. A whole colony of minuscule ants carried torches through her veins.

"I'll probably be tired." Vivienne knew it was a lousy excuse as soon as she heard her own words. She had to say something, a last attempt to keep him away from her.

"You don't know yet what tired feels like. But you will."

Theodor opened a portal, and after she grabbed her purse, they both stepped in. It was dinnertime.

Chapter 17

Vivienne nervously squeezed Theodor's hand the instant they entered his parents' home. She'd thought it would be the four of them and maybe Theodor's sister. She looked forward to meeting her. Instead, the whole family and their closest friends, about twenty people, waited for them.

A few times, anxiety got the best of her. Theodor covered her hand with his under the table. The gentle touch infused her with calm.

She managed to relax, and by the time they finished eating and went to sit with drinks in the spacious living room, Vivienne could put words together in sentences. Theodor stood by her side most of the time, except when his mother took her away for a surprise.

Vivienne stared at the cream dress and the matching shoes in the box in front of her. Without knowing how or why, she accepted the invitation to attend the New Year's Ball. Queen Emelia, Theodor's grandmother, insisted she couldn't miss it. As one of her favorite events, the queen had hosted it every year for centuries.

Vivienne managed to relax under the welcoming atmosphere.

One exception made her nervous—Theodora. She seemed reserved, polite, and to some degree, cold.

Close to midnight, at the first sign she started to get tired, Theodor excused both of them, and they left.

When they stepped out of the portal, Vivienne glanced at her surroundings.

"Um . . . Why are we at your place?"

Theodor set the box containing her outfit on one of the couches in his living room and turned to face her. With agonizingly slow movements, he took off his blue shirt.

His body seemed chiseled in granite, strong and magnificent. The sharp angles and lazy curves could've made the Gods jealous. His intent gaze answered her question before he closed his arms around her.

A loud pulse roared in her ears. She could swear everyone in a mile radius could hear it.

"We have unfinished business"—he purred his words—"and it's been on my mind all night."

Vivienne tried to tear her eyes away from his tensed muscles under the tanned skin. His kiss numbed all her senses. She wasn't sure it was real.

Somewhere in the back of her mind, one thought formed like a tiny drop. It floated closer and closer, and hit her with the force of a tsunami.

She was about to sleep with him.

Vivienne broke the kiss and backed away from him. She hadn't noticed when he'd unbuttoned her blouse, and she scrambled to wrap it around her. "Please stop."

Theodor stared at her, confusion shadowing his eyes. "Viv, what's going on? I thought you wanted this, too."

"I did, I do, I just can't . . ." Vivienne struggled with the words, or with the lack of.

Her eyes studied the rug under her feet. It had a geometrical design—dark-blue lines intersecting only to split again. She tried to find a pattern, but she couldn't.

"Are you still afraid of me?" Anger surfaced in his tone. "Do you think I would hurt you?"

Vivienne shook her head. "No. I'm not."

"Then what are you afraid of?"

She didn't need any enhanced senses to detect the tension. It sparked around them like invisible forks of lightning.

"I'm not—"

"Do not lie to me."

She fought back the tears flooding her eyes. "I can't. Please understand." With trembling hands, she opened the screen on her bracer. "I have to go."

Theodor interrupted the dial, holding her wrists apart.

"I deserve an explanation."

Tears ran down her cheeks. She couldn't answer his justified request.

"What are you afraid of?" He repeated his question, forcing her to look into his eyes.

Deep silence stood between them, uncomfortable, prickling her skin.

"Myself," she whispered.

Theodor's brows furrowed, but he released her and stepped back folding his arms over his wide chest.

The muscles tensed and relaxed under his skin in a mesmerizing dance. *I want him, but I can't. It's wrong.*

"Care to elaborate?"

She didn't want to. "No. Maybe . . . Not now." Vivienne shook her head. "Please, I have to go."

She finished dialing, and the portal opened in front of her. After the first step, Theodor caught her arm in his hand. Lightning and ice blades cut and burned her deep, all the way to her soul.

"You can run all you want. I'm not giving up. I never have and never will."

Vivienne expected some adverse reaction from him, but nothing quite so harsh. She gazed into his deep-blue stormy eyes. *I have to get out of here. Now, before it's too late.*

"I know." Her whisper caused Theodor to release her arm.

~ ~ ~

The portal closed behind Vivienne. *What the hell just happened?*

His frustration and hurt converged into anger. Theodor grabbed his shirt off the floor and threw it across the room. The soft, silky fabric opened in the air and floated. It landed on the stone floor soundlessly, leaving him unsatisfied with the result.

His fangs descended, and he glanced around. He wanted to hit something. Theodor ran out on the terrace and jumped on the stacked boulders.

Questions without answers avalanched in his mind, feeding his fury. Why did she run? What happened in that one split second that freaked her out?

If Theodor could've only kept his calm, he might've thought of peeking in her mind to get answers. But he'd lost it. *I can hardly recognize myself. What the hell is she doing to me?*

He didn't notice how far he'd run until the clouds dissipated and the moonlight shone on his surroundings. Outside the city limits, millions of stars blinked in the sky. Wilderness all around, not a soul in sight. The song of a timid ribbon of water running down smooth stones failed to calm him.

Theodor rushed into thick trees, uprooting them. Broken branches added to the tumult in his ears. The hard impact with the solid trunks broke his skin in a few places. Bleeding scratches didn't stop him. He needed to feel the hurt on the outside of his body, to match the pain inside.

Levitated fragments of trees hit others, causing splinters to fly in all directions. The side of the mountain, made of colossal boulders, didn't escape unscarred.

Theodor punched and kicked the rocks. His knuckles left blood imprints on the rubble.

Afraid of herself? What is that supposed to mean? She's good at confusing the hell out of me. I know she wanted me as much as I wanted her. Until her fear spiked and blinded me. He stopped and acknowledged the destruction around him.

A new wave of frustration and anger overtook him. Huge blocks of stone flew through the air as if they were weightless. Heavy thuds shook the ground beneath his feet.

A pair of bright eyes glowed between broken branches—a small fox. Theodor faced the critter and hissed. The poor creature turned tail and ran.

"Yeah, run. It's all you know how to do. You and Vivienne. Run!" The rushed steps of the fox over leaves and twigs mixed with the loud drumming of his pulse.

Theodor sat on a fragment of a boulder and held his head in his hands. The hurried beat of his heart resonated in his ears. *Is she playing with me?* He stood and punched the block of stone he had just sat on. Hundreds of shards flew, cutting into his flesh.

Straightening his frame, Theodor closed his eyes and took a few deep breaths in an attempt to calm himself. He healed all the cuts and bruises marking his body.

The first signs of a new day colored the sky in hues of blue. *This looks like a damned warzone . . .* In the faint light of the morning, the broken trees and smashed boulders revealed what his uncontrolled anger had done. *With no winners.*

A sigh left his lips. He'd fought himself and lost. Nature had paid the price.

~ ~ ~

From his suspended terrace, Victor stared into the new morning sky.

Three days until I'll have the damn locator. His request, to be hidden inside a small champagne-colored gem with certain specifications, would take an extra day and a half, but it was worth it.

When he'd seen Theodor and Vivienne kiss in her office, his plan to win her trust flew right out the window. She'd been avoiding him for a couple of days, had locked her doors. It was time for action.

Theodor already had an advantage. If Victor wanted Vivienne, he needed to hurry. With or without her compliance, he would take what he wanted from her. At any price.

Breaking the rules, he searched for her address in her personnel file. His indiscretion could be tracked, but he didn't care. The address listed was in Vienna. It was a cover-up, most likely set up by Theodor. Vivienne lived on Crete, and he had to find out where. The locator he'd ordered would take care of it.

Vivienne had stirred something deep inside him like no other mortal had in centuries. She made him feel hungry for her body and thirsty for her blood. He had to have her.

"She's going to be mine one way or another," he growled between fully extended fangs.

His promise disrupted the silence blanketing the mountains.

~ ~ ~

Vivienne wrapped an oversized red wrap around her body, over a same colored two-piece bathing suit. A walk on the beach in the refreshing breeze would help her think. She'd been crying for most of the day and part of the previous night.

The coarse, pink sand welcomed her steps, and she occasionally stopped to pick up pieces of sea glass. She gathered the frosted glass in a multitude of colors every time she was on the beach. Her collection neared two jars.

A patch of white sand attracted her, and Vivienne ran to it. Unlike the pink ones, the white grains were fine like a powder. It tickled the bottoms of her feet and between her toes.

She sat in the warm sand and let out a deep sigh.

How could I let things get this far? We are wrong for each other. Maybe I should run away. Go somewhere else. It doesn't have to be Paris. Especially not now that I know some crazy Malvina vamp is on the loose.

"Vivienne."

She turned her head in the direction of the unfamiliar voice. The last person in the world she would have expected ran toward her—Theodora.

What is she doing here? She waved her hand. Only seconds later, Theodor's sister sat beside her.

"Hi."

"Hello. What are you doing here?" Vivienne studied in detail the woman beside her.

Long hair, pulled into a high ponytail, cascaded down her back in ebony waves. She looked like her mother, but at the same time she reminded Vivienne of Theodor. She had the same deep-blue eyes with bright glowing lights.

Theodora resembled a genie with her suede shorts and tiny top barely covering her perfect body.

Instead of leather, boots made of silk rose high to the middle of Theodora's thighs. A long and ample tulle coat completed her outfit. *She sure doesn't dress like most vampires.*

"We need to talk."

"About what?" A bad vibe crawled up Vivienne's spine. She remembered the previous night, the other woman's coldness and distance.

"About you and my brother." Theodora turned her gaze to Vivienne, abandoning the view of the sea.

Vivienne felt her cheeks burn. *I'm probably as red as my wrap.*

"There isn't much to—"

"Look." Theodora's hand covered Vivienne's tight fist. A few pieces of her precious sea glass, nested inside her hand, grind against each other under the gentle squeeze. "I love my brother, and I like you. If I didn't, I wouldn't be here." She remained silent for a few seconds.

She must be searching for her words.

"You don't know me yet. Hopefully, that'll change soon, and we'll be friends."

Vivienne kept quiet. She had no idea what to say, or how to react.

"I'm not one to beat around the bush. I've come here to find out why exactly you don't want to become one of us."

"I don't know what to tell you," Vivienne hedged, trying to get out of talking about a subject she didn't even want to acknowledge.

"Don't even think about trying to lie to me. It won't work." Theodora touched her own right temple. She had a kind smile, like her mother's.

"May I ask you to stay out of my head?" Vivienne asked with a shy voice.

"I need to know the truth. I see something has happened since I last saw you."

Vivienne stood quickly with the intention to leave.

Theodora, as fast as any vampire, followed, stopping in front of her.

"My brother let you run away from him last night, and that's his problem. I'm not him." She rested her hand on Vivienne's shoulder. "He doesn't know I'm here, and this will stay between us." Theodora pointed to the sand between them. "I came to talk to you, and we are going to do so."

Theodora's determination made Vivienne lift her tearful eyes to the other woman. Words refused to form.

"Why do you think Theo brought you over last night to meet the whole family?"

Vivienne shrugged. "Your mother invited me a few days ago."

"Why?" Theodora's hold on her shoulder tightened.

Do they all like this stupid question? She never thought about the reason behind the unexpected invitation. "To have dinner?"

"No, silly." Theodora paused and another smile bloomed on her lips. "Theo introduced you to the family. He wanted everyone's acceptance, and he got it." She withdrew her hand.

Vivienne moved her gaze to the setting sun. It melted into the water. Only a thin sliver still visible. The sky ignited in fire around it.

Low, timid waves caressed her feet. She took a few steps in silence, with Theodor's sister by her side.

Theodora stopped and picked up a piece of bright-blue sea glass, handing it to Vivienne.

"I can't begin to tell you how sorry I am for everything that happened to you in the last year. I wish I could kill that bastard who hurt you myself, over and over again. But you have to understand it's over, in the past." Theodora stopped again.

"Maybe, but it will always stay with me."

"I know, and I can see how hard you try to overcome it."

Vivienne tightened her fist around the colorful glass pieces.

"I know my brother can be difficult at times, a real pain in the butt to deal with." She snickered. "Believe me, we grew up together. He can be stubborn, harsh, and don't get me started on his hostility toward compromise. To be honest, I miss him the way he used to be." Another warm smile stretched her lips.

"What do you mean?" Vivienne's attention focused on the woman beside her.

"He's spent the last four hundred years fighting some of the most vicious vampires in the world." Theodora picked up another piece of sea glass, this time a rare red one. She kept it in her hand, playing with it. "His life wasn't easy. It changed him. I haven't seen Theo smile in over two centuries, until last night."

Vivienne lowered her head, her eyes preoccupied with the rough, wet sand.

"Against all odds, he kept one thing from his old self." Theodora moved the glass from one hand to the other. Dried grains of sand slipped through her fingers. "He kept the hope that one day he'd meet the woman destined to him—"

"Malvina," Vivienne whispered.

"Who the hell's Malvina?"

"I overheard Theo talking about her with George. Apparently, they're engaged." Vivienne's voice fluctuated. "For whatever reason, he wants to kill her."

"I doubt my brother is engaged to anyone. Whoever she is, if Theo wants her dead, he must have a reason. However,"—she waved her hand as if dismissing the other woman—"she's irrelevant. He is crazy about you."

Vivienne lifted her eyes to Theodor's sister. Hope mixed with a trace of fear and accelerated her pulse.

"I saw it last night, and before you ask if I'm sure, yes, I am." Theodora gave Vivienne the piece of glass she's been playing with. "It's why I came to talk to you today."

"It's wrong. We can't be together." Vivienne shook her head. She didn't want to think about a possible future with Theodor.

"Why not?"

"You don't understand." Vivienne gathered some courage from within. "We belong to different worlds. We're wrong for each other."

"Says who?" Theodora threw her hands into the air. "Nothing's wrong."

"Theo's a vampire. I'm human, and I will never become one of you." Panic returned to Vivienne's tone.

Theodora stopped and crossed her arms over her chest. "Why?"

Here we go with that damned question again. Vivienne struggled to take a couple of deep breaths.

"I can't. I don't want to. I . . ." She hesitated. "I don't want to become a monster."

"Come again?" A deep crease marked Theodora's forehead. "Is that what you think we are?"

"Not you, or Theo . . ." Vivienne touched Theodora's crossed arms. "Not your parents either. None of your family." She'd offended the woman in front of her, and her whole species with the one word. "I'm sorry. That came out wrong"

"Then make it right." Theodora's unblinking eyes sparked with tiny lights.

"All my life I thought vampires were imaginary, blood drinking monsters." Vivienne withdrew her hand. "Then I met Theo, your family . . ." She paused, searching for her words. "I'm still trying to get used to everything." Her voice dropped in volume.

"So, you need more time?" Theodora uncrossed her arms.

"I'm not sure time has anything to do with this." Vivienne lowered her head.

"Becoming a vampire won't change who you are. The transformation is physical, not moral. You'll still be you, keep your personality, values and knowledge."

Tears streamed down Vivienne's face. "It's been almost a year since I became a GeM. I still don't know who I am anymore. I can't handle more changes."

Theodora wrapped her arms around Vivienne's shoulders in a hug. A sweet hint of jasmine filled the air.

"This is where I'm confused." She stepped back from the quick embrace. "You're already a GeM. Just like us, you need blood to survive. Would it be so awful to be also fast, strong, and immortal?"

Vivienne wiped away the tears, avoiding Theodora's inquiring gaze. "I'm afraid. I was thinking of running away," she admitted. Hearing her own fears out loud, she realized how bad it sounded.

Theodora's perfectly groomed brow arched, and a smile spread from her lips to her blue eyes. "And that is going to solve all your problems how?"

Vivienne shrugged and turned her absent gaze to the sea. Without direct sunlight, the water appeared dark.

"Think about it. First, Theo will find you. I can guarantee you that." Theodora closed her fist and straightened her thumb. "Second"—the index finger followed—"you need to reconsider your decision to stay human just because you're afraid of some myths. And third"—her middle finger rose—"turning into one of us will give you an eternity with Theo. You're a smart woman, Vivienne. This is a once in a lifetime chance." Both her hands opened in the air. "Don't blow it."

Vivienne let out a sigh. Her whisper sailed into the soft light of the dusk surrounding them. "I'll think about it."

Chapter 18

George tried for hours to make sense of the lists of names received earlier that day from his contacts in Paris. He hoped one of the names would jump off the screen and bring some answers.

"This is ridiculous." Theodor paced in his living room.

"Trying to find a name we don't know?" George's, half-amusing, half-sarcastic question, failed to dissipate the tension.

Theodor kept quiet for a few more seconds. "I love her."

He'd suspected as much. George stared at Theodor's back, at his tensed shoulders. Sadness lingered around him. His friend had all the symptoms of a man in love.

If being over two millennia old ever taught him anything, George knew not to poke at a wounded lion, especially not the one right in front of him. He detected the absence of enthusiasm in Theodor's voice. From experience, George knew that love always came with pain attached, like a warning label.

"I hope you are not talking about Malvina."

George's joke had the desired effect. Theodor laughed and turned around.

"No, I'm not."

"Phew. It would've been awkward to have to kill her."

With the tension diffused, Theodor returned to his seat.

George and his group of almost fifty people were the first ones to join their prince. He'd helped Theodor set the foundation of the Old Coven, witnessed him signing the contract coming close to its expiration. George and his group, *The Sentinels of the Sacred Grounds,* had been the only ones Theodor hadn't had to fight. He had their loyalty and unquestioned devotion.

George had laid all his knowledge and experience at Theodor's feet since the day the chosen prince entered the world. The bond between them had stood the test of time and was stronger than ever.

~ ~ ~

"Do you have any plans for tonight?"

Theodor's question made George arch a brow, amused.

"I hope you're not asking me out. I would hate to have to tell you that you're not my type."

They both needed a break after almost five hours of reading useless lists of names.

"I'm not. I can do a lot better." Theodor smiled, joining the joking mood George seemed to be in that night. "I'd like you by my side at midnight in the *Sanctum*. Malvina is bringing her people here to meet with me."

"Of course, but I have a date at three. You think we'll be done by then, or should I move it?"

It was Theodor's turn to raise an inquiring brow.

"A date? Who are you, and what have you done with my friend?"

"What can I say? Seeing you and Vivienne together inspired me. I think I'm ready to give myself another chance."

"That's great." Theodor wished he could have a date with Vivienne, too. "As for the meeting, it should be over by one. I already told Malvina, one hour is all the time I can take from my busy schedule."

George couldn't help but laugh. "Do you want me to focus on someone in particular?"

"Yes, her." Theodor's answer held harshness within.

"I never get the easy job, do I?"

George was right—he always got the jobs Theodor wouldn't trust anyone else with. "She insists the shield surrounding her mind is permanent. I'm not buying it, and you have the most experience with shields."

"Shield or not, I have to agree with you. All our abilities are trainable." George rose to his feet and took a couple of steps. "We control when, how, or if we're using them. Something being permanent is unheard of. She's either very special, or she's lying."

"I'm going with the latter."

"I'll keep an eye on her. Anything else?" George resumed his walk.

"No. That's all. I'll make sure her people are worthy."

"Does this mean you're thinking of accepting her offer?"

"No. I'm thinking I'd like to find a way to convince her people to join me without her." Theodor leaned against the backrest of the cream-colored couch. "I only have to keep her around until I come up with something."

"I have to admit, I'm surprised that you're going to play games." George pushed back from his face a strand of auburn hair. "Usually a short fight settles things for you."

A sigh escaped from deep within Theodor's chest as if a pressure valve had been opened. "I'm getting tired of fighting at every step. Besides, I want to see if I'm any good at these games."

A few seconds of comfortable silence floated in the room. George took a few more steps, stretching his legs after hours of sitting.

"What if we get our guys to run background checks on all the women on those lists? Pictures, previous addresses, known names, and everything they can find. This isn't getting us anywhere." George pointed to the records still displayed on the translucent screens.

"That might work. It'll take time, but we'll have a better chance of finding something. Let's do it."

"I'm on it." George hastily picked up his datapad and left the room.

Theodor rested on top of the cushions. His thoughts swept in one direction, and one word formed on his lips.

"Viv . . ."

He wanted to see her, but unsure she was ready for a new confrontation, Theodor controlled his urge. The way she'd run away the previous night troubled him. He wasn't ready to face her either.

~ ~ ~

A couple of minutes after midnight, Malvina and her group stepped into the *Sanctum*. They all lined up, and Theodor noticed admiration in their curious glances.

The *Sanctum* always had an overwhelming effect on anyone seeing it for the first time. Even Vivienne was impressed with it. *Viv, I wonder if she's asleep yet. Damn it, I need to focus here.*

George stood by him, a step back, as his loyal right hand, consultant and friend.

Theodor nodded quietly to every one of Malvina's people who bowed their heads. He stood tall and proud in front of the long table. His black sword rested on top of the smooth surface, a reminder for everyone that although this was intended as a peaceful meeting, if need be, he was ready.

The black stone embedded at the bottom of the long handle appeared as an ordinary decoration. It only flared to life under Theodor's touch, glowing bright blue.

Two elevated, black candelabras decorated the ends of the table, contrasting with the white slab of stone. They'd both been modified to accommodate, according to rituals, the two sacred burning fires.

As soon as the portal closed, Theodor clasped his hands behind him. Each calculated step brought him closer to the men and the three women in the group before him.

High in the air above them, the luminescent spheres glided on their path, flooding the room with a bright, cold light.

"There's one missing?" Theodor glanced at Malvina for the first time that evening.

Unlike before, she'd dressed appropriately for their meeting. Instead of a low-cut, revealing blouse, she wore a leather tunic. Even her boots seemed more combat-ready, with lower, sturdier heels. Her bright red hair was just as flashy as always, but gathered in a long braid, over her shoulder.

"Yes, My Prince. We had a strong disagreement, and he chose to walk away." Malvina handed him the twenty-one folders she held. Each of them contained confidential information about her people.

Even if her voice still scratched Theodor's ears in the most unpleasant way, she was tolerable, and her gesture appreciated. Her eyes had a different color, a rich brown, playing well with the rest of her features. *Even those were fake. Why am I not surprised?*

"I see." Theodor handed the folders to George, who placed them on the long table.

He continued to inspect the group in front of him, and their minds, making sure of their intentions. A married couple among them attracted Theodor's attention and stirred his interest. The husband had cheated on his wife, with Malvina.

He considered the information useful and chose to keep it for himself, in the event he might need it later. Out of curiosity he read minds to see how many of these men had been sleeping with Malvina. Every single one.

Theodor hid his disgust behind his gloved hand covering a pretend cough.

"I'm assuming he's the one named Serge?" Theodor asked out loud after he picked up the name from the minds of three different individuals.

~ ~ ~

Malvina bowed her head.

"That's correct." She smiled inside, grateful to her uncle. He'd made sure that nobody would ever know the two of them were related.

Her anxiety grew with every passing second. She could only hope Theodor would keep his word and not control the minds of her people. *If it were me, I'd take advantage of the situation.*

She glanced at the amphitheater. The navy-blue pillows were lined on the stone benches. *One day, all this will be mine. I can't wait to see the other Sanctums, in the rest of the covens.*

For a couple of seconds, she imagined herself leading all the vampires in the world, ordering them to start the war against humans. A grand parade would celebrate the victory. *Everyone will know my name and kneel before me.*

Malvina already wished the meeting would end.

"What kind of disagreement?"

Theodor turned around quickly to face her again.

"He opposed joining your coven." Practicing her lines proved to be helpful. She'd never sounded more convincing, not even to herself. *Thank you, Uncle Serge.*

Malvina moved her gaze to Theodor's friend. *Hm. The head of the Sentinels doesn't look like much.* She tilted her head to the side. *But he can be useful. And he keeps checking me out.*

She shifted her weight from one leg to the other, making sure her hip stuck out. The moment George glanced in her direction, Malvina flashed the most irresistible smile in her arsenal.

To her disappointment, George didn't seem interested. *Is he playing hard to get? Who cares. I don't need him.*

~ ~ ~

"Is that true?" Theodor asked the next man in line and focused his attention on him.

"I wouldn't know, Your Majesty. I've been living in Chicago for the past four years. I only come here when summoned." The smell of his fear incited Theodor's senses.

The man spoke the truth, and Theodor continued his inspection, stopping in front of the next person in line.

"Have you sworn your loyalty to Malvina?"

"Yes, Your Majesty. I swore my life to her, and anyone she chooses to serve, at any cost."

Pleased with the answer, Theodor moved on.

Malvina's lying. I can smell it from a mile away. Without the slightest glance toward his friend, Theodor sensed George's effort in evaluating her abilities.

"Sooner or later I'll find out what she's hiding. What about her shield?" he asked George, using their link.

"Just as I thought, it's not permanent. But her control is impressive. It took some serious training," George replied, confirming his suspicions.

Theodor took the time to speak with each of the twenty-one people. He wanted to make sure they had no hidden intentions.

If Malvina lied, and she did, the group had no idea. After the meticulous exam, Theodor concluded they would serve him with loyalty. Their vows would be honored.

"I'm pleased to see you were truthful, and your people bound by honor. I'll think about your proposal and let you know." Theodor closed the meeting with a cold, indifferent tone and opened a portal for the group. He wanted them gone.

Malvina stopped before stepping into the portal. "May I ask when you think you'll have an answer?"

Theodor decided to have some fun. "A couple of months at least."

Malvina tilted her head with grace and continued on her way, surprising him with how composed she remained. He expected her to make a scene. The blue and purple swirls of the gateway swallowed her and her followers.

The meeting had gone better than he'd expected. Even with Malvina's lies, her people sparked Theodor's interest.

"I want them in the coven." He turned to George as soon as the portal closed.

"You'll figure out a way." His friend took the pile of folders and placed them in the cabinet behind the table. "You always do."

~ ~ ~

Serge waited for Malvina's call. When she finally let him know how the meeting went, he let out a relieved breath.

The old-style winged chair covered in brown leather, a replica from a few centuries ago, squeaked under his weight. His gaze traveled to the mantel of his fireplace. The few objects thoughtfully arranged on its surface always brought a sad smile to his face.

A couple and two young, identical boys smiled at him from an old, black-and-white photo. Serge had carried the picture with him for centuries, until he had it encased in glass to prevent any further deterioration. He remained the last survivor of his long-gone family.

The tiny lock of light-brown, almost blond hair enticed him. He rose to his feet, and with a trembling hand, he touched the transparent box. Even near the fire, his fingertips detected the cold, smooth surface.

A delicate, lavender silk ribbon held together the thin, wavy hairs. Serge remembered collecting them one by one from anywhere in the house he could find them. They belonged to her.

"Heather."

The sound of the crackling fire covered his painful whisper. His gaze traveled to the ring he had bought for her. He'd wanted to ask her to marry him. She'd run, scared, before he could do so. The oval-shaped amethyst sparkled in a multitude of shades under the dancing light in the room.

Serge remembered the exact moment he'd met her. Her eyes had fascinated him, made his heart beat faster and his blood rush through his body from the very beginning. Heather had been born with deep-brown eyes, but she'd wanted them to be blue. She'd decided to undergo cosmetic surgery before he'd even met her.

Something had gone wrong during the operation, and her body partially rejected the pigment. She'd been left with lavender eyes, and she'd hated how people had stared at the unusual color. It had been what charmed him.

Another sigh left his lips, and Serge glanced to the last of the glass boxes arranged between the two large candlesticks.

One single rose, withered and dried, lay under the cold glass. Every time he would bring her roses, her favorite flowers, Heather would break the stem of one. She'd used to kiss the soft, lush petals, and attach the flower to his lapel. This had been the last one he'd given her, before what had become their final night together.

Now the rose was black, dead as his dreams. He had nothing but memories left. Serge turned his back to the mantel displaying his mementos and glanced absently around the room.

On one whole wall, floor-to-ceiling shelves held hundreds of old-fashioned books. Another memory flashed through his mind.

Heather had loved to read. Some days, they would sit

together and read for hours in each other's arms. She used to say that there was no such thing as too much knowledge.

Another sad smile. Serge gave up.

Even if he helped Malvina, it wouldn't end well. He had made his peace. He'd watched over her, trained her, and taught her everything he could. The promise he'd made his brother centuries ago had been honored.

Since he had found out about her plans, Serge had tried to accept that sooner or later he would lose her too. She refused to listen to him this time. Her thirst for power clouded her judgment.

Serge sensed the end nearing. Losing the woman he loved left him with no desire to live.

One ultimate plan would be his last stand, and he was ready for it.

~ ~ ~

The next morning, Vivienne woke up determined to get out of the house.

Hot pink lipstick and light makeup masterfully hid the signs of a whole day spent crying. After a frugal breakfast of coffee and a slice of toast, she grabbed her purse, ready to leave, when a knock rooted her in place.

"Viv, it's me. Open up." Theodor's voice echoed in the quiet living room from the other side of the thick door.

A sudden tremor coursed through her body. *Maybe if I don't open, he'll leave. What if he overrides the entry panel again?* But she missed his mesmerizing eyes, the soothing sound of his voice, and the intoxicating scent of his cologne.

After a deep breath, she worked up the courage to open the door. Vivienne had a smile prepared but froze under his gaze.

The sapphire never-ending vortexes in his eyes lured her in.

Theodor claimed her lips and wrapped his arms around her body without a word. He kicked the door closed behind him when Vivienne's hands closed in fists on his vest.

Passion wiped away any thought.

"I love you." The three little words melted her bones.

The surrounding world ceased to exist. The floating sensation overtaking her ended on top of her bed. The covers cradled her body like soft clouds. *Am I dreaming?*

She surrendered in his arms. Theodor wasn't a vampire prince that moment. He was the man who saved her life and stole her heart.

Chapter 19

Her pulse accelerated at the memory of the past few days. Vivienne hid her face in her hands. It had been four days since Theodor had declared his love.

Vivienne tried her hardest to focus on the screen in front of her, but failed. *It's so surreal.*

She glanced at the flowers filling her office and lab. Twelve black vases holding a dozen roses each spread a heavenly scent in the otherwise sterile lab.

The white petals with red tips, as if dipped in blood, tempted her to touch them, just like the man who sent them.

I can get used to this. The conversation with Theodora sparked to life in Vivienne's mind. She'd never been that happy before. The concept of immortality, of a never-ending life with Theodor, didn't seem like such a bad idea after all. But turning into a vampire still scared her.

The glass doors opened with a familiar hiss, and Victor entered, staring at the flowers surrounding him.

Even if the orchid plant he'd given her as an office warming gift outlasted the flowers from Theodor, it now looked pathetic on the corner of her desk.

"Is it a special occasion?" he asked, motioning to the flowers.

"No," Vivienne answered and rose to her feet. *Perfect timing. I needed a distraction.*

"I see. Ready for lunch?"

~ ~ ~

She nodded, and he let her walk out the door first. Victor peeked back one more time before exiting her office. *I might be already too late. Theodor has guts, and a hell of a way of marking his territory.*

Victor patted his pocket, making sure the locator hidden inside the champagne-colored gem was ready to serve its purpose.

He hadn't seen Vivienne for days. She'd worked from home, or at least it had been her excuse to avoid coming into the office.

"How is everything going? Did you have more problems accessing the data you needed?" He did his best to sound casual. They both sat with their food at one of the tables near the floor-to-ceiling windows.

Victor had to keep their conversation as light as always and work-oriented to make sure he didn't raise any suspicions.

Vivienne's unusual glow of happiness alerted him. He suspected Theodor had something to do with it.

The thought of her, in the arms of the other man, made the muscles in his jaw twitch. His determination to make her his pushed him further. He couldn't afford to lose any more time.

"No, everything is going well. I think I'm going to direct my research toward what happened to me."

"What do you mean?" He was genuinely interested to find out more.

"Before I got infected, I used to wear glasses—"

"Really?" He lifted his sandwich from his plate, but stopped halfway to his mouth. "I can't imagine you with glasses."

Vivienne finished chewing a mouthful of food. "The infection somehow corrected my vision." She pointed to her eyes. "I think the *smart virus* not only fights an anomaly when induced, but also cures, or corrects, an existing one in a host."

"Interesting. Can you prove it?" Victor recognized the potential in her research and admired the idea. She lived up to her reputation.

"I'll have to run some tests, do more research, and go from there."

He stared at the excitement animating her eyes.

"If I could isolate the exact component responsible for the improvement of my sight, we might just come up with a cure for many human diseases." Her smile brightened the whole room. "The trick is to cure people without turning them into GeMs."

Victor hid the small gem in his right hand. With an affectionate gesture, he grasped her left wrist, the one with the bracer, and discretely attached the disguised locator.

"If you can pull this off, you might qualify for the *New Age Prize*. You'd be the youngest winner ever," he said, leaning forward, closer to her, as if he was divulging a big secret. "Let me know what you need. Sounds like a good cause, and I'd like to be a part of it."

~ ~ ~

Vivienne reclaimed her hand from his. Unlike Theodor's, Victor's hands were always cold. A slight shiver tingled her spine, causing her discomfort. The closeness felt inappropriate, and she made sure she put some distance between them.

"I only came up with the idea yesterday. It's a long way ahead, but I have hope." She took another bite of her veal sandwich.

Victor didn't need to know she'd been in bed, with Theodor, when she'd had the idea. Theodor had encouraged her to pursue the research, between kisses and whispers. Her heart picked up speed at the memory.

She couldn't wait for this evening. They were supposed

to have dinner at his place at seven. She peeked at the screen displaying the time above the door. Six more hours to go.

After lunch, Vivienne returned to her office and focused her attention on the lit-up screen. Her bracer vibrated, and after a quick glance, she hurried to answer.

"Theo."

"Viv, I'm sorry, but I have to go to Paris this evening." He sounded half furious, half guilty, about ruining their dinner plans. "It's about those so-called accidents George had been investigating."

"It's okay. I might stay late, too. I'm searching for some more information." She managed to hide her disappointment. "I guess I'll see you tomorrow."

"I should be back early morning, maybe three, four o'clock." The suggestive gaze and the irresistible half smile made Vivienne laugh.

"I'll be sleeping. Tomorrow I have to be here early." She waved toward her surroundings. "Victor offered to help, so I have to make a list with materials and everything else I need."

"Do you have to involve him? I thought it was your idea." A crease marking Theodor's forehead deepened.

"Genetic material and all the other things I'll need aren't easy pickings from the side of the road." She tilted her head, slightly amused by Theodor's dislike of Victor's involvement. "He'll have to procure them for me."

"You should sleep at my place. It's safer, and my bedroom is a little more comfortable," Theodor suggested.

Vivienne felt the tips of her ears burning. The mention of his place revived intimate memories of the two of them, forever etched in her mind. Her heart back-flipped in her chest.

Theodore was right, his bedroom was a whole lot more comfortable, an oasis by itself.

The bed alone, as big as her whole office, had ten-foot tall posts surrounded by soft silks. It was a shame he barely used it, since he only slept a few hours a week. *We've probably used it more in the last four days than he has in years.* Vivienne controlled a giggle.

One whole wall of his bedroom offered unobstructed views of the sea. In between double panels of glass, black screens opened and closed the ceiling at a touch of a button.

"I'll be fine at my place."

Vivienne loved her modest home. She preferred to sleep there when alone.

As soon as they terminated the connection and the comms were off, Vivienne focused her attention on her work. It remained the only thing that kept her mind away from Theodor.

~ ~ ~

Victor stepped out of the portal and observed his surroundings. A simple living room, with décor close to austere, welcomed him. He sniffed the air, recognizing her familiar scent. Vivienne's presence was strong.

Some of the roses he'd seen earlier in her lab were spread throughout.

The locator had worked, and he was in her home. Victor had waited until past midnight to make sure Vivienne was asleep. He was close to turning his plan into reality.

In the kitchen, on a drying rack, one single coffee mug waited upside down, ready to be used. *That's not going to happen.* He continued his way toward the hallway in front of him.

With every step, he sensed her closer. Fangs descended, and he grinned in anticipation. Victor couldn't wait to taste her blood, to touch her skin. Desire made him dizzy.

First, he had to take her out of here. He'd already made the necessary preparations at his place. The room he'd reserved for her, completely isolated from the rest of his house, had all the imaginable luxuries.

The only way in and out was through his bedroom. She would live in a golden cage and have anything she could possibly wish for, except her freedom. *Maybe in time I'll even give her a lab somewhere in the house. She's smart, and it would be a waste to keep her from research work.*

The night, cooler than usual, bathed the island in crisp, refreshing air which entered her home through the opened windows. Clouds danced with each other in the black sky. The moon, covered most of the time, fought the pesky puffs. Short intervals of clear skies allowed the silver coin to shine.

The bedroom door was wide open, and he advanced like a shadow sweeping along the walls.

Victor heard her steady heartbeat, smelled the blood flowing through her body, and had to hold back a hiss. He was finally only steps away.

He imagined Vivienne in his bed and licked his lips at the thought of tasting her. Black silk scarves were prepared in case he would have to bind her. With her acceptance or without, that night, she would be his.

Another break in the clouds filled the room with soft silver light, and he gazed at Vivienne. Only inches away, he hovered. Her lips seemed so soft, so inviting, he could hardly wait to kiss them. Sweet breath brushed against his skin and set it ablaze.

A few strands of wavy hair covered the side of her face, and Victor gently brushed them away. He didn't want to wake her up before the right time.

Vivienne moved slightly, and he licked his lips again. Desire filled his body. She turned her head to one side, and he focused on her pulse throbbing under the delicate skin of her neck.

For a few moments, he fantasized about sinking his fangs into the tender flesh, breaking the smooth skin. *I can almost taste her blood.* He leaned over, closer to her, and brushed away yet another rebel strand of hair.

"Vivienne," he whispered soft and tempting, like the compelling song of a siren. A couple of seconds of silence and no reaction from her, assured Victor she was in deep sleep.

He called her name again, with the most alluring tone in his arsenal. The soft skin on her cheek begged to be touched, and Victor brushed the back of his hand over the side of her face.

She moaned and turned her head. Vivienne blinked a couple of times. Recognition settled in her eyes, followed by confusion and fear.

"Victor?"

~ ~ ~

The whole evening Theodor had a gut-feeling lurking inside him. He hardly focused on the job in Paris. Information, file after file streamed in front of his empty eyes, his mind absent at the task. Something didn't feel right.

When he couldn't endure it any longer, he turned to George. "I need to go. Please finish here for me."

"What is it?"

"Vivienne . . . Something's wrong."

An unusual sense of imminent danger made him teleport straight into her home.

Theodor recognized Victor's presence as soon as he stepped out of the portal. All his senses shifted on high alert, and he rushed to Vivienne's bedroom, making it just in time.

With one quick movement, he yanked the other man away from Vivienne's bed.

Victor flew across the room, hitting the wall behind him with a deep thud. The hanging mirror he landed on shattered in hundreds of shards, bouncing and breaking on the stone-tiled floor.

Vivienne jumped out of her bed and hit the button on the side. The small luminescent globe floating only a couple of inches from the ceiling flooded the room in a cold, white light.

"What are you doing here?" Victor rose quickly to his feet and turned to Theodor.

"I told you to stay away from her." Theodor's fangs descended, and his growl filled the room with threat.

He glanced toward Vivienne—she was terrified, but unharmed.

In only her black lace nightie, she shook against the far wall beside one of the cream draperies. Her bare feet on the cold floor attracted his attention. She curled her toes at the contact with the stone, and wrapped her arms around her body. Tears pooled in her eyes.

With one step, Theodor placed himself between her and Victor.

"How did you know where she lives? How did you get in?"

~ ~ ~

Victor's eyes darkened in front of the threat. "That's irrelevant." He drew two daggers from under his long coat. "She's mine."

Vivienne covered her mouth with her left hand, trying to stop the yelp that escaped anyway. Her right arm, still wrapped around her body, tightened. She could swear she was living yet another nightmare.

The tears she tried to hold back started to run down her cheeks the instant Theodor removed his sword from the scabbard on his back.

Through blurred vision, she noted the blue glow of the stone embedded on the handle of the ancient weapon. It mirrored in his eyes. Sharp, silver-coated edges contrasted with the black metal and shone in the cold light.

"I warned you." Theodor's voice sounded different from what she had gotten accustomed to in the last few days. "I told you I'd kill you if you touched one hair on her head, and you just did."

Theodor's controlled calm sent a cold tremor through Vivienne's body. Before her very eyes he morphed into the beast she feared. The vampire came to life.

~ ~ ~

As much as he tried to tame the beast inside him, Theodor had to free it that night. He needed to be again one with the powerful demon inside him. With one sweep of his sword, he put Victor on the defensive, forcing him to take a couple of steps back.

Taking advantage of the brief moment, he glanced toward Vivienne again. She closed her eyes for a few seconds. He heard her thoughts—she hoped this was a bad dream and wished the scene before her away.

Her terror escalated to new heights. She'd seen, for the first time, the side of him she feared. The determination to protect the woman he loved was stronger than his resolution to keep his demon at bay. *I'll deal with this later. I have to protect her. At any cost.* Theodor shifted his attention back to Victor and parried a strike.

~ ~ ~

The sound of splitting wood made Vivienne reopen her eyes. Victor had avoided another one of Theodor's hits, and his sword had slashed the footboard of her bed in half.

With surprising agility, Victor closed the distance to Theodor. A flurry of stabs in the air made a sinister, high-pitched whir. A couple of his hits pierced the mattress and ruined her sheets, but the last one slashed though Theodor's left arm.

The cut glowed in bright amber for a second, before deep red blood filled the straight line.

"Theo." Her yelp pierced the brief moment of silence.

She couldn't imagine him dying in a fight, protecting her. Fear and guilt wrapped around her heart.

Under Vivienne's frightened gaze, his wound vanished. *He healed himself.* A relieved sigh flew between her lips. Another hiss brushed against her ears, and Theodor lifted his sword above his head.

One fluid movement caused the blade to swoosh through the air. A cut across Victor's chest slashed his black tunic. He growled with what Vivienne first assumed was pain.

She was wrong. The injury enraged him, and he threw himself in Theodor's direction.

Victor marked another small successful hit, and his adversary took a step back.

Theodor checked the deep gash on his right thigh. A predatory grin covered his face.

Vivienne wished she had never seen it.

A wild beast protected her from a man she'd never thought would hurt her. Theodor, or rather his beast, stood between her and the darker-than-hell monster she'd mistaken for a friend.

Theodor's mesmerizing sapphire eyes were a distant memory. Bright, luminescent azure globes replaced them, emotionless. His fangs seemed longer, more terrifying than ever, and Vivienne shuddered against the wall behind her.

For one split second, her attention moved to Victor's eyes—black pools of malevolent darkness. Demons lived inside them.

With his second wound healed, Theodor appeared to have lost control of himself. He launched at Victor with a roar.

They both leaped again, their bodies twisting in the air. Theodor landed first. His feet touched the ground with a thump. His right arm, holding the sword, extended in front of him the same instant Victor landed.

Both men stood still. The tip of Theodor's sword protruded through Victor's back, and another yelp escaped her lips. She covered her mouth with both her hands, bending over. Her earlier light dinner flipped in her stomach.

The unnatural glow in Theodor's eyes faded away. Life returned to them and vanished from Victor's.

"I didn't want to kill you." Theodor closed his left hand on the other man's shoulder. "You should have backed away."

Victor's skin glowed as if lava melted him from inside out. His body smoldered brighter and brighter, until it exploded without a sound. Amber droplets filled the air only to extinguish the next second. Black ashes floated slowly, landing on the cold stone floor and over the ruined bed.

~ ~ ~

Theodor placed his sword on his back and ran to Vivienne, hugging her close to him. With his control regained, he became himself again.

"Viv . . ."

"What happened? Where did he go?" Vivienne's unblinking eyes still followed the tiny pieces of ashes.

"He's gone. He left me no choice but to kill him."

"Where's his body?" Vivienne's question assured Theodor that she had focused her reading and learning about vampires on their way of life, not on how they died.

"We don't leave a body behind when we die." He nodded toward the black dust surrounding them. "We just turn to ashes."

Vivienne stopped trembling and freed herself from his arms. Her bare feet avoided the ashes littering the floor.

"I need to get out of here," she whispered, exiting the bedroom.

Theodor shook his head and followed her. Her calm worried him. "I'm sorry you had to see this."

Vivienne lifted her gaze to him. She seemed petrified. Quiet tears dried on her face.

He knew that instant, his odds of changing her mind to let him turn her had just been reduced to zero.

Chapter 20

"You were right, again," George whispered with sparkling eyes. "Malvina owns a penthouse in Paris."

Theodor had already told him what had happened earlier that morning after he'd left in the middle of their mission. Vivienne was sleeping in the next room, and he didn't want to wake her up.

"I knew it." Theodor jumped off the couch. "Have her apartment under strict, but discreet, surveillance."

"I've already taken care of it." George rose to his feet. "We'll know all her movements."

Theodor nodded a couple of times. "If she is the one hunting in my territory, we'll have the proof."

"And if she's not doing it alone, we'll catch whoever else is behind it." George took a few steps toward the door when Theodor stopped him.

"You haven't told me how your date went?"

His friend stopped near the door. "I guess I'm still not ready to date. I didn't go with any expectations, but I was surprised by how guilty I felt."

"Or maybe she simply wasn't the right girl to get you out of your shell."

"Since when are you so wise?" George opened the door and stepped over the threshold.

"I've learned a few things." Theodor felt the tug at the corners of his lips.

George shook his head with amusement and closed the door behind him.

Theodor's smile melted away. Vivienne's reaction to the previous night worried him. He'd had to use his magnetism on her and put her to sleep when she wouldn't come out of the shock. She had stared at him with tears in her eyes and her body shaking out of control.

Silently, he entered the bedroom and joined her in the oversized bed.

Vivienne stirred in his arms. Her head rested on his shoulder. Dried tears still marked her cheeks. If he hadn't left Paris early, it would've been too late.

He had underestimated Victor. His arms tightened around Vivienne instinctively, and he had to fight back an angry hiss.

Nobody will ever touch you again. I'll die before I let anything happen to you. I swear.

She turned her head, interrupting his thoughts. Her long, thick lashes fluttered open, revealing light caramel, almost golden eyes. Theodor smiled at her initial confusion. She wasn't used to his bedroom yet. "Good morning."

She loved to see him smile. Lately, he couldn't wipe that damn smile off his face every time they were together. That morning wasn't any different.

"Theo." She closed her eyes when he kissed her forehead. Her body molded against his.

From the depths of her mind, he heard her scream and sensed her fear. She remembered the previous night and withdrew from his embrace, blinking a few times.

"Everything's okay."

"You said I would be safe here." Tears threatened again, and Vivienne fought them back. "Why did Victor come after me?" Every muscle in her body tensed.

"You're safe. I didn't expect him to become obsessed with you."

"I thought he was a friend."

Theodor sensed her fear turning into anger. The sting of betrayal hurt her.

"I know, and I'm sorry. When I first noticed his interest in you, I warned him to stay away, to leave you alone." He gently touched the side of her face with his fingertips. "I can only guess that us being together threw him over the edge."

Vivienne wrapped herself in the silky sheet, her hands closing on the embroidered edge. She slid out of his arms.

Theodor missed her before she even reached the bathroom. After a quick shower, she returned wearing one of the soft towels. Theodor waited for her with a late breakfast.

She sat beside him on the loveseat. They had made it a habit to stay close to each other, and not on opposite sides of the table.

"Are you all right?" Theodor wrapped an arm around her.

She nodded and reached for her coffee.

Theodor waited for the smile she always displayed after the first sip. He loved seeing genuine joy reflected in her luminous eyes. It never came.

"How did he know where I live?"

"Did he ever visit?" Theodor asked. "Maybe he followed you?"

Vivienne shook her head a few times. Soft, still-damp ringlets of honey danced and tickled his arm. "No. I always used the portal, just as you told me."

She reached again for her coffee and Theodor followed the movement of her thin hand. Light reflected off her bracer.

"Did you lose one of the gems?" He pointed to it.

"No. It always had nine, the oval one in the middle and four round ones on each side," Vivienne answered and checked quickly to see if she missed one.

"Then why are there five on this side?" Theodor's hand closed around her wrist with suspicion.

"He touched it"—Vivienne lifted her gaze to him—"yesterday." Her whisper made Theodor pay increased attention to the gems. One of them was a slightly darker shade, and not perfectly lined up with the rest.

It detached easily, falling into the palm of his hand. The tracker blinked inside, and he crushed the disguised equipment, showing it to Vivienne.

"This is how he found out where you live."

A tremor coursed through her body, and both his arms closed around her. Vivienne leaned her head on his chest.

"Viv, we need to talk." Theodor decided to open the subject hammering in the back of his mind.

She nodded silently, waiting for him to continue.

"I know you love your place. You like to be on your own, but . . ." He paused until she looked at him. "I think you should move here, with me."

Vivienne blinked a few times. In spite of his expectations, she didn't reject his idea on the spot.

"I don't want you to feel rushed or pushed to do anything against your will." He tried to ease any suspicions. "You might think we're moving too fast, but I want to spend as much time with you as possible," Theodor pushed further, taking advantage of her indecision.

A timid smile curled her lips, and he kissed her.

"Do you think my home isn't safe?" she asked.

"Not at all. I will continue to watch over you every night you decide to sleep there. It just makes more sense for you to be here."

Theodor followed her hesitant thoughts. She twisted a strand of hair around her finger, and absently played with it. A part of her wanted to move in with him. The other part, the one screaming in her mind to run, he chose to ignore.

"How about we compromise?" she suggested under Theodor's disapproving gaze.

"I don't do compromises. Things always go the way I want them to, and if they don't, I make them."

"Then maybe you should start." Vivienne's tone reminded him she wasn't an average woman. "I'll keep my place and have some of my things here for when I spend the night." She abandoned the curled, dampen hair and placed her hands on his chest, making his heart jump. "Please, don't rush me."

The part of her he ignored earlier had slapped him in his face. *I should've known it was coming.*

Theodor held back a growl in the back of his throat. *I don't like it. Not one bit.*

"Viv."

"I'm trying really hard not to move back to the mainland." She withdrew from his arms. A determined look sparked in her eyes. "I'm starting to have doubts that Crete was, or still is, the best option for me."

Her stubbornness interfered with his plans again, and his persistence would push her away.

He lifted and kissed each of her hands.

"If you promise you'll spend more time here than at your place."

Vivienne's laugh filled his heart.

I can't lose her.

"Fine."

His kiss stopped her from saying anything else, and they both ignored for a while the world around them.

~ ~ ~

Day after day, Theodor got used to the routine falling into place. Vivienne barely went to her home. She split her time between her lab and him.

With only days left until the *New Year's Ball,* the celebratory mood spread worldwide.

The New Year had remained an important holiday, even after the Flood. Throughout the years, many religious holidays had been forgotten.

When the alien ship crashed on Earth and wiped out nearly three quarters of the population, faith in many of the old religions was shaken to the core.

A new year had always represented a new beginning, and Theodor planned his own, with Vivienne. In his office, he took the black box out of his pocket. Like all vampires, he kept alive traditions from long ago. Humans moved on through time, and from generation to generation they lost many of the old ways.

The square box held a ring. Theodor would ask Vivienne to marry him on the first day of the new year. Only vampires still offered engagement rings to their brides to be.

The princess cut diamond in the middle glimmered to life. He'd rejected four other stones, the ones that failed to match the color of her eyes. A multitude of tiny lights reflected from the multifaceted gem.

With the box closed and safely away, he faced the window.

What if she rejects me? Every time he mentioned turning her, her fear hurt him. Vivienne accepted him, but not the beast inside him.

Theodor ran his hand through his hair. A couple of onyx locks fell on his forehead.

Trying to imagine his life without Vivienne always saddened him. He didn't want that life. He'd lived it already. Without her, he would turn back into *Theofrost*. She was the only one that could make him smile so much his cheeks hurt at times. She made him feel alive.

He did not want to lose her, or the happiness she brought him. A month after Victor's death, having her in his arms every day elicited thoughts about the life he wanted.

Theodor based his hopes in a future together on her unpredictability. After all the time he'd spent in her mind, he still couldn't guess her reactions. She surprised him at every turn.

Three more days until my dreams may come true or crash and burn in hell.

~ ~ ~

New Year's Eve filled the air with excitement. Theodor tuned to the opening door. Vivienne entered the room as always— bringing animation in his life.

"Do I really have to wear these . . . ?" Vivienne lifted her gaze to him.

She stopped fumbling with the gloves giving her so much trouble.

His exceptional hearing picked up her galloping heartbeat. It was the first time seeing each other in formal evening attire.

Theodor stared at her smitten. Vivienne's dress was the sweetest shade of buttery cream. Smooth, velvety silk hugged her curves, making him want to slide his hands over every one of them. With a sweetheart neckline, and a high slit on the left thigh, the dress followed the lines of her body closely.

Vivienne held over her shoulders a long shawl from the same exotic fabric. Extremely conscious about the scars on her back, she always covered herself. Theodor was the only one she allowed to see them.

Strands of creamy pearls held some of her hair up, only to let the rest cascade on her back in bouncy curls. The mixture of different shades of light brown and blond mesmerized him, and Theodor ached to touch them.

"You look stunning . . . Breathtaking." He finally recovered from the quiet admiration.

Vivienne blushed lightly, under very little makeup. Her eyes sparkled in a multitude of gold tones.

"You're not bad yourself."

Theodor closed the distance to her.

"Troubles with the gloves?"

"A little." She hesitated. "Why do I have to wear them again?"

Theodor laughed, and Vivienne reacted in a most unexpected way. She drew him down to her in a kiss that temporarily numbed his mind.

"It's customary to wear gloves and to go weaponless to these parties." He managed to translate his almost coherent thoughts into words, holding her close to him.

"I understand the no weapons part, but these things are a pain." Vivienne took a couple of steps away from him, fighting with the second glove.

Her high heels whispered on the hard floors, attracting Theodor's gaze. The shoes perfectly matched her dress. He already missed her from his arms. The side slit gave him a peek at her legs, and his whole body tensed with want. He had to tear his eyes away from her.

How the hell am I going to make it through the night? Maybe I should ask her now. Theodor dismissed the thought as quick as it formed.

"Just as we're not allowed weapons, we're also encouraged not to use any of our special abilities." Theodor hoped to shake the desire taking control over his body and mind. "These gatherings are a reason for celebration. We're supposed to relax and enjoy." If he didn't control himself, they would never make it to the ball.

Vivienne whirled on her heels to face him. Her second glove was almost on.

"The special powers some of us have can only be exercised through skin-to-skin contact." He found it harder and harder to stay focused on any topic. "The gloves came into the picture long ago, when for most, those powers were difficult to control. In time, they became customary."

A crease appeared on her forehead. "But your abilities have nothing to do with touch. With or without them, you can still get in people's minds or do all the other stuff." She waved her gloved hand. "Well, except healing."

"True, but as I told you before, just because I can do those things, doesn't mean I will."

Her trembling hands assured Theodor he wasn't the only one having difficulties controlling urges.

For a second time, he walked close to her. He picked up the jewelry box from the low table and held it leisurely in his left hand.

"Viv, please accept these." He opened the box in front of her.

A pendant dangled from the choker made of the same cream pearls as the ones in her hair. In the middle, a champagne diamond hung by a thin gold ring.

Unlike in the Old World, pearls were extremely rare, a luxury. The vast majority of humans had never seen any real ones. The bracelet completing the set had six matching diamonds all around.

"I can't accept this." Vivienne adjusted her second glove. "It's too much."

She stepped back at the sight of the unique jewelry.

"Please." Theodor knew the effect his gaze had on her. She couldn't resist it. "I insist."

"Only because you insist, I'll wear them tonight. But I'm doing it under protest."

Theodor clasped the choker around her neck and the bracelet on her wrist. His right eyebrow arched.

"Your protest"—he tossed the empty box on the nearest table—"is duly noted." His arms coiled around her.

Another kiss endangered their resolution to leave in a few minutes.

"Thank you. I have never seen anything this beautiful," she whispered, her fingertips running over the smooth, round pearls.

Theodor tilted her face to him with a gloved hand and smiled the way she loved it: with his heart.

"I have. You."

~ ~ ~

Theodor wrapped her hand around his arm as soon as they stepped out of the portal. She observed her surroundings with excitement and eagerness. The majestic castle belonging to the Third Coven towered before them.

Guards flanked the spacious entry and welcomed them with respectful bows.

"Do they know you?" Vivienne asked in a whisper, and Theodor nodded silently.

Wide-open double doors led to the entryway into the ballroom. Heavy, red draperies were held to the sides with gold tassels.

Before they entered, Vivienne heard the animation of the party, clinking glasses, and voices melting into the music. Mixed scents of various perfumes and colognes made her take a deep breath. She tried to identify them in her mind.

Tens of luminescent globes patrolled the air halfway to the three-story ceilings. Their light revealed a completely different world to Vivienne.

Her fascination with the Old World had mostly been sated with pictures and documentaries seen in libraries. Here, now, it came alive before her eyes.

If someone told me a few months ago I would spend the New Year at a ball, with vampires, I would've laughed. But there she was transported into a long-gone world.

Over one thousand people mingled around in elegant evening wear and white gloves. She didn't know where to look first. Thick, marble columns decorated with red and gold ribbons supported the vaulted ceilings.

Trays with champagne glasses and finger foods floated

around, powered by minuscule batteries. Servants in black-and-gold uniforms assisted everyone's needs.

"Is everyone here"—she had to search for the right words—"like you?" Vivienne whispered in Theodor's ear. His cologne tickled her nostrils and warmed her.

"No. Most are vampires"—Theodor stared at her—"but there are also a few humans, and even GeMs. Why?"

Her hand tightened on his arm. "Just curious."

Surrounded by hundreds and hundreds of vampires, she wished for the first time she didn't fear them. Unfortunately, it remained wishful thinking.

The rest of his family waited for them a few steps ahead.

Theodor's hand covered hers on his arm. The warmth and calmness went through the gloves and settled deep inside her. She sensed an invisible shield, like a protective bubble, closing around them.

"Relax, you're safe."

Vivienne heard the smile in his words before she saw it on his lips.

"You're with me."

The shimmer in his eyes, the touch of his hand, and the sound of his voice flooded her with confidence, and desire.

Chapter 21

Theodora had already raised a few eyebrows with her dress in the few minutes since she arrived. Her light-blue gown, completely translucent, had intricate embroidery placed strategically to keep her covered, more or less.

Vivienne couldn't help thinking that ironically, Theodora's gloves covered the most flesh.

"How the hell did she get in here?" Theodor's growled question revealed the depth of his anger, interrupting Vivienne from her thoughts.

"Who?" his father asked first, scanning his surroundings.

"Malvina."

The name of the woman who was supposedly going to marry Theodor sent a shiver through Vivienne's body. Her earlier confidence melted away.

She followed his gaze.

Somewhere, deep inside, Vivienne hoped Malvina would be ugly and laden with deadly weapons. She hoped the woman deserved to die, as Theodor implied. To her surprise, she didn't see a hunched back or a crooked nose, not even an ugly mole.

The fabric Malvina's dress was made of seemed wet and tight on her magnificent body, like a second skin. *I wish I had her curves.* Vivienne tightened her hold on the edge of her shawl.

Malvina appeared like a siren, risen from the deepest, darkest black waters of hell. Breathtaking beauty mixed with elegance and evil. She swayed her hips in an alluring dance-like walk, making many heads turn in her direction.

"Your Majesties." Her gracious bow made Vivienne more insecure.

The glare the other woman shot her way reminded her of Greg. She felt inferior, unwanted, like a pest that needed extermination.

"How did you get in here?" Theodor kept a low tone, and Vivienne assumed he tried not to attract unwanted attention.

"Just like everyone else, with an invitation." Malvina's smile could melt all the ice in the world, except the glacier in his eyes.

"Did you steal it?" Theodor earned himself a disapproving glance from his father.

Vivienne's gaze moved from one person to the next, following the conversation.

"Of course not." She turned to Theodor's parents. "I'm honored to meet you, Your Majesties. My name is Malvina."

"They know who you are." Another growl left his lips.

Princess Ana and Prince Andree smiled politely, but coldness sparked through, like sun reflecting off ice.

Malvina turned to Theodor's sister next, with a flashy smile. "You must be Princess Theodora."

"Aren't you observant? What was your first clue?" Her sarcasm would have been enough to make anyone run, or at least be embarrassed, but not the stunning Malvina.

For one fraction of a second, Vivienne saw her deep brown eyes charged with hate.

"A human." She measured Vivienne with superiority. "I don't think we've met."

The rest of the family moved closer. "Oh, I see. The family's latest toy."

Vivienne closed her hands into fists, furious and frustrated. Malvina could easily overpower her or any human. Tears threatened, but she blinked them away. She wouldn't let anyone see her fear, especially not *that* woman.

"What did you call her?" Theodor's hand closed around Malvina's arm. "Apologize, right now, or I'll break it."

Vivienne couldn't tell if it was his threatening tone, or the pain Malvina must've felt in her arm, that convinced her to fabricate some sort of excuse.

"Sorry, I didn't realize you were someone important."

A sudden urge to gouge her eyes out of their sockets made Vivienne inhale deeply.

"What kind of lame apology is that?" Theodor continued to squeeze her arm.

Vivienne remained petrified, unable to make any sound. Insulted and terrified, she wished she could disappear. Her fear surrounded her like a torture device turned to maximum, suffocating her.

"Theo, you're hurting me." Another fake smile stretched her lips. "With our impending wedding, I didn't think you would show up here with a human."

"Our impending wedding?" Theodor accentuated each word. "I haven't accepted your terms. And considering your behavior, I never will," he spat with disgust.

Theodor released her arm with a push, and Malvina stepped back to regain her balance. One of her high heels cut into the seam of her dress, but she recovered quickly, with grace. His hand closed into a fist.

"Let's not discuss this right now." Prince Andree stepped forward. "This is not the time, nor the place for it."

"Is there a problem here?" Mihai and Gabriel Veres, Theodor's uncles, stopped behind Malvina. They both appeared serious and tense.

"She insulted Vivienne," Theodora answered quickly and nodded toward her, now surrounded by the family.

Mihai's eyes narrowed, his nose twitched, and a slight crease marked his forehead. *Is he sniffing Malvina? Or does he just not like her?*

"It's not my fault that Theo is making a show out of—"
"You want a show?"

Theodor's coldness sent shivers down Vivienne's back. It reminded her of the night he killed Victor.

"I will make one, of your death. If you want to live through this night, stay away from us." His index finger pointed to her chest with enough threat to make her retreat.

A few curious heads turned toward the group.

"Miss, have we met before?" Mihai offered his arm to Malvina.

"I don't think so." The stunning woman turned her attention to Mihai. "I would have remembered." She accepted his arm with another charming smile, and both walked away.

Theodor let out a hiss, and Gabriel placed a hand on his shoulder.

"Theo."

"I'll kill her."

"Let me know if you need help. I'm in." Theodora's offer brought smiles all around.

"Are you okay?" Theodor turned to Vivienne.

"I'm fine." She tried and failed to smile.

Theodor wrapped his arm around her. "Let's dance."

"I don't know how," Vivienne whispered, allowing him to direct her to the dance floor.

She'd never enjoyed going to parties as a teenager. Vivienne always focused on her studies, and the few attempts at participation usually found her hiding in a corner and watching everyone. Most times, she tried to solve formulas in her head. Later, she found refuge in her work.

"Just follow my lead." Theodor gently guided her through their first waltz together.

~ ~ ~

Only steps away, Malvina studied Vivienne and Theodor. With every passing second, she grew more hateful and desperate. *I should be dancing with him, not that worthless human.* During that first dance, Malvina made up her mind—she would get rid of any obstacles in her way, including the weak mortal.

Her first ball, a total failure when it came to her plans, brought excitement otherwise.

Malvina hadn't anticipated Theodor being interested in someone else. She waited patiently until he stood alone, and she approached him again, hoping to salvage some of her plot.

"Is she the reason you haven't accepted my proposal yet?" She nodded toward Vivienne.

Theodor turned to her. His gaze glided over her pendant—a tear-shaped ruby on a black chain.

"No. You are."

"Oh, Theo, you're not nice. If she's so important to you, I'll let you keep her." Her fingers closed on the gem. "You can play all you want, as long as you marry me."

The muscles in his jaw twitched, and his eyes glowed. Neither of his reactions were a good sign.

"You don't get it, do you? My answer is *no*. I will not marry you."

Malvina tried her hardest not to lose control.

"Are you going to give up your dreams and ambitions, your coven? For a human?" She couldn't hide her disgust. "Are you serious?"

"You have no idea what you're talking about." Theodor's shoulders relaxed, and he glared at her with disdain and his well-known coldness. "Stay away from me and my family. And stop spreading rumors." His index finger stopped about an inch away from her chest. "If you ever come within ten feet of Vivienne, I will kill you. And enjoy it. Are we clear?"

Malvina gulped. The sudden lump in her throat interfered with her thinking. Theodor's words, colder than ice, left no doubt he would follow through. With one last spark of pride, she squared her shoulders and stared into his dark, narrowed eyes.

"You will regret this. I'm going to make you beg for forgiveness."

Malvina whirled on her heels and left. She peeked behind once, to see him standing like a statue rooted into the marble floors. She had just declared war, and she needed a quick and efficient plan to ensure victory.

~ ~ ~

Theodor had no idea how long he stood there. Sounds around him melted into one another. Between the music, voices and laughter, the clinking of the glasses, and the footsteps, he could barely hear his own thoughts.

The sense of danger crawled up his spine. His breath became shallow, and inside the gloves, his hands covered in sweat.

With too many people around, locating Vivienne proved to be quite a task. He glanced toward one of the floating screens displaying the time—a half hour until midnight.

A sudden urge to find her, the need to hold her in his arms, overrode everything else. *It feels like Paris all over again.*

He panicked and swept the whole ballroom in a long glance. Every single color ever invented popped in the sea of guests. The multitude of faces, all the thoughts he could hear from everyone around, made him dizzy.

"Theo."

He suddenly tensed when a hand closed on his shoulder and spun around, with a growl. "Mihai," he whispered with slight relief.

"This Malvina . . . There's something about her." His uncle walked alongside Theodor.

"Yes, she's about to die."

Mihai's laugh made Theodor turn his head. Over his uncle's shoulder he saw Vivienne and stopped, changing direction. His sister stood by her side.

His relief only lasted a fraction of a second. Malvina had joined them. He had to hurry. With all the people in his way, Theodor resisted the temptation to charge through all of them.

Out of nowhere, his parents cut in front of him.

"Theo, she's safe." His father's hand closed on Theodor's arm.

He didn't answer, suspecting everyone could sense his agitation. Vivienne seemed uncomfortable, scared, but his sister talked to Malvina, and he focused his attention on the conversation, listening to every word from about thirty feet away.

"Princess Theodora, I'm sorry, but I think we might've started on the wrong foot." Malvina's voice still annoyed him, in spite of all the distance.

"No. We started right." Theodora stared at the other woman. "I don't trust you, and I don't like you trying to extort my brother into marrying you."

"It's not what you think."

"Then drop your shield and prove me wrong," Theodora challenged her.

"I wish I could." Malvina lowered her gaze. "My shield is permanent."

"That's bull, and we both know it." Theodora's raised voice attracted a few curious glances. "Now, if you will excuse us, some very nice people are waiting for us."

Without another word, Malvina stepped aside, allowing Theodora and Vivienne to continue on their way. She exited the room with anger coiling around her like a tornado. Theodor's attention focused back on Vivienne.

His eyes met hers, and they smiled at each other. Only seconds later, his hand finally rested on her waist.

One by one, the whole family gathered together and started to move toward the terrace. With minutes left to midnight, they didn't want to miss the fireworks.

~ ~ ~

Malvina watched them from behind one of the plush draperies.

Her uncle taught her to always be ready and have a safe getaway. She knew how to hide, how to make herself untraceable. The few calls made earlier assured her everything was in place. All she needed now was to execute her plan.

The last seconds to the beginning of the new year had a different effect on her. Most of the guests were excited about the countdown to midnight. She only grew angrier and more determined to eliminate the obstacles.

Her fury escalated when Theodor kissed Vivienne. *Oh, she's dead. I'm not going to let a human ruin my plans.*

The desire for power and revenge grew stronger than ever. Malvina prepared for the boldest move she had ever attempted.

~ ~ ~

A couple of hours later, back into the ballroom, Vivienne started to feel tired, but she didn't want to go home yet. Instead, she excused herself to the ladies' room. At Theodor's insistence, his sister went with her.

"I can handle going to the bathroom by myself," she objected when Theodora opened the door.

"I would hope so." Theodora winked. "My brother asked me to come with you."

"Please, I would really like a moment to myself." Her insistence won. Theodora closed the door and remained outside.

Vivienne took her time and splashed some cold water on her face. Soft, plush towels rolled and arranged in a partial pyramid decorated the countertop. She took one, patting herself dry, trying not to smudge what little makeup she wore. A lemon fragrance, fresh and invigorating, made her smile into the mirror.

The smile froze on her face. Malvina stood right behind her, with a malicious stare. Vivienne knew she was in trouble. Her first instinct was to run and scream for help. Theodora waited right outside the door.

With one quick movement, Malvina grabbed Vivienne's hair and pulled her back. "If you make one sound, you die."

Vivienne's heart stopped. Tears filled her eyes. She heard the strings of cream pearls in her hair breaking. They poured in a thin stream, bouncing off the white marble floor with tiny sounds. They rolled away, as if scared to stay in one place.

"Stop twitching." Malvina yanked her closer. "You're coming with me."

"No. Please, let me go," Vivienne whispered, terrified at the sight of Malvina's fangs.

"You're in my way. Theodor's mine." Malvina's growled words burned her ears.

"He loves me." Vivienne tried to free herself.

With the back of her gloved hand, Malvina hit her across the face, releasing her hair. Thrown back by the force of the hit, Vivienne lost her balance. She fell backward. Her head hit the cold floor, and she lost consciousness.

~ ~ ~

"What's taking so long? Why aren't you in there with her?" Theodor stood in front of his sister.

"Relax, nobody went in or out. I was right here at all times, guarding your future wife."

"Will you stay out of my head for once?"

"That's no fun. Theo, she's a smart girl, she'll say *yes.*" Theodora squeezed her brother's arm.

Her encouragement brought a small smile to his lips. "I would prefer if she said yes because she loves me. I already know she's smart." He still doubted his chances.

"Her feelings for you are strong enough." Theodora smiled at him and withdrew her hand.

In all the time they'd been together, Vivienne never said to him the three most important words. He still waited for them.

"Please go in and see what's taking this long."

Tingles went up and down his spine, and for the second time that night, he felt uneasy.

"You have to learn to let her breathe, you know? Don't suffocate the poor girl." Theodora's right hand closed on the handle and she opened the door.

She stopped in the doorway and turned to her brother with guilt written all over her face. "She's gone."

Her whisper reached Theodor's ears like a nightmare. His worst fears were coming to life. He pushed past his sister into the room, and his gaze fell on the pearls littering the floor. The few drops of smudged blood made his heart stop.

Theodor dipped the tip of his finger in one of the drops and sniffed. He recognized the scent of Vivienne's blood. "It's hers."

"Are you sure?" Theodora approached him. "I don't mean to doubt you, but I want to make sure we don't jump to conclusions."

She won herself one of the deadliest glares from her brother, and Theodora bowed her head.

"I swear that nobody went in after her."

"There." Theodor pointed to the opposite side of the room. "It's another exit."

He ran and opened the second access door, revealing an empty hallway. A lone pearl shone on the dark-colored carpet covering the floor.

Slowly, with his fists tight, Theodor turned to face his sister.

"I'm going to find Vivienne and kill Malvina."

Chapter 22

Theodor threw the champagne bottle against the far wall, about twenty feet away. It had been waiting on ice for him and Vivienne to celebrate their engagement. *This isn't what I had in mind. It can't be happening.*

The glass shattered into hundreds of shards, and the bubbly drink splashed against the immaculate light-blue paint. The liquid ran down in a stream, soaking and staining the now dented wall.

"No!"

His scream resonated through the whole house, all the way into the palace. With uncontrollable fury, he exited the living room with a roar, fangs fully extended.

A couple of servants ran in to clean the mess. They trembled in front of his fury.

Theodor stormed into his office, and with hurried but steady movements, he accessed the security cameras from the ball. He saw with his own eyes Malvina carrying an unconscious Vivienne through the dark hallway, and disappearing into a portal.

They could be anywhere in the world.

Head between his hands, Theodor rested his elbows on the edge of the massive wooden desk.

Only three hours ago, happiness filled his heart. He relived every one of those last seconds with Vivienne.

They had just finished dancing, and she'd gently pulled him to her level, letting him know she would use the ladies' room. He could still sense her breath brushing against his skin, setting his body ablaze.

The discreet kiss she'd planted on his cheek made him touch the spot and close his eyes. Hundreds, thousands of blades stabbed his heart at the same time.

Ten minutes later she'd been gone. Without Vivienne at his side, without her luminous presence, he fell back into the darkness.

Stone, ice, terror, all surrounded him like an invisible funnel, dragging him into the dreadful abyss. The lair of his inner beast, the same place he's been trapped for centuries.

Before he hadn't known what happy meant, now he did. Vivienne had showed him the way out of the terrible pit.

"I want her back."

Theodor rose to his feet. A cold calm covered him. He readied himself for anything and everything to bring Vivienne back into his life.

~ ~ ~

Serge paced his library for close to an hour. He stopped in front of the fireplace and stared at the precious objects on the mantle.

He'd known all along, all those years, that Malvina would make a mistake. His earlier conversation with her haunted his mind. At first, she'd tried to lie and convince him she had a great time at the ball.

She could trick anyone in the world, but she could never fool him. He knew her too well. Serge insisted, and his niece finally admitted what she had done. A mix of anger and fear set in his heart. The end neared, and Malvina's actions only drew it closer.

He begged her to let go of the woman she'd kidnapped. They could still run away to safety. Set on satisfying her thirst for power, Malvina ignored reason. Not even he could talk any sense into her any longer. *She's a lost cause.*

He tried to find out where she went, but his niece terminated their connection. *She could be anywhere.*

With Malvina gone rogue, beyond any hope of redemption, he had one last option—his final plan.

After spending almost two hours in his greenhouse, Serge readied himself for the ultimate sacrifice. He glanced around one last time, convinced he wouldn't come back. The fire burned in the fireplace with the same crackling sound he found relaxing. Outside, the blizzard raged against the lofty windows.

Serge touched his mementos as a farewell. With a long, loud sigh he shrugged into the long, hooded cape and opened a portal.

Blue and purple swirls swallowed him.

The mention of Malvina and Theodor's names opened all doors, and only minutes later, Mihai Veres agreed to see him right away.

Serge entered the long reception room and walked with his head down and his face hidden. A few steps away from the famous Veres descendent, he stopped and bowed with respect. "My Lord."

"Who are you, and what information do you have?"

Mihai cut straight to the point and took a step toward the man in front of him.

Serge stood tall and lowered the hood, revealing himself.

"Ivan," Mihai murmured with disbelief.

"No." He shook his head. "I'm Serge. Ivan was my twin brother. Malvina is his daughter."

Serge's eyes followed Mihai's right hand grabbing the handle of his sword. All the information contained in only a few words seemed to still be processing in his mind.

"How is it possible?"

"My Lord, I will explain everything, but please, take me to Prince Theodor. I'm not here to fight." He lifted his hands in surrender, showing the other man he wasn't armed.

Serge and Mihai stepped out of the portal at the same time, inside the Sanctum belonging to the Old Coven. There was no time to let his surroundings impress him. He needed to focus on what lay ahead of him—the strong possibility he was living his last moments.

At his request, Mihai had called everyone in the family, and they all gathered in only minutes.

As soon as he approached with Mihai, they pulled weapons, except Theodor and his sister.

His brother's name echoed in the room on a few different tones, but Mihai stepped between him and the others.

"He's not Ivan."

They all stared at him in disbelief, holding their threatening stances.

~ ~ ~

"Who are you, and what information do you have?" Theodor figured the responsibility to ask fell to him since they were in his house.

The weapons swished back into their scabbards, and Serge faced him.

"My full name is Serghei Drago. You may know me as Serge. Ivan was my twin brother." A new round of loud hisses filled the Sanctum, but he continued. "I'm here to beg you for my niece's life. Malvina is Ivan's daughter."

He recognized the name of the man who allegedly left Malvina's group. It appeared there was more to it.

"You're too late." Theodor puffed out his chest. "As far as I'm concerned, she's already dead."

"Please, My Prince. I'm here to volunteer my life in exchange for hers."

The beast inside Theodor twitched with excitement. Blood was always welcome. He stared into Serge's eyes with curiosity.

Out of nowhere, Vivienne's image appeared in his mind. She smiled, happy. He remembered the lightness and joy she had brought to his life.

"Do you know where she took Vivienne?" he asked, holding back an angry growl.

"No. She wouldn't tell me." Serge lowered his gaze.

Theodor walked away from him. He stopped after a few steps and turned to face Serge.

"You haven't wronged me. She did, and she will pay."

"She's blinded with anger. The thirst for power and revenge has overtaken her mind."

"Revenge for Ivan?" Theodor's father broke his silence.

Serge nodded toward Prince Andree.

"What does Vivienne have to do with Malvina's father?"

Theodor returned his attention to the man in front of him, still confused by the half explanations.

"What she did last night wasn't supposed to happen. Your relationship with this girl threw her over the edge . . ." Serge hesitated. "Permission to speak freely, My Prince?"

Theodor checked the other man's mind quickly.

He understood the weight of Serge's sacrifice. "Granted, and you may rise. Start with the beginning. I hate when I get half the story."

~ ~ ~

Serge bowed his head one more time. The prince lived up to his reputation. His actions, so far, proved every bit of the man rumored to be—fair, but unforgiving. Serge had admired him for years.

"When we were in our late twenties, Ivan disappeared for about a year. He visited me one night and told me what he'd become, offered to turn me too." Serge figured it was just as good as any point to start his story. "Even if we appeared identical, we were very different people. We grounded each other, completing one another. At the time, it seemed like a good idea, and I accepted."

Serge stopped for a second and glanced at everyone. He had their attention, and the hostility seemed to diminish.

"After a few years, for reasons I will never know, Ivan developed a hatred against humans. We started arguing. We fought against each other a few times."

The smooth tiles under his feet served as a screen for the rapid images flashing through his mind. "Last time we did, I barely made it out alive after I gave him a scar." He lifted his hand to the side of his face. "We both decided to go our separate ways. I hadn't seen him for about two centuries."

"You didn't hunt with him?" Queen Emelia's surprised tone caused Serge to turn to her.

"Never." He shook his head. "I'd heard about his habits, how ruthless he had become. I was ashamed to admit we were brothers." His gaze returned to the ivory tiles. "After two hundred years, only days before his death, he contacted me and asked to meet in Paris."

After a deep breath, he took a few steps and continued. "He surprised me with Malvina. Her mother, a human, died during childbirth. He never even mentioned her name. Malvina had just recovered from transition, days before—"

"The hypocrite." Prince Andree's growl interrupted him.

Serge nodded in agreement. At the time he'd thought the same thing.

"He knew he might not survive the battle against the Third Coven, and asked me to take care of his daughter." He stared into Theodor's direction, but he could only see the images playing in his mind. "I trained her, taught her everything she knows." Serge's voice dropped to a whisper. "I tried my best to raise her right. I failed." He turned again toward the man that had killed his brother centuries ago, Prince Andree De Croix. "There's too much of her father in her. She hates humans as much as he did." His shoulders drooped.

Prince Andree mirrored his son's image and crossed his arms over his chest, as if he dared Serge to continue.

"It wasn't until recently that I found out about her plans. I tried to stop her, change her mind." His voice fluctuated again. He wished he could've at least appeared stronger in front of the most powerful family in the world. "All this time I managed to keep us safe, away from all of you. I knew we would both be killed if you discovered us."

A new glance around the room brought doubt in Serge's mind. Maybe if he had come to them long ago, he and Malvina wouldn't be in this mess now.

"Again, what does Vivienne have to do with any of this?" Theodor's patience seemed to be thinning.

"The human girl just happened to be in her way. Malvina's plan was to kill all of you and take over leadership of all vampires, turn them against humans . . ." He had never felt more of a failure as he did that instant.

"You were supposed to be the first one to die, Prince Theodor. She wanted to marry you, so she could get close and catch you with your guard down."

"That would've never happened." His brows furrowed. "I've never trusted her."

Theodor's words drew another sigh from Serge.

"Next would have been you." He bowed his head before Princess Theodora. "With both of you dead, she figured your parents would have been easy to take out next." Serge covered his chest with an open hand. "Queen Emelia, you would have been crushed with your family gone, and next in line."

Serge turned lastly to Mihai and Gabriel. They stood beside each other, which reminded him of the long-gone times when he'd stood by his brother.

"Lord Gabriel, you would've followed and you, Lord Mihai, would have been last."

"I'm not sure if I'm flattered or offended." Mihai's remark, intended to loosen nerves, failed.

"She's a lousy strategist." Theodora ran a hand over her wavy ponytail. "If she would've done her homework properly, she should've known that our family doesn't get weaker when one of us is in danger, or hurt. We become stronger, and more united than ever."

Serge bowed his head in front of the princess with blazing blue eyes.

"So, you knew Malvina's plans all this time and did nothing?" Princess Ana's revulsion was loud and clear in her voice.

"I only found out about all of this about a month and a half ago, and tried to prevent it from happening. Unfortunately, she is beyond stopping." Serge had a hard time keeping his voice level. "Malvina has lost contact with reality. She's . . . hopeless."

A heavy silence covered the Sanctum, like a scratchy, uncomfortable shroud.

~ ~ ~

"Who would know where she is?" Theodor couldn't afford to waste more time. He needed answers.

Serge lifted his head and straightened his shoulders. "If she followed what I taught her, she should be in a safe house, somewhere isolated, surrounded by loyal people."

Theodor took a few steps in deep thought. *Her group. Which one? I know.* He ran behind the long table and opened a cabinet. With trembling hands, he searched in the pile of files Malvina had given him and picked one.

"Would he know?" He showed Serge a picture.

"Chris is one of the closest to Malvina, almost a fanatic."

"Perfect. I'll talk to him."

"He won't tell you." Serge's tone revealed sadness and hopelessness.

"Oh, he will." Theodor moved to the side, dialing the frequency written in his file.

A couple of rings later, Chris answered. Surprise filled his beady green eyes. He quickly checked his surroundings, fearful and agitated.

"Your Majesty."

"Where's Malvina?" Theodor didn't waste time with pleasantries.

"I don't know," he answered, too quickly to be truthful.

"You're lying. I'll only give you one chance." Theodor's voice thundered in the Sanctum. "You're either telling me where she's holding Vivienne, or I'm calling your wife and telling her you've been cheating on her."

Theodor couldn't care less about his family's shock. He had never blackmailed anyone before. This was a special occasion, and he had to act accordingly.

Vivienne's life is on the line. I will do whatever it takes to save her.

"Your Majesty, please." Chris's winey voice reminded Theodor of Malvina's. "My wife would kill me. She's the best fighter in our group."

"Then talk."

"If I do, Malvina will end me."

"Take your pick. You have ten seconds. Nine . . ."

Theodor didn't back down. He noticed his sister and both his parents trying to read Chris's mind. He was a great distance away. They couldn't reach deep enough.

The other man faltered, and Theodor figured he needed a reminder.

"Six. Five. Four."

"Fine." The man lowered his head. "We're in Alaska. I'm sending you the coordinates."

Theodor terminated the connection as soon as he obtained what he needed. "Easier than I expected."

He turned to face everyone, adjusting his sword on his back. His father spoke first. "Let us come with you."

"No. This is my business. I'll take care of it." Theodor pulled his leather gloves on.

"She won't be alone, Your Majesty. Please, let me come with you. I can talk to her," Serge pleaded.

Something in his eyes, in his voice, softened Theodor. He mulled the idea over for a couple of seconds. Serge's presence intrigued him.

"Fine. You may come with me. The rest of you, please go home. I'll let you know when I have Vivienne back."

Mihai's head jolted up. "You're entering my territory, and I'm very particular about intruders." Mihai stepped forward and closed his hand on the handle of his sword. "I'm coming with you, and don't bother arguing with me."

Mihai's determined tone left no room for negotiations, and even if displeased, Theodor accepted.

~ ~ ~

"Wait." Prince Andree stopped them before activating the portal. "I think it would be smart to give this man a weapon." He gestured toward Serge.

Andree had sensed the other man's unique, yet familiar presence. It felt different from Ivan's and Malvina's.

"A sword would suffice, Your Majesty."

Without any hesitation, Andree grabbed his sword and offered it to Serge. When both their hands met on the handle, he didn't let go, forcing Serge to lift his gaze to him. They stared at each other until Theodor's father nodded and released the sword.

"I want it back. I'm very attached to it." The same instant he whispered in Serge's mind *"Redeem your family's honor. Make sure my son comes back home."*

Serge bowed his head without a word. The next second, the portal opened for them.

~ ~ ~

Cold. Vivienne's eyes opened to darkness. She blinked, trying to see something, anything. There was nothing but pitch black all around.

The air smelled stale and cold. She tried to move and lifted her hand. Pain throbbed through her body. Her temple, where she hurt most, was sticky.

Suddenly she remembered everything: the ball, Theo, Malvina.

Vivienne made another attempt to move, but her body wouldn't budge, as if it weighed a ton. She opened and closed her eyes a few more times, trying to focus on something. Darkness, heaviness, and pain were all her senses could detect.

"Theo." She'd meant to scream his name, instead she barely whispered. The raspy, low sound made her throat hurt from the effort. Silence cocooned her and could've been comforting if it wasn't so terrifying.

"Help." Another whisper moved the air around her.

Vivienne closed her eyes, exhausted. She gave up trying to move or scream. Stillness became her friend, slowly dissipating the pain. One word screamed in her incoherent mind—death.

She could swear she floated in the darkness with nothing holding her down. There was no direction.

With one last attempt to stay awake, Vivienne tried to open her eyes again. She wasn't sure if she did or not. It was just as dark. The sweet gliding feeling enveloped her. She remembered experiencing the same sensation right before falling unconscious in Greg's chains.

She flinched at the memory, but the darkness drew her in. One more image flashed in her mind. Theo gazed at her with a half-smile and the bluest eyes in the world. She smiled and surrendered, allowing nothingness to swallow her.

Chapter 23

Malvina glanced nervously around her. All her people were gathered in the underground hideout, one of her safe places. *Nobody knows where we are. I didn't even tell Uncle Serge. I should be safe, at least in theory.*

She feared Theodor would find them sooner or later. She had to prepare.

Malvina wanted Vivienne dead. She hated her. But without the girl locked in the cellar, Theodor wouldn't hesitate to kill her. The weak, disgusting human was her ticket to staying alive.

Malvina turned to one of the women in the group. "Vicky, check on the human."

Vicky quickly left the room, and Malvina continued to pace in front of the fire.

Her people talked to each other, scattered in the vast underground space. Their voices hummed, echoing in the stale air. Malvina couldn't focus on understanding the words, her mind too busy to process anything.

The dirt floors were hard and frozen. After all, they were in Alaska in the middle of winter. *This isn't what I had in mind for the first day of the new year.*

Behind her, the wood paneled wall hosted an oversized fireplace. A roaring fire added a homey glow to the otherwise lifeless room. An almost five-foot-tall stack of firewood was piled to the left side.

In the far-right corner, a massive, antique armoire held basic supplies. The ceiling, supported by thick, strong beams, waited for the second layer of insulation.

She had started building her place not long ago. It would take time to finish since she didn't want to attract attention. They were in Mihai Veres' territory, and she was considered hostile at best.

"Malvina. We need to warm her." Vicky ran into the room, carrying the inert human body. There was panic in her voice. "She's almost frozen to death."

A few of the others glanced at her, only to return to their interrupted conversations.

"You do that. I need her alive." She waved at the storage place. "There might be some blankets in that armoire." Malvina's flat, cold voice rose above the others.

Her disgust for humans was well-known. She referred to humans as pests. They were weak, high-maintenance and useless, except for their sweet blood.

Vicky hurried and grabbed a few blankets, placing Vivienne on top of a couple of them near the fire and quickly covering her with the rest.

Malvina inspected Vivienne's pale, gray skin with a passing glance. It seemed as if no blood was left in her body. *Meh! She'll warm up. Eventually.*

Her attention returned to her people. Malvina made sure each one knew their assignments, especially the two able to use stealth, making themselves invisible.

Footsteps on the top floor reduced everyone to silence. She knew it was Theodor, sensed his unique powerful presence, and he wasn't alone. *Uncle Serge? No. It can't be.* Fear and excitement mixed inside her, accelerating her pulse.

"We have company. Everyone, take your positions." Malvina indicated a couple of strategic points. "Vicky, how's the human?".

"Still unconscious, but alive." Vicky's few words sufficed.

Malvina didn't care about anything else but her plan.

~ ~ ~

Theodor sensed Malvina and her group's presence nearby. He searched for Vivienne's unmistakable signature. Something interfered.

"Keep your eyes open. There should be a secret entrance somewhere," Serge whispered, earning an arched brow from Theodor and a frown from Mihai. "If she listened to anything I taught her." A bookshelf on the back wall captured his attention.

Something about the man didn't quite add up. Theodor stared at him for a few seconds. Serge wouldn't betray him. He'd sensed his pure intentions from the second they'd met. *What do I sense? What is blocking me?*

Theodor made his sword ready for yet another fight. The handle felt good in his hand, and the weight of the weapon familiar.

Mihai followed his example, and they both stood behind Serge. He finally found what he searched for and pushed a group of books deeper into the shelf. The wall behind the shelving unit slid to the side with a heavy grinding sound. A dark opening with stairs carved into the rocky soil revealed itself, spiraling downward.

"Before we go." Serge stopped them. "You should know that two of the guys we will confront can use stealth." He took the first step down the stairs.

"Great. Nothing like fighting what you can't see," Mihai muttered, following Serge.

Theodor remained quiet. The imminent fight needed his undivided attention. He didn't know if Vivienne was still alive or even if she was there.

The beast inside him stirred with eagerness. He needed

to become one with the dark demon again. It was the only way he could take on twenty vampires and survive.

At the bottom of the stairs, on the landing, he stopped. Massive double doors with solid metal hinges towered in front of him. A thin strip of light underneath the crude wood planks broke the darkness.

Mihai stepped to the right and Serge to the left, leaving Theodor in the middle. After one more glance toward the other two men, Theodor nodded.

One hard kick, and the doors burst open. His group advanced into the room as one.

Two men disappeared. *The stealth guys were slow, and Chris is one of them.*

From the first step, he located Vivienne under the blankets. Her heartbeat was just as slow and faint as the night he first found her. She lay unconscious, but alive. His gaze traveled to the woman kneeling by her side—the wife Chris had cheated on.

"She's alive, Your Majesty. Look out for the two stealth guys. You can see them distorting the view." Vicky pushed her thoughts in his mind the instant their eyes met.

"Thank you." Theodor didn't expect a new ally in Chris's wife.

Hisses filled the room and weapons unsheathed. His ancient sword glimmered in the low light, and the stone resonated with him. Theodor connected to his power, to his beast, to his darkest depths.

~ ~ ~

Serge noticed his niece at the far end in front of the fire. *She's nervous.*

"Malvina, you have one chance. Let Vivienne go." Theodor's voice boomed against the dirt walls.

"No. You have one chance. You marry me, or she dies."

Malvina took a few steps back. Her foot touched Vivienne's body. Fangs descended, and a hiss escaped her lips.

"Don't be stupid, people. You can't win this." Serge hated fighting. It reminded him of his brother. Some things were better left in the past.

"Traitor!" Malvina's scream broke Serge's heart.

She had no idea he'd willingly offered to give his life in exchange for hers. Still, sadness filled him. Serge bowed his head, defeated. He finally understood he had cradled a snake who now shed its deceitful skin.

"He's not a traitor. But you wouldn't understand." Mihai's intervention seemed to leave her indifferent.

Serge saw her discreet signal, a nod and a long sweeping gaze across the room. The first two of Malvina's people jumped at the same time, starting the inevitable fight.

~ ~ ~

Theodor expected the attack. He slew one of the two in the middle of his jump, before the man touched the ground. His trusted sword sang a song of death in the stuffy air, and the first ashes floated in their macabre dance.

The second one managed to lunge at Theodor, but he parried the attack. Ashes still floated around them when he separated the head of the second attacker from his body.

Mihai and Serge turned at the same time, covering Theodor's back and the sides. A couple more attacked from behind.

They had only been in the room about ten seconds, and already four were dead. Each kill set Theodor back, further and further from his goal. He was killing possible covenants.

"Anyone else?" His growl echoed in the empty space. He hoped he didn't have to kill them all.

The low light of the fire didn't stop him from noticing some of Malvina's people retreating.

"Fight, you cowards!" she screamed at them all the way

from the back of the room. She appeared as a sinister black silhouette against the bright fire behind her.

Instead of listening to her, six advanced with their hands up and laid down their weapons kneeling in front of Theodor.

He didn't have time to indulge in their fear and resignation. Three more came toward him with swords and daggers.

Theodor reacted quickly and reached to one of the daggers on his belt. The sharp blade flew straight into the heart of one of them. The man took two more steps, unable to stop, glowing in bright amber. More ashes.

Two more attacked from the sides, and Mihai took one of them. Serge fought the other, one of the women in the group.

Theodor finished the two in front of him with only a scratch to himself and his vest sliced on the left side.

Vivienne stirred under the blankets. The barely noticeable movement attracted his attention.

"Viv!" His call traveled the thirty-some-foot distance.

Theodor smelled Malvina's fear. He had gained the advantage faster than expected. In a desperate move, she knelt, and grabbed Vivienne, holding her up. Vicky rose to her feet, a few steps away from Malvina.

"Let her go." Theodor's voice thundered over the sounds of the swords and daggers clashing against each other.

He had already killed five men. Mihai and Serge finished off their own adversaries and caught up with him.

Simple math told him he could still reach his goal. It wasn't up to him. If they preferred to die, so be it. Vivienne's life was most important, more than his own ambitions, his coven, his centuries-long string of fights.

Theodor kept advancing toward the back of the room, and Malvina licked her lips. She held Vivienne's body against hers. A river of honey, tangled, and blood-stained ringlets covered Vivienne's face. He couldn't even see her eyes.

Instead, he saw Malvina's. Sheer terror and pure insanity burned in them. *She won't stop.*

"You're not going to have her," Malvina hissed. Her fangs ripped into the delicate skin on Vivienne's neck.

"No!" Theodor scream filled the room.

Everyone froze. Not a breath disturbed the frigid air.

Time itself stopped for Theodor. The most insignificant details became important. Vivienne had lost her shoes somewhere, and her bare feet must've been cold. The elegant creamy dress she loved, hung on her body, ripped, stained with her own blood.

Her faint heartbeat slowed to an alarming rate. Blood trickled down her neck, staining the dress farther. Scarlet droplets ran around the cream pearls, coating them in a sticky layer, one by one.

Theodor sensed movement behind him and turned his head just in time to see one of the two men materializing from stealth with a dagger in his hand. He aimed for Theodor's heart.

Mihai's and Serge's swords skewered Theodor's attacker from two different directions. His dagger fell on the ground and bounced a couple of times. The two blades remained in his body until he soundlessly exploded in black ashes.

Theodor returned his attention to Vivienne, and without any hesitation, he ran to her. She didn't have much time left. He had wasted precious seconds.

The instant he stopped, only a step away, another of her men emerged from behind Malvina, holding a pistol toward Theodor.

The bullet fired from the gun had the unmistakable shine of silver. With a quick reflex, Theodor threw his sword into the man's chest. He ducked the projectile, and the other man flew backwards, pushed by the force with which the sword impaled him. For a couple of seconds, he hung on the wooden wall by the fireplace, about a foot off the ground.

He resembled a tasteless decoration, igniting in amber and matching the color of the flames.

Without his weapon, Theodor grabbed Malvina's hair, yanking her head back and forcing her to release Vivienne.

The woman that meant everything to him fell to the hard, frozen dirt at his feet. Life slipped out of her body at a worrying speed.

Another movement to the right caught Theodor's attention. Vicky, his unexpected ally, threw one of her daggers toward him. The trajectory, slightly over his right shoulder, assured him he wasn't the target. He checked behind him.

Chris was ready to strike when his wife's dagger plunged into his heart.

"The bastard has cheated on me for long enough," she muttered. "I've been waiting for an opportunity."

Theodor heard her words from afar. Everything seemed distorted. His right hand held onto Malvina's brittle red hair. With his left hand, he grabbed her shoulder, and she hissed.

The usual makeup covering her face was smudged with Vivienne's blood. Demons ran and laughed in Malvina's eyes, a party in hell. She tried to bite him, to fight him off in a desperate attempt to escape his grip. Her hands scratched the skin on his forearms. It didn't matter.

"Your end," Theodor growled in a low tone and drank in her fear, satisfying his beast's demands.

With one single, vicious movement, Theodor separated her head from the rest of her body. He stared at it with disgust one more time. Tendons hung broken, and blood still sprayed around after the sudden severance. His fingers unfurled from the bright hair, and let her head fall with a thud in the dirt beside the slumped body already ignited in flames.

"No." Serge's voice rose from somewhere behind, and Theodor glanced over his shoulder again. The other man's knees hit the dirt the same second Malvina's remains disintegrated in burning amber.

Theodor rushed to Vivienne and hugged her body to him. Her eyes blinked opened.

"Theo." Her hand tightened on his arm, her nails digging in his flesh.

She recognized him. Too weak to remain conscious, Vivienne closed her eyes. Her hand slid limply to her side.

He faced another impossible choice. Saving her life meant turning her.

How am I going to live with myself if I break my promise? I've always kept my word. I can't lose her. I can't.

"Forgive me. It's the only way."

Theodor hesitated one more second. He closed his eyes and hoped his destiny guided him in the right direction. Four-centuries-old ambitions mixed with ashes on the floor, sacrificed for one life, Vivienne's.

His fangs sank into her neck, right beside where Malvina had bitten her. He started to count the seconds.

~ ~ ~

One last attacker hoped for a killing blow and ran behind Theodor. During the turning process, with all focus on the human, any vampire would be most vulnerable, completely defenseless. And so was Theodor.

Mihai saw the rebel attacker from the corner of his eye. Every living cell in his body tensed. Old memories sparked to life in his mind. The day he almost died was as vivid as five hundred years ago. His inexplicable bond with Ana was clear now. She saved his life so he could live that moment. He had to be there, to protect Theodor.

He launched himself in the air, and his sword slashed through the other's man body before he could even come within striking distance of Theodor.

Mihai landed on one knee near Serge and rose to his feet. With the last of the ashes settling on the ground, Mihai turned to the remaining survivors. His sword cut through the air in a circle, taunting them.

Malvina was dead, half of her group gone. The last ones remaining bowed their heads and knelt.

"I thought so," Mihai whispered with a victorious undertone.

Serge lost his balance, and Mihai hurried to steady him. "What's wrong?"

"I don't know. A presence . . ." His words faltered. "I'm not sure." Serge labored for air.

His gaze stopped on the honey-colored hair fanned over Theodor's arm.

On shaky legs, Serge took a couple of steps. "Heather," he murmured, stunned.

"No, her name is Vivienne." Mihai tried to hide his confusion in front of Serge's unusual reaction.

~ ~ ~

Theodor heard whispers and noises behind him but focused his attention on Vivienne. He couldn't afford any mistakes. This was his first time turning a human. The seven seconds seemed the longest in his life. Vivienne's death, or her immortality, both rested in his hands. *Seven . . . Six . . .*

Fragments of his memories mixed with hers and flashed through his mind. Her blood tasted sweet and warm in spite of how cold her body was. He'd stopped Malvina just in time. *Five . . . Four . . .* His mental countdown continued, and his venom worked its way into her body. Traces of her ocean breeze scented shampoo reached his senses.

The room started to spin around him, and Theodor closed his eyes. *Three . . . Two . . .* Everything mingled in an alluring desire, and the beast within him surfaced again. He feared he wouldn't be able to stop in time. *I have to.*

He subdued his inner demon, and with one more second left, another thought crossed his mind. *Is she going to hate me for what I've done?*

At the exact seven second count, he released Vivienne and healed her wounds. Sweet blood still coated his lips and hands. He lifted her in his arms and held her close to him. Her heart picked up its pace. The transition had started.

You may hate me, but at least you'll be alive to do so.

Theodor rose to his feet and turned around. Serge stood right by him. He trembled, and his right hand lightly touched Vivienne's hair.

"Heather."

His whisper surprised Theodor. "Heather was her mother's name. Did you know her?" Theodor remembered one of the discussions he'd had with Vivienne.

"Was?" Pain, longing, and lost love clearly mixed in the other man's eyes.

"Yes. She died when she gave birth to Viv."

~ ~ ~

Serge took a sharp breath. His heart broke all over again in a million pieces. He stared at Vivienne, the source of the strong current he had sensed earlier.

A powerful and indisputable bond tied them together, and he finally understood. An unexpected joy bloomed and pieced his heart together one more time.

"What color are her eyes?" They couldn't be lavender, but he had to ask.

"She has . . ." Theodor stared at him. "Your eyes."

"My daughter," Serge murmured, lost in his inner world. "I have a daughter . . ."

"She's going to be all right. I had to turn her. There was no other way." Theodor tightened his hold on Vivienne. "You're welcome to join us. I'll take her home."

Serge nodded. His shoulders dropped. It was official now—his Heather was dead. Pain gripped his throat, he couldn't make one sound.

But he had a daughter. Like a phoenix risen from the ashes, hope sparkled one more time, offering him yet another reason to live.

"Your Majesty." Vicky stopped Theodor before he opened a portal. She presented him with his own sword.

He turned toward her and nodded. With both hands holding Vivienne, Theodor glanced to his uncle. Mihai grabbed the sword and placed it in its scabbard on his nephew's back.

Vicky stood surrounded by the surviving members of the group. Only nine had made it out alive.

"Thank you for your help."

"We want to join your coven." She gestured to the others. "All of us."

"I can't fight you right now." Theodor glanced at Vivienne.

"You don't have to. It's been a while since we wanted to join, but we were bound to Malvina." Vicky pointed her thumb behind her.

"In that case, you are all welcome to follow me. We're going home."

Theodor opened the portal, and one by one everyone stepped in.

Serge remained last. He glanced back one more time to the ashes. Malvina's tiny mound of black dust brought a sad smile to his eyes.

"You're at peace now."

He had lost one part of his life in that room and discovered another.

~ ~ ~

Vivienne had been in transition for two days.

Theodor sat by her side all the time, except one hour. He had to be present for the admittance ceremony. Serge, Vicky, and the rest of the group joined the Old Coven.

He had dreamed about that moment for centuries. Now, his coven finally reached one thousand members.

All his ambitions seemed suddenly unimportant. Underwhelmed, Theodor stood in the center of his Sanctum, numb. The moment his contract annulled, a weight had lifted off his shoulders. All his thoughts flew to Vivienne.

His dreams, his efforts, all but faded. He understood the power of destiny. *It was her, all this time. Everything that happened was supposed to unfold the way it did.* As soon as the ceremony ended, he ran back to her.

Every time Vivienne experienced pain, Theodor eased it. He held her tight in his arms, close to him, infusing her with strength. The moment when she would wake up a vampire neared, and his anxiety intensified.

"You love her, indeed." Serge had stayed with her for hours, too.

"I had planned to ask her to marry me right after the ball. With everything that's happened, I didn't have the chance, but I still intend to do so." Theodor moved his gaze from father to daughter. "I do love her, more than anything in this world."

Serge displayed a coy smile. A shadow crossed over his face and settled in his eyes.

"Since you are her father, I should probably make sure first that you don't have anything against my plans." Theodor glanced at the other man.

"I have no right to interfere. I didn't even know she existed until two days ago." A sigh left Serge's lips. "We're two complete strangers with a powerful bond. I fear her reaction to me."

Theodor nodded. He appreciated Serge's honesty. Not everyone would admit their fears out loud.

His own doubts, hidden deep inside, surfaced.

"I fear her reaction, too . . . at what I've done."

Chapter 24

Vivienne blinked her eyes open. Theodor sat on the edge of the bed, holding her hand.

"Viv."

She snuggled into his arms and rested her head on his chest.

"I love you so much." Theodor inhaled her sweet scent. "I've missed you." He closed his eyes, trying to conceal his anxiety.

He had to tell her she was now turned, a vampire. There was no easy way to do it. All the time she'd been transitioning, three and a half days, he'd run through all the possible scenarios.

Her unpredictability messed up every single plan he'd imagined. After all this time, he still didn't know what her reaction would be. His breath quickened.

The sudden lust he sensed washing over her made him inch his head back, just enough to gaze into her eyes.

Golden lights, like tiny wildfires, flickered from the depths of her irises. Vivienne had inherited his family's trademark, as he'd suspected she would.

A passionate, mind-melting kiss made him forget the reality for a short while.

~ ~ ~

Vivienne didn't remember going to bed. Her body hummed with an unusual energy all bundled up inside. She had never awakened so full of life before.

Her ears registered the waves brushing over the sand,

splashing against the boulders, and glanced to the windows. They were closed against a gloomy sky. Footsteps outside the room shuffled over the stone floors.

Somewhere far off, whispers and laughter mixed together in a background noise. Sounds from what she thought would be the kitchen followed, mingled with metal clinking against metal.

She shook her head, trying to get all the noises out of her mind. Instead, they intensified, grew louder.

Theodor appeared more attractive than ever. He smelled like power and cologne, playing havoc with her senses. Vivienne tightened her hold on his hard body. She enjoyed the sensation of his muscles in the palms of her hands.

An array of aromas worked their way to her nose. They must've been busy in the kitchen, and chicken was definitely on the menu. Some dessert's sweetness and fresh-baked smell brought a tiny smile to the corner of her lips.

It seemed all her senses ran out of control.

"I'll teach you how to block them." She heard Theodor in her mind, but she ignored him for the moment.

Her gums hurt, and she checked them quickly with her tongue. The sweet-salty taste of her own blood surprised Vivienne. Her canines elongated into sharp fangs. A hiss escaped her lips, and she quickly covered her mouth with her hand.

"What's happening to me?"

Theodor hugged her closer. "You've finished your transition. Please, forgive me."

His voice sounded different, as if demons tortured him. A strong grip stopped her from retreating from his arms. Vivienne sensed his tension.

"Transition? I have fangs. Theo, please tell me you didn't . . ."

Theodor nodded and inhaled loudly. "It was the only way to keep you alive, Viv."

Her mind emptied of all thought. Tears refused to form. Theodor gazed into her eyes.

"No. I trusted you." She slowly moved her head from right to left and back. "You promised me you wouldn't turn me against my wishes." Vivienne hoped she misunderstood him. The guilt in his deep, mesmerizing eyes told her otherwise.

"What's the last thing you remember?"

Fighting all the noises and smells, she searched her memories. His hand holding her head and his thumb caressing her cheek didn't help.

"The ball. We were at the ball, right?" A brief moment of excitement. Then she remembered the rest. "Malvina. She came after me in the ladies' room . . . And cold, it was so cold . . ."

Theodor kissed her forehead. His lips felt hot on her skin, as if he breathed fire.

"Yes. She kidnapped and almost killed you. She bit you, Viv. I had to turn you."

"No!" She yelled at him and hit his shoulders with her fists. "You promised me."

Theodor held her closer to him and forced her head onto his chest. "Shhh. Everything is going to be okay."

Vivienne grew more incensed. She wanted to scream, since she couldn't cry anymore. A claw tightened around her throat.

When she stopped hitting him, Theodor kissed her hair. A deep exhale burned the top of her head.

"I couldn't let you die, Viv. I love you."

Vivienne shut her eyes tight and wished to awaken from the nightmare engulfing her. It had worked so many times before. *Please be a nightmare. I have to wake up.*

"It's not a dream." His whisper brought her back to the terrifying truth.

Her deepest fears had turned into reality. She knew the change was irreversible.

"You turned me into a monster—"

"Is that what you think I am? A monster?" Theodor's hands grasped her shoulders, pushing her an arm's length away from him.

She avoided his stare. Vivienne didn't want to see him. "Let me go."

Her whisper, half-threatening and half-defeated, caused Theodor to loosen his grip.

"It's your choice what you'll become. I only did the *monster* thing and saved your life." His hands slid along her arms, completely releasing her. "Again." Hurt froze the wisps animating his irises.

Vivienne climbed out of bed.

"I need to go home."

~ ~ ~

"This is your home. Viv, I love you." He paused briefly and drew in a deep breath. "Marry me."

"What?"

I couldn't have possibly chosen a worse moment to ask her. Theodor tensed, following all her reactions. Her heart skipped a few beats, bringing him hope.

"We can now spend eternity together." He rushed to her side.

"I hate you!"

Theodor felt his heart breaking. The moment he feared most was there. He refused to accept her words without a fight. *This can't be real.*

"No, you don't." His thumb caressed her cheek. "You are mad at me for now. I understand and accept it." Theodor closed his hands on her arms again. "But you don't hate me."

"You're crazy if you think I'll ever marry you." She freed herself from his hold. "Not after what you've done to me."

"I'm crazy, for you. I will ask you to marry me every day until you say *yes*. I don't care how long it takes." Theodor cupped her chin in his hand. "We have all the time in the world." He released her and stepped back.

Vivienne didn't respond. She grabbed her bracer from the nightstand locking it onto her wrist.

Theodor stopped her before she could touch any of the buttons.

"What are you doing?"

"Going home. I don't want to see you anymore. Ever." Golden sparks glowed with fury in her eyes. *She's beautiful even when she's angry.*

"Too bad, you will see me every day. You need to start training." He reached for her.

"No, I don't. I didn't ask to be what you made me." Vivienne avoided his touch. "I don't want to be like you. I won't train." She stood her ground, and another hiss escaped between her fangs.

He had a long road ahead of him. Theodor took a breath in and let it out slowly, preparing himself for yet another fight.

~ ~ ~

All the new reactions confused her. She couldn't control them, or herself.

"As a young vampire you need to learn about your body, your senses, how to control your emotions." He waved his hand in her direction, up and down. "Now you're extremely vulnerable. It's my responsibility to—"

"Consider yourself free from any obligation. I don't want you to train me." Vivienne hissed and opened her bracer.

Theodor grabbed her wrists, stopping her from opening a portal. "There is someone in the living room waiting to meet you."

She couldn't resist appeasing her curiosity. "Who?"

"Your father." He freed her hands.

Vivienne closed her eyes. She wasn't sure she'd heard him right. "I don't have one."

"Yes, you do. He discovered you."

She massaged her temples. Her shoulders slumped, defeated, overwhelmed by everything happening to her in such a short period of time.

"I feel like I should go back to sleep and try to wake up again. This is a never-ending nightmare."

"I know it's a lot to take in."

"You do? I wake up a vampire." Her arms wrapped around her waist. "You ask me to marry you, after you turned me. Against my wish." She needed to remind him about the broken promise. "Now you're telling me I have a father? No, you have no idea." Vivienne ran out of air. "There are all these noises in my head, the smells around here are driving me insane, and I have all this energy bundled up inside me." Her hands went up in her air with frustration. "You don't know."

Vivienne took a few steps away from Theodor, trying to calm herself. *I have a father only a few steps away? Where was he until now? Why didn't he ever let me know he existed at least?* Questions started to roll in her mind, like the waves on the beach. *And what in the world are they baking? It smells divine.*

"He'll explain everything. As far as I understand, your mother ran away from him before either of them knew she was pregnant.

"Get out of my head." She hissed again, whirling on her heels toward him. Her hands squeezed her head between them.

Theodor's eyes narrowed on her, and for a few seconds, they battled in silence. Vivienne turned her back at him. She still couldn't believe the reality. *Is that cinnamon I smell?*

A few steps after she entered the living room, Vivienne stopped in front of the waiting man. After all, she'd agreed to meet him.

He had shoulder-length, dark hair pulled in a low ponytail, and a sword on his left hip.

Black tailored clothes made him appear slim and distinguished, like an old-time noble, with a kind smile. *I've seen him before.* His eyes surprised her most, identical to hers, as if she gazed into a mirror.

"Baby girl, please forgive me." He hurried over and wrapped his arms around her. "I didn't know you existed."

She remembered the few moments when she'd regained consciousness, during her transition. He and Theodor had stood by her side, cooling her heated body with icy-cold water.

Vivienne recalled Theodor's embraces, the strength he'd offered her, and his whispers, telling her everything would be okay. *Well, it's not okay. Not by far.*

The strong, unexpected, and undeniable bond with her father shocked her.. He'd called her *baby girl*. Nobody had ever called her that. Vivienne tried to reject him, but she couldn't. Her stiff attitude against him melted away.

She remembered her childhood. Every day she'd envied other kids with parents, wished she had at least one. Vivienne loved her grandmother, but she could never fill the void left by the absence of her parents.

Now, her father embraced her. Warmth spread calmness in her body, fuzzy like a brand-new blanket. Her childhood dream became reality.

"Are you sure you're my father?" Vivienne feared her own question and held her breath.

"I am. You must feel the connection, too." Serge took a step back, staring at her.

She just nodded. Another question appeared into her mind, and Theodor answered, using their link.

"*Yes, he's a vampire.*"

Another growl escaped her lips. She couldn't control herself. "I asked you to stay out of my head."

No matter what he said or did, it only served to anger her more. She wished him out of her head so badly her whole body tensed. Her hands curled into tight fists. Teeth ground and a sheer layer of sweat covered her body.

Theodor tilted his head to the side and took a step toward her.

"How did you do that?"

"Do what?" Vivienne shot back.

"You kicked me out of your mind. And I can't get back in. It's like a . . ." He stopped for a moment, glanced at Serge, and then back to her. "You've inherited Malvina's shield. When she bit you, she transferred her power to you."

"Whatever you're talking about, I don't care and don't want it." Vivienne voice grew louder with each word..

~ ~ ~

The invisible shield dropped leaving Vivienne's mind exposed. Theodor caught her thinking about running away, somewhere far, where he couldn't find her.

She thought she'd made a big mistake accepting the invitation to come to Crete in the first place. Her thoughts pierced straight into his heart like sharp blades.

Theodor grasped Vivienne's shoulders forcing her to face him.

"Don't ever think about running away from me." An uncontrollable growl escaped him. "We belong together, and you know it."

"I—" She tried to free herself, but Theodor's hold on her tightened.

"I won't let you destroy what we have, and condemn both of us to misery.

He released her and walked away from her. Vivienne stared at him speechless. He meant every word.

Only seconds later, she opened a portal and left with her father. Theodor didn't try to stop her. He stood like a statue until she disappeared into the swirling gateway.

She needed some time alone with her father. And she would think twice before trying to do something stupid. Like running away.

Hmm. That shield is going to give me trouble. I just know it. I wonder what else she's inherited.

Theodor's gaze roamed over the gray sky. The cloudy, windy day matched his mood. A storm brewed inside him as well. She refused to be his wife, furious at him for turning her. *I'm not surprised.*

~ ~ ~

The initial bond with her father only became deeper and stronger with every hour, every minute, every second spent together. Vivienne had a lot easier time adapting to being a vampire than she ever had as a GeM.

Hours and hours of talking to her father made her understand what had happened to her mother. It turned out, she and her mother both shared an inexplicable fear of vampires.

Vivienne finally accepted she had entered the world half vampire. Maybe it was her destiny after all. She didn't mind her new strength, the energy, or all the new powers.

Following through on his word, Theodor had been asking her to marry him every single day. It became harder and harder to keep rejecting him.

All of her attempts to decline his training were reduced to mere nothing by his insistence. He was more stubborn than her. After the first few days, Theodor discovered that somehow, they now shared all of his powers. Vivienne could read minds and control them, heal, and levitate objects or people.

Vivienne started to run tests on herself. She knew from what she had read before that she should have gotten only one of his special abilities. Never mind Malvina's shield. *Why did I inherit everything?*

Day after day, Vivienne trained and divided her time between her father and her lab. Away from everyone, in the isolation of her office, Vivienne couldn't ignore how much she missed Theodor, being with him. Finally, she had figured and accepted her feelings for him.

"I love him." Her whisper had no witnesses other than her quiet office. Unfortunately, it was too late. She couldn't forgive him for what he'd done.

More often than not during her training, Vivienne fought temptation. When he touched her, showed her how to breathe or how to move, she wanted to forgive him.

Vivienne could have admitted how much she loved him and agreed to start their lives together, at least in theory. But in reality, every time she stopped herself. He'd broken her trust.

About a month later, at night, Vivienne worked in her lab. For the first time since her turning, fatigue overwhelmed her.

Vampires don't get tired. She suspected something was amiss.

With trembling hands, she hurried to draw some of her blood and ran a few more tests. The simple act of walking between one piece of equipment and her desk exhausted her.

In spite of her attempts not to, she fell asleep. The beep from one round of tests woke her three hours later. She had slept for the second time in the last two days.

"Something is definitely wrong," she muttered.

The only light breaking the darkness in the lab came from the one globe floating over her desk. From the first glance at her datapad Vivienne noticed the unusual readings.

Her hurried steps echoed over the cold floors. She input the data into another one of her terminals.

One sheet of paper slid out of a thin opening only a couple of minutes later. She read the results of the tests and sat on the floor, unable to make it to a chair. "No . . ."

Hours had passed when she finally threw the crumpled piece of paper she had been staring at into the wastebasket. Her mind jumped from empty to so busy she couldn't keep up with her own thoughts, to empty again.

Vivienne managed to organize her thoughts and fabricate a plan. If she wanted to succeed, she had to hurry.

~ ~ ~

"Baby girl." Her father welcomed her the second she stepped out of the portal. "This is a nice surprise."

Vivienne wore for the first time the suit Theodor had insisted she accept. Fashioned of the softest tan suede, it perfectly matched her skin tone, making it hard to tell where the leather stopped and her skin began.

The tiny top hugged her body, leaving her back exposed. With her turning, all the scars on her back had disappeared, and she loved showing it off now. Just another upside of being a vampire.

The tight-fitting pants resembled a second skin. She was best balanced in heels, and her thigh-high boots gave her the perfect posture.

Against any expectations, Vivienne was most proficient with dual swords, the trademark of a born fighter. Theodor had ordered a scabbard for her. Temporarily, she wore a belt with two daggers.

"Father, we need to talk." Her voice sounded tired, and

her head hung low. Her shoulders dropped under an invisible weight.

Serge wrapped an arm around her, and they both walked into the greenhouse. Vivienne loved it. She enjoyed sitting there with her father for hours, both of them watching the hologram of her mother twirling above the flowering bushes.

"You look as beautiful as your mother."

Vivienne smiled and followed his glance toward her oversized duffel bag.

"Thanks. But just like her, I have to go."

A few seconds of silence enveloped them, interrupted by her mother's laugh.

"Do you see how happy she was?" Serge asked and covered Vivienne's hands with his. She just nodded. "You could be just as happy if you would accept the man you love. He loves you so much, Vivienne."

"He turned me," she growled, her anger directed toward Theodor.

"He saved your life. Would you rather be dead? I witnessed everything. There was no other way, baby girl." Serge patted her golden ponytail cascading over her shoulders. "He risked his own life to save you, opening himself to danger with enemies still surrounding him."

Vivienne averted her eyes and let out a deep sigh. She knew that already. He had told her before all the details. Her decision became harder to follow through.

"I can't trust him anymore. And now there are complications."

"What do you mean?"

"I'm pregnant."

~ ~ ~

Serge turned to his daughter. *She must be in an early stage since I can't even sense it yet.*

"How is it possible? Your turning would have killed the baby if you were pregnant for less than eight weeks."

Sadness covered her luminous eyes, like a glaze made of gloomy pain and dark suffering.

"Yes, it would have, in normal conditions." She nodded a few times. "I've been working on some tests. I'm the first GeM to evolve into a vampire." She lifted her head to her father. "At least the first one in any records. According to my research, GeMs inherit all special abilities. They can also preserve a pregnancy through the transition process." Her hand covered her still flat abdomen. "I'm almost six weeks."

"Baby girl, listen to me." Serge grasped Vivienne's shoulders in his hands and stared into her eyes. "You're a smart woman. I'm not going to tell you how to live your life. It's your choice. But, is this what you really want?"

"I can't get over what he did." She lowered her head.

"Prince Theodor has been known for his word, and honor, for centuries." He released her. "Do you have any idea how much breaking that promise is eating at him? He had to choose between his conscience and your life. He chose you."

Vivienne rose to her feet as if his words burned her.

"He figured he would rather live with his broken promise than without you," Serge stood. "He chose his love for you over his own honor and peace of mind."

"I'm sorry. I have to go. We'll keep in touch," Vivienne whispered and ran out of the greenhouse.

Serge let out a deep and heavy sigh. His eyes returned to the happy hologram twirling atop the pink heather.

"Out of everything you could have passed down to her it had to be this fear."

His painful whisper flew in the warm and sunny-looking greenhouse.

~ ~ ~

Vivienne always loved winter but hated the discomfort

it brought. Now, for the first time, she stood in the middle of the falling snow without shivering from the cold. Her body adapted to the temperature. *I wish I could've adjusted just as easily to the pain stabbing my heart.*

She stood in the exact same spot where almost three months ago she'd lain unconscious. Her plan, made in a hurry by her analytical mind, was already set in motion. Vivienne would disappear, fall off the face of the earth without a trace.

But she needed to make one last stop before saying goodbye to her old life. Facing the place where everything had changed was her ultimate test.

The dark alley welcomed her as deserted as the last time. The empty crates were stacked in the same place. She could see, with her mind's eye, her old human form running with erratic steps, and finally collapsing from pain and cold. The ground was covered in a thick layer of white, clean snow as frozen as she wished her heart would be.

Vivienne enjoyed each of the snowflakes melting in contact with her skin. The rest of them fell on top of the others with a whispered song she could now hear. The speeders hummed far behind her in their traffic lanes. *I always thought they were silent.*

Memories from the last couple of months flashed through her mind. She missed Theodor. Her arms wrapped around herself as if they had a mind of their own. For a short while, Vivienne fantasized about forgiving him for turning her.

They could live their lives together, have their baby. She had promised herself a long time ago, that her kids wouldn't have her sad childhood. Yet, her determination to run away had set in motion that exact future for her unborn baby. She would deny him the right to know his father.

Her craving for Theodor hurt her body and messed with her mind. She could sense his presence.

"I hope you aren't doing what I think you're doing."

Vivienne whirled around, startled. He stood behind her, only steps away. *My senses aren't that bad after all.*

"Theo. What are you doing here?"

"The better question is what are you doing here?"

She should've been furious at him for finding her. Instead, the old butterflies made their round inside her body. Their incendiary wings reminded her how much she loved him. "How did you know I was here?"

Theodor stared at her with an impish smile. *That smug air always suited him so well.* Vivienne had to tear her eyes away before she gave into temptation and jumped into his arms.

"You missed your training," he reminded her. "By four hours." The additional remark made Vivienne purse her lips. *Damn it. I forgot about training.*

"I searched for you. I even visited Serge."

At the mention of her father's name, she gazed at him.

"Did he tell you—?"

"No. He didn't." Theodor walked closer. "Your father kept your secret, but his memory preserved your short visit. I also tracked the signal on your bracer." He pointed to her wrist. "Where do you think you're going?"

His hand closed on her arm.

Vivienne knew she could trust her father, but had completely forgotten he didn't have to say a word. Or that her bracer was traceable.

"Theo, please understand." Snowflakes stuck to her eyelashes. She had to blink a few times. The blue lights in his eyes, just like always, mesmerized her, making her decision questionable.

"Viv, I love you."

Theodor tilted her face to him.

Vivienne's lungs turned uncooperative.

"I'm sorry . . ."

Theodor's fierce kiss numbed her. She expected him

to threaten her, to make things more difficult. Instead, he showed her how much he loved her.

"Don't leave." His whisper touched a deep level she didn't even knew existed.

"I'm sorry, Theo." Vivienne's hand cupped the side of his face.

"Viv." He covered her hand with his.

"I'm so, so sorry for everything I've put you through. I hope you can forgive me." Vivienne paused for a second. "I love you . . . Will you marry me?"

His kiss left her breathless. She couldn't leave him.

~ ~ ~

Theodor stared into her golden blazing eyes with a half-smile and his eyebrow arched.

"No. *You're* marrying *me*."

"I can't wait," Vivienne whispered and kissed him, wrapping her whole body around him.

Same as the first time they both had been in that alley, a speeder approached. Theodor lifted her duffel bag on his shoulder, and with her in his arms, he hurried to open a portal.

"Where are we going?" Vivienne's question brushed warmth against his skin, made him smile.

"All three of us are going home."

"You know?"

"Did you think I wouldn't?"

Vivienne's lips covered his.

Theodor realized that very second, he held in his arms everything he ever wanted: the woman he loved, their family. His destiny was finally fulfilled.

He glanced one more time to the dark sky sifting light snowflakes over them. Without another word, he stepped into the swirling portal.

Thank you for reading Bloodline Destinies. I hope you enjoyed reading Theodor's story as much as I loved writing it.

Please feel free to join my newsletter at <u>www.iulianafoos.com</u> for future releases, updates, and news.

You may also find me on Facebook, at <u>www.facebook.com/Authoriulianafoos</u>, or follow me on Twitter at twitter.com/iulianafoos

On Amazon, at <u>www.amazon.com/Iuliana-Foos</u> you can also find Bloodline Origins, first book in the series, the story of Theodor's parents.

Also from **Iuliana Foos** and **Soul Mate Publishing**:

BLOODLINE ORIGINS

Determined to turn her fantasy into reality, Ana starts her journey to become a vampire. Along the way, she learns the truth about their secret society, discovers her prestigious bloodline, and falls in love.

Not all vampires are accepting of humans and war looms in the shadows. An ancient tome reveals the vampires' alien descent and sparks war.

An army bent on eradicating her coven's existence threatens her new world. Survival or annihilation will be in Ana's hands.

Available now on Amazon: **BLOODLINE ORIGINS**

CPSIA information can be obtained
at www.ICGtesting.com
Printed in the USA
FFHW010117250519
52633747-58139FF